THE BALLERINA AND THE REVOLUTIONARY

BY CARMILLA VOIEZ

Cover art by: Nicola Ormerod
Edited by: Vanessa Knipe

This is a work of fiction. All of the characters, organizations and events portrayed in this novel are a product of the author's imagination. Any resemblance to persons, living or dead, actual events, or organizations is entirely coincidental.

This story is dedicated to everyone, whatever their gender identity and sexuality. May we all find beauty in our diversity.

Thank you to Vanessa, Karl, Sarah, Gabrielle, Ann and Trish for your help in bringing Crow's story to life.

1

(London, England - 2013)

My body was like flotsam, tossed about in the crowd. My throat, dry from shouting, felt full of razorblades. Where was everyone? The bodies, bouncing beside me, crashing against me, were strangers. All my friends scattered in the first surge, not long after the rioting started and the police descended. Above our heads, damp with sweat and water spray, towered a dozen mounted police. Glossy, chestnut mares gazed haughtily down at the crowd as their riders tapped batons against body armour, menacingly. The bodies of fellow anarchists and others pressed in around me. The tide was turning. We were moving back, retreating, scurrying away like frightened rats.

A sweaty chest crushed my face. As the man moved so my jaw and nose moved too, pinned between it and an arm behind me. I gasped for breath.

It was always the same. Two steps forward, one step back. Our comrades had been occupying the closed school for months, providing free education to adults and children alike in this deprived area of London, but the landlords wanted them out.

Answering their call for help, we stood with them.

Dressed in black and red, we created a buffer between those grass-roots heroes and our moneyed oppressors with nothing other than property values, profit and fast turnarounds on their minds. Our stand-off displeased the Metropolitan police, and here they were again, determined to move us on. Comply or die – that should have been their motto.

Amidst the chaos, I heard a shout and recognised the voice. Jumping, I accidentally bludgeoned a man's ear with my elbow as I rose. He yelped in pain and shock then acknowledged my existence, at last.

'I need to see,' I told him.

He supported my weight, lifting me above the crowd. Outside the tightening ring of protesters was Chrissie. She was being tackled by three policemen and wrestled to the ground.

The man withdrew his support and I slid between bodies and dropped to my knees. Beyond the forest of legs, Chrissie's face was being pushed against concrete, a heavy boot pressed between her shoulders. Our eyes met. Wrapping my fingers around a rock from the ground, I rose to my feet, leaned forwards and pushed my way towards the front of the crowd, weaving between hot bodies. The smell of anger and fear tainted the air. Sweat and tears dripped like rain.

At last, my body fell clear of the crush of protesters. Chrissie craned her neck and stared back at me. My shout of rage was cut short as a riot shield slammed against my cheek and I crumpled on the ground beside her.

In the flashing lights of my dazed vision, her face faded. I reached out and grasped her wrist. A smile lit up her face and she mouthed one word, 'Crow', before all light extinguished and I passed out.

My name was Crow. I was nineteen years old and had spent most of my life trying to escape all forms of hierarchy, most accurately portrayed for me, by the image of the matriarch, i.e. my crazy mother.

Mother's name was Vivienne. We didn't look alike, we didn't act alike and we certainly didn't think alike. Vivienne was a prima ballerina before she gave birth to me and I had all the grace of an elephant. She wore long, floating skirts and big jewellery, while I felt more comfortable in combats and t-shirts and hated the long hair she made me wear as a child, a symbol of begrudging femininity that never felt comfortable. My head was shaved now, much easier.

As far as I could remember I had always hated her, and she me. I never figured out what she wanted from me and simply assumed it was my unhappiness. Once free of her oppression, I naturally transferred this simmering animosity to other unworthy authority figures, but things were rarely as simple as they seemed.

I survived the blow from the shield, although the crowd were moved on and the building cleared. A pity really, another community space handed over to the country's rich elite. It made my head spin. I never understood the principle of profit over people. There were a lot of things I didn't understand, but in the end I was a fighter and I guess I existed outside of society. It was easier that way, less complicated, and I could keep my priorities in check. I liked to think of myself as a freedom fighter, like my dad. The squat had everything I needed and I did a bit of this and that to make enough money to feed myself. All I had ever wanted was to survive and be free.

It's why I left home when I did, at thirteen.

2

(Bristol, England - 2007)

There was barely enough space for my single bed, wardrobe and chest of drawers in my tomb-like room. Every inch of wall was covered with posters and ink drawings - faces whose features were twisted into grotesque parodies of themselves. I moved quietly around the room, dragging long, black hair back from my soft-brown skin. Muddled piles of clothes, books, and CDs waited in a stolen suitcase. The case was half full when the door opened and my mother strode across the room.

'Where do you think you are going, Giselle?' Vivienne asked.

I blushed and stared at the floor.

'Giselle?' Mother asked again, softer this time.

Her gaze dropped to the brown, leather suitcase, and she pushed the lid closed, hissing between her teeth. 'What are you doing with my case?' Her voice was quiet, but each word was pronounced carefully as if to avoid any misunderstanding.

I watched, wide-eyed and terrified, as she brushed invisible dust from the suitcase. Her neck twisted until it appeared as though her head was almost parallel with her left shoulder. It was her most unnatural, freakish and intimidating pose and she used it sparingly. Her eyes blazed with fury as I shuddered within the fragile armour of my skin, struggling to maintain eye contact.

'I'm leaving? I can't stand ... it anymore.' I backed away towards the small window.

'It's those junkie friends of yours, isn't it?' Vivienne spat. 'They've poisoned you against me. Well, you can't leave. You're only thirteen years old.'

'Stop it! I keep telling you. They aren't junkies.'

'I knew you were up to something. Nanny told me.' Vivienne jutted out her chin and pursed her lips.

'Nanny's dead!' I screamed. 'And you're a fraud. She'd never have told tales on me, even when she was alive.'

Vivienne's head snapped abruptly back to the correct position. She picked up the case and emptied my belongings onto my bed with a few sharp shakes. Suitcase tucked under her slender arm, she marched out of the room, leaving the door open behind her.

Exhausted, I fell to the floor. My hair covered my face as I sobbed. I spat strands of it out of my mouth, snarling as I tore at the roots. I kicked my bedstead then winced with pain. I kicked it again, harder.

'I hate you,' I whispered.

I stood up and pulled my hair back again, knotting it at the nape of my neck. I tiptoed across the room, clutched the doorknob in my shaking hand and pushed it closed without making a sound. At last it felt safe to exhale and I sighed, hugging my torso tightly with one arm for comfort. I chewed the fingers of my other hand and stood, swaying, for a few minutes then rushed across to the window and pushed it wide open. The lawn stretched out about twelve feet below. I climbed onto the windowsill and crouched there for a moment, crow-like in my dark clothing, then I jumped, rolling as I hit the ground. Testing my limbs and finding nothing broken I ran, away from Vivienne and away from home, empty-handed.

I glanced back at the dark windows of Vivienne's house as I reached the end of the street and blew a goodbye kiss to my brother. I felt as light as air, free. Of course I wasn't free. I could never be free. It was always the same. Two steps forward, one step back.

3

(London, England - 2013)

In a dark room, under a filthy blanket, my body stirred.
In my dream, I lay on the ground, next to a man with blue eyes; he was smiling. We were in a forest. A zephyr whipped up brown and red leaves, making a rotating fence around us. The circle of leaves grew tighter and tighter until they scratched my skin as they rushed past. Sitting up, trying to bat them away, I realised I was naked and wrapped my arms around my chest, pushing my flesh taut against my ribcage.

The wind stopped and the leaves fell to the ground, burying the blue-eyed man. I dug up leaves in handfuls, but the pile was too deep. Angry buzzing emanated from the mound. The leaves were alive with bees and wasps. I yanked back my hands and saw they too, were covered with hundreds of insects.

The buzzing became louder until the sound of an alarm clock woke me. My blanket fell away as I sat up, revealing my khaki t-shirt. I always slept fully dressed. Scratching my fuzzy, shaven head, I winced. A week after the beating and my bruises still troubled me. My entire body throbbed with pain. My face was scratched and sore and my right cheekbone bruised and swollen. As I glanced around the room the movement made my earrings jangle together; the sound soothed me.

Six other bodies lay on the floor, wrapped in blankets. Two pairs of bodies snuggled together, limbs entangled, sharing their heat. The remaining two slept alone, like me.

The alarm next to Matty's body was still buzzing. I yawned, padded over, switched it off and checked the time – fourteen hundred hours. I shook Matty's shoulders to wake him. He peered at me, through eyes rimmed with red. His sour breath made my stomach churn.

'It's time to wake up,' I grunted and slouched out of the communal bedroom, into the kitchen.

With an exaggerated yawn, I pulled a saucepan out of the sink and rinsed it under the tap. I filled it then lit a camping stove to boil water for coffee. The two cleanest cups found, I rinsed them, half-heartedly, before spooning in coffee granules. By the time Matty joined me, there were two coffees on the windowsill and I was smoking my first cigarette of the day, inhaling the smoke and exhaling the memories of my nightmare.

We stood in silence, drinking and smoking until a knocking at the front door startled us.

'Giz,' my brother's voice called through the letterbox.

I ran to the door and peeked through the opening. 'Tom!' I beamed. 'Go round to the back of the house.'

Matty was already unbolting the back door when I returned. As usual he was late for work. 'Bye, Crow!' He saluted me, grinning.

I directed my wave at Matty's retreating back. Tomas walked through the door a moment later. I smiled and took a step towards him. He grabbed and squeezed me, lifting me from the floor. At six feet tall, Tomas was almost a foot taller than me. His short, dark hair was carefully styled and his skin much paler than mine, with only the hint of a tan. His eyes were hazel. From looks alone, it was hard to see any family resemblance between us.

'What you doing here, Tom?'

When Tomas stepped back from our embrace tears gathered in his eyes. My fingers tingled, as if they were directing me to comfort him, reach up and stroke his cheek. I couldn't. Instead, I asked, 'What's wrong?'

'Didn't you get my letters?'

'Vivienne again,' I answered, stiffly, turning away to roll another cigarette.

'She's responding now. Most of the time she seems ... lucid.' He sighed, wiping his face brusquely with the back of his hand. 'But it's hard, seeing Mum like that ... so weak.'

'Oh. But, Catherine and Melissa are okay?'

He nodded. 'I have to bring you home. Mum needs to see you.'

'No.'

'When Mum woke up ... she asked for you. She's desperate to see you, to apologise. She never meant to hurt you.'

Anger made my arms shake. Trying to steady them, I

reached out and squeezed my brother's wrist.

He pulled away. 'Giz, for Christ's sake, it's been six years. Isn't that punishment enough? You know, Mum's life wasn't easy either.'

'It's Crow, and don't do that. Don't stand up for her. Yeah, maybe she loves you now, but she's never loved me. I was always too clumsy, too ugly, too angry ...'

'Look ... G-Crow ... it's just ... come with me. Do this for me, please.' Lines of pain, like spiders' webs, were etched across his skin around his damp eyes.

'I don't know.' I sighed. My shoulders dropped in resignation. I did know. I knew I would always provide the stability my brother needed, however unstable I felt myself and I knew I could never be free of his need for me. One step forward, two steps back.

'Just for a couple of days, please,' he begged.

I remembered how fiercely I shielded my big brother while we were growing up. He was always the sensitive one, too easily hurt. I realised how much he still needed me.

'I'll try,' I whispered, shuddering.

Packing to leave the squat involved no more than picking up my backpack from beside my pile of blankets. My khaki rucksack had, for years now, contained my life: my clothes, my belongings, even my dreams – stored for travel, small and easy to transport.

I kissed Chrissie's cheek and placed a note, beside her sleeping body, to explain where I had gone. I left the

blankets where they were; I would be back in a couple of
days.

4

The journey, from London to Bristol in Tomas's Volvo, seemed to take forever, yet somehow we only had time to talk about how Melissa was getting chubby now she had started on solids. The subjects of Vivienne's health or my return home were, apparently, verboten. So it came as a shock when Tomas dropped me outside Vivienne's house.

'Hang on, why the fuck, have you brought me here? Listen, I'll just kip on your floor, Bro.'

'Oh Giz, I'm sorry, we don't have room. Mum's house is empty.'

'How many times? The name's Crow now, not Giz, not Giselle – Crow, and anyway ... empty ... where's Vivienne?'

'In the hospital. I wrote ...'

Of course he did. I shook my head and pressed my fingertips to my mouth, holding back a stream of obscenities.

'Look. See how it goes. Just for one night,' he negotiated; his voice oozed confidence. 'If it doesn't work, I'll sort out a B&B for you, if you want. I'll pick you up tomorrow, when I finish work.'

He handed me a small bundle of keys and a mobile telephone. 'Here's the keys and Cathy's mobile in case you need anything. Our number's stored here, see. I almost forgot ... here, take some money for food.' Thrusting two crisp ten pound notes into my open palm, he turned to leave.

I stood there, confused, too much information too quickly. My brain needed chance to catch up. 'Tom,' I called after him.

He turned and smiled.

'Want to stay for a cuppa at least?'

'I'd love to, but Cathy and Melissa. I better check they're okay. See you tomorrow, Sis!'

'It's just Crow,' I grumbled. 'Crow.' But he wasn't listening. He was already indicating to pull away.

Fuck! Home for two minutes and already I felt powerless. I couldn't find the strength to argue with his logic, so instead I waved goodbye. It was getting dark and the building loomed bigger than I remembered, silhouetted against the blood-red and violet sky.

A flash of blue in one of the windows reminded me of the eyes in my dream, but it was just the reflection of Tomas's car.

The paved path to the front door was hemmed in by walls of grass on either side. The late-spring garden was heavy with flowers; roses and geraniums fought with dandelions and cow-parsley for supremacy. Grime covered the windows.

My chest felt tight and adrenaline surged through my nerve endings preparing me for fight or flight. My hand shook as I reached toward the keyhole. I placed my left hand against the door, steadying myself, not wanting to fall. The wood seemed to vibrate as if I was feeling the rapid heartbeat of the house itself. I pressed my forehead against the narrow glass panel at its centre. I had to do this. *Do it for Tom.*

I opened the door and edged inside, wiping my feet on the mat before stepping onto the parquet floor beyond. It was a generous hallway; a space designed for welcoming guests, laying open the entire soul of the house. Except, all five doors joining it were closed and I felt I was intruding.

I wandered into the kitchen to make coffee; my feet found the way from memory. Beyond the dirty window lay the garden in which I'd played as a child. Forgetting the coffee, I unlocked the back door and stepped out. Birds and grasshoppers filled the fresh air with the sound of their chirping.

Little had changed, although the grass was longer. The swing in the far corner squeaked a soft greeting, the wooden shed glared its warning and the vegetable garden was so full of life it reminded me of an Amazonian jungle. I smiled, remembering times spent digging this earth with my Nanny, before she died. The memory was so vivid; I could see it just in front of me. Almost close enough to touch.

In the empty garden, knelt a white-haired lady and beside her, a small girl with black wavy hair - me. We were digging up weeds together, talking animatedly, so close our arms kept brushing against each other.

'Look, Nanny.' I held up a fat, wriggling worm and giggled.

'If you pop the worm here, in the soil, he'll help Nanny's flowers grow.'

'Why?'

It was my favourite word when I was three. Why does the worm help the flowers to grow? Why is my skin brown while yours is white? Why do you love me more than Mummy does?

Nanny patted my hand.

'Why are you crying, Nanny?'

'Just a touch of hay-fever, darling.' She wrapped her arms around me and sniffed my head.

'Your Mummy's feeling better now. She's coming tomorrow, to collect you and Tomas.'

I clung to Nanny's thin body, burying my face in her floral blouse.

'Mummy's very excited about seeing you, sweetheart. She really misses you.'

I let go of my grandmother, and walked, slowly, to the far corner of the garden then sat down on the earth, facing the wall.

'Giselle, darling, come here. Let me give you a kiss.'

I didn't move. I heard Nanny groan with pain as she stood up; one arthritic knee locked and she stayed there for a moment her body shuddering, gathering strength before she pushed her legs into a stronger position. She hobbled across the lawn and sat on a bench to my right.

Tapping her lap with her palms, Nanny called out. 'Shall I tell you a story, Giselle? Shall I tell you the story about the ballerina?'

Unable to resist the lure of my favourite fairytale, I toddled over, climbing onto Nanny's lap. She stroked my hair as she recited the story. Her touch calmed me.

'Once upon a time there was a beautiful little girl, with hair the colour of ravens' feathers, eyes the shade of rain-clouds and skin like newly-fallen snow. Her mother was as wild as the deer, but she wanted a different life for her daughter. So she left her in the arms of a man and woman who could not have children of their own.

'The little girl grew into a woman, as tall and graceful as the willow tree. She became a famous ballerina and travelled the world, dancing for kings and queens.

'One day, a man told her she was not meant to be a ballerina at all. He said she was a river, able to bring life and freedom to the people of his country. They fell in love and travelled the mountains of his homeland together. He was a freedom-fighter and they ran hand in hand, giving hope and love to the poor.

'Soon the ballerina discovered they were going to have a baby and they were happy. But, they lost each other in the mountains. She searched and searched, but never found him. Heartbroken, the ballerina returned to her family.

'When the baby was born, she was every bit as beautiful as her mother, but with the sun-kissed skin of her father and eyes like coal. The ballerina looked at the baby through a veil of tears. She was the image of her lost father. While the ballerina could not show it, she loved her daughter very much.'

Shocked by the vividness of the memory, I stood still, gripping my forearms. I listened to the sounds of life: bird, insect and human, within and outside the garden walls. I sniffed. I couldn't forgive Nanny for dying. She had left Tomas and me alone with Vivienne. I had been a child, unprotected and unloved, or so it had felt. I shuddered, unfolded my arms and reached into my pocket. I rolled and lit a cigarette, but felt too tired to finish smoking it, so I threw it onto the patio and wandered back into the house.

It was only nine o'clock, but I felt a stupor I couldn't seem to shake, as though the house itself was draining my energy. I was here because Tomas asked, but where was he? One step forward, two steps back.

As I carried my bag upstairs, the paintings on the wall seemed to move around me. The cold, grey eyes of Vivienne's portraits watched me, judging me, as they always had.

I wondered about my old bedroom. Would it be as I left it: a shrine to the child who stormed out six years before, vowing never to return? More likely it would be full of boxes or paintings.

My old bed waited inside; the covers had been changed to pristine white cotton and broderie anglaise and the walls had been repainted in soft lilac, but I recognised it as mine and embraced its familiarity. My old indie band posters and line-drawings were gone; replaced by framed press-clippings and theatre posters of Vivienne as a young prima ballerina. I wrinkled my pierced nose in disdain, remembering how beautiful Mother was, and how vain. Vivienne's long black hair was bound tightly in the images - flawless. How many times had I wanted to strangle her with that hair? I rubbed my head and snorted. Lifting the pictures of Vivienne off the walls, I stacked them together in the wardrobe, before taking off my Doc Martens and curling up in bed, fully dressed and, as always, ready to run.

5

'Nanny. No don't go. Don't leave me ...'
I woke with a start. My head jerked from side to side as I looked around the room, trying to remember. Sitting up, I felt the soft bed beneath my legs. The room was brightly lit, in spite of the still drawn curtains. I recognised my childhood chest of drawers. Everything came rushing back and I started to cry.

Not willing to be weak for long, I reached inside my bag and drew out a five inch blade, sheathed in black leather. Part protector, part controller: a replacement parent. The cut I made across my forearm was short and shallow, but enough to calm me.

Pain always calmed me: the explosive pain in my jaw when a police shield hit me or the pain of binding my body, altering it to reflect how I felt on the inside. The agony of watching people I loved get hurt, move away, die, all of these disconnected me from my thoughts, thoughts that hovered in waiting whenever I felt a move towards contentment or self-acceptance, thoughts I wasn't strong enough to face. Two steps forward, one step back.

The modern bathroom, full of perfumed soaps and expensive shampoos, offered me the first hot shower I had experienced in months. I thought about my arrival the day before. Part of me felt trapped, pushed into coming here by my brother. While the other part felt curious, eager to meet my niece and Tomas's wife. The hot, running water was definitely a bonus, but I wasn't certain I could stay for long. I would meet my brother's family, poke my head around the door to Vivienne's ward then return to London. I didn't feel I owed Mother anything.

Gradually, the stroking of my soapy hands over my body, tracing scars across my arms and thighs, calmed me. I stepped out of the shower and dried myself roughly with a large white towel, wincing as it rubbed against bruises. I replaced the bandages around my chest and put on a clean t-shirt.

I sauntered into the kitchen. Finding a jar of instant coffee, I made a bitter tasting cup, rolled a cigarette, smoked it and decided to use some of Tomas's money to go grocery shopping.

The local grocer's was quiet and I bought the few items I needed, quickly. I glanced up and saw a wiry, blond man walk past the shop window. His long hair was unbrushed. I couldn't see his face, but he seemed familiar. The checkout girl coughed, attracting my attention and I scowled at her. Paying the glossy, impatient girl, I grabbed my bag of shopping and hurried after the man.

In spite of his relaxed gait, I had to run to catch up with him. As I got closer, I noticed his feet were bare and caked in mud. Needing to jog to keep moving at his pace, I tried to ignore the pain of the shopping bag slamming against my leg; tins of baked beans dug into my calf each time it hit me. Adjusting my hold on the bag, I was distracted for a moment and lost sight of him.

I raced to the next corner, hunting for him. Light traffic whipped by at a steady pace. I studied the signposts: Redland Crescent and Clifton Road. I remembered the parents of a school friend had a big old house on Clifton Road and wondered whether they still lived there then checked myself. What would I say to them?

I looked around, but the man had gone. I balled a fist and shook the shopping bag aggressively. A low, frustrated growl rumbled in my chest. Across the road, I spotted a rank of shops - a post office, a hair dresser called Top Style, a purple fronted shop bearing the legend Healing Ways, a greengrocer and a chip shop. Intrigued by the purple shop, I picked my way through a break in the traffic and across the road. Crystals, in the shop window, caught and refracted light into a myriad of dancing rainbows, self-help books nested below them between stacks of tarot cards. I noticed an advert stuck behind the glass: "Crystal healer, medium and clairvoyant - Vivienne Nightingale." A mobile number was listed below her name.

I sighed. Everything always came back to Vivienne. I walked inside the shop, just to check whether the blond-haired man was inside. A smiling, bald man in a red satin shirt appeared from behind a beaded curtain. I blushed, glanced around the shop then left.

The heavy smell of fish and potatoes frying made my

hollow stomach ache and groan in protest. I rested the shopping bag on the floor and tried to tame my hunger with a cigarette, but it didn't work so I headed back to the house to make lunch.

6

Tucked between the wall and the kitchen table, eating beans on toast, I thought I heard footsteps in the room above - Vivienne's room. At first I assumed it was the sound of old water pipes shaking until I heard the sound again, more clearly than before. Hackles up, I silently put down my cutlery and pulled the knife from my bag. I slipped off my boots and crept up the stairs.

Portraits loomed over my head. I shrank beneath the weight of their stares. My ears grasped echoes of resentful whispers and I hung my head in shame. Ashamed of what? I couldn't remember, not really, perhaps it was purely that I wasn't more like her.

I faced her door, shaking with fear, expecting her to rush out at any moment, screaming my name or slapping my face. I concentrated on my breathing, trying in vain to calm down. I was grown up now. She couldn't hurt me anymore.

Mastering my fear, I opened her bedroom door and inspected the empty room. Vivienne's huge bed crouched in the corner like a monster ready to pounce. Shadows lingered at the edges, a dark audience to mother's regular performances. The air smelt stale. It reeked of old perfume, sweat and sex.

I marched to the wardrobe and opened the door. Frills burst forth from its bowels. I moved soft, delicate fabrics and checked behind them. No one lurked there. I pulled back the curtains and opened a window. Sunlight poured through the smeared glass, bouncing off Vivienne's full-length mirror and flooding the room.

Breathing slower now, I sheathed my knife and strolled to the bedroom door. Already the air smelled fresher. I turned around as I reached the hallway, glancing back at the rich fabrics and heavily patterned wallpaper - a true boudoir, a shrine to her pleasure. I sighed and moved to walk away when something caught my eye. Turning back to the room, I watched as the décor altered.

Subtly at first - the colour of the light-shade, a change of carpet then everything looked different. And there was Mother, centre stage, on the bed, naked, legs splayed and mounted by a huge man. Her flushed face fixed on me and I was a terrified ten-year-old girl once more.

'What do you think you're staring at?' Vivienne demanded.

'Maybe she wants to join in,' the oily-voiced stranger suggested.

My body shook. The man didn't break his rhythm as he spoke. His flabby body still pounded between Vivienne's thighs. Mother's eyes looked cold and empty. I shook my head, denying what I saw, and turned away in horror. I fled to my own bedroom, chased by my mother's laughter.

7

After slamming my door, I placed a chair against it and sat down, hyperventilating.

I sat for ten minutes or more, sobbing silently. Still shaking, I stood up and opened my window to breathe. In a replay of years past, I started the mental ritual of packing my things, before realising they were already safe in my backpack. The thought calmed me. I could leave. Tomas would be disappointed, I wouldn't meet my niece and I might always wonder whether Vivienne had ever loved me, but I could go. I had power now, the choice was mine, and she could not stop me. Two steps forward, one step back - it was my dance and I trusted it not to fail me.

Recognising the shift in power adulthood had brought, I dried my tears and sat on the edge of the bed. Gradually my heartbeat slowed and the painful pounding in my chest, dissipated. I considered the pros and cons of heading home. I could tidy up, close the windows and curtains once more, lock the doors, and leave. I could keep the house keys and phone with me. Tomas would ring when he arrived at the house this evening and found me gone. I could try to make him understand, reach beyond those emotional blinkers. The remaining grocery money might be enough to pay for a bus ticket home. I wondered whether I should take a walk to the bus station to see.

Bus stations - I remembered the first time I had arrived at one. I was thirteen and the place reeked of urine. I walked, head bowed, past two young men, hovering by the entrance, blowing smoke into the rain. There was a queue at the information window. I glanced through lowered lashes at the other people waiting to travel. A child tugged on her mother's hand, hurrying her to the kiosk for sweets. An Asian family sat on one of the benches; the father spoke loudly, not in English. His family seemed mesmerised by his every word. Entranced, I remembered standing and watching them, until the man noticed me and frowned.

The bus fare was too expensive and I needed to beg for more coins. I wondered what I would do and where I would sleep once I reached London. The motorway was just a short walk from the bus station, but I dismissed the idea of hitch hiking; the thought of being so close to an unknown man for hours terrified me. Instead I headed towards the shopping centre to beg as a pervasive drizzle replaced the rain. Pigeons swooped overhead as people rushed past, never quite touching me. Chilled air moved between us, causing the hairs on my arms to stand on end. At that moment I realised I was, and would always be, completely alone.

Six years later I knew that would never change. Being alone was part of who I was. I could be alone here as easily as I could be alone in a squat in London. Without returning to Vivienne's room to close her window, I left the house and walked aimlessly, until I reached a park then wandered over grass and between trees before sinking onto a bench, watching the empty swings.

The ringing phone startled me.

'Hey Giz, where are you?'

I frowned. *Crow and fuck you!* But instead of articulating my thoughts I simply answered. 'Westville Park.'

'Oh, okay. See you in thirty minutes.'

Tomas hung up and I was left alone with my thoughts once more. I stared at my grubby combats, withdrawing deep inside myself and only looking up again when I heard my brother's quick footsteps.

'What's wrong, Giz?'

I shook my head. 'What do you think?'

He stared at me blankly.

'Okay, first you refuse to acknowledge I shed that name years ago. What gives you the right? Then you abandon me in the place I hate most in the world. What were you thinking, Bro?' I turned from him and stared at the ground between my knees. 'Nothing in the house seems real. I see ...' I rocked myself as I struggled to find the right word. 'Ghosts.'

Tomas's eyes flashed and his face reddened as he clenched and unclenched his fists. He sat quietly for a moment. 'You haven't even seen Mum yet.' He looked up at the clouds then turned to face me. 'Cathy's made dinner for us ... Melissa's excited to see you.'

I didn't tell him I'd seen far more of our mother than any

child would find comfortable. Instead, I nodded and followed him to the car park, wondering when I had become submissive.

Tomas's house was smaller than Mother's. It stood on a modern estate not far from Vivienne's cottage, surrounded by communal greens and as Tomas pulled up outside, an auburn haired woman, holding a flame-haired infant, opened the front door.

I climbed out of the car and rushed to see them. 'Cathy, she's beautiful.'

Tomas's wife smiled. 'Come on, you two; the spaghetti's getting cold.'

The front door led straight into a large sitting room, dominated by a huge television. White walls were covered in family photographs and a large oil painting of Brunel's famous bridge. Wooden floors were polished and clear of clutter. A square, pale wood table protruded from beneath the staircase. It had been set for dinner with woven navy place mats, large wine glasses and carefully folded napkins.

Catherine carried spotless white plates full of food through the kitchen door and placed them on the table. Her Italian speciality had been adapted, at Tomas's suggestion, for me with a Quorn mince base. The food was delicious and it felt good to be part of a functional, loving family for a few hours.

8

'Thank you, Cathy. The food's lovely,' I told her.

She blushed. 'It's just something I threw together. It's a bit drier than usual though. Different mince I guess.'

'It's great, babes,' Tomas said, nodding. 'Not dry at all.'

Catherine frowned and took a large sip of wine. 'I don't normally drink,' she explained.

'Oh?' I asked.

'Breast-feeding.'

I nodded. 'Of course. Melissa is beautiful. She looks so big and strong.'

'She's already moving about,' Catherine said, proudly. 'We've had to cover all the spare sockets. She's way ahead of the other babies.'

I smiled. 'I can tell.' Truthfully, I had no idea. Vivienne and I had never spoken about babies and as the youngest child, I had no experience, but it seemed like the right thing to say.

'Do you plan to have any?' Catherine asked.

I coughed and a mouthful of wine burned my oesophagus. I shook my head, trying to catch my breath. Catherine looked disappointed.

'You okay, Giz, sorry Cr ...?' Tomas asked.

I nodded. My face was burning and my eyes were damp.

'I'm fine,' I croaked.

'We've been talking about having another. Haven't we, Tomas darling?'

Tomas nodded. 'The house is a bit too small, though,' he said.

'Why don't you move into Vivienne's?' I asked.

'Don't even try,' Catherine answered. 'I've asked the same question a thousand times.'

'Mum won't be in hospital forever,' Tomas said.

Catherine shrugged.

'How is she?' I asked.

Tomas's eyes darkened. 'You'll see her tomorrow. She'll be fine. She just needs a bit of peace and quiet. You know Mum.'

'Not really,' I whispered.

'Did you tell ...' Catherine frowned and looked at me for a moment, ' ... her what happened?' Her voice sounded sharp.

The words made me uncomfortable, but I was sure that hadn't been Catherine's intention.

Tomas flinched. 'Sure.'

'I know she had an accident,' I said.

Catherine laughed. I looked at her and she turned away but not before I caught a hint of malice in her icy eyes.

'I should settle Little Missie for the night.' She stood up and lifted Melissa from her rocker beside the table. The baby was fast asleep and didn't make a sound. I expected Tomas to tell Catherine to wait until she finished her dinner, but he continued to eat in silence. I looked from one to the other, confused, but decided not to pass comment.

'How's work?' I asked Tomas, after Catherine climbed the stairs.

'Great. Top salesman almost every month.'

I smiled. 'Well done, Bro.'

'What are you doing?'

'This and that. Portraits mostly.'

'Does it pay?'

'I don't need much.'

He sighed. 'You know you'll have to grow up at some point, Sis.'

'This sis thing, it kinda bothers me, you know?' I blushed and concentrated on my food.

'Not really. What do you mean?'

'I ... I don't identify as female.'

'Huh?'

'Have you heard of gender-queer?'

He shook his head. 'Is it okay, you know, if we don't have some deep and confusing discussion about this shit right now? You know with Mum and ...' He sighed.

This shit? One step forward, two steps back. I stared at him coldly, trying to control my breathing, but he didn't seem to notice. I wanted to rage at him, tell him how his dismissal of me and my identity made me feel, but I saw a tear glisten in the corner of his eye and forgot my words. He still needed me. I was his rock and a rock cannot change, not in his eyes. I watched as he brushed the tear away with the back of his hand and sniffed. We sat silently for the rest of the meal as I tried to figure out the least confrontational way to explain myself to him.

Five minutes later, as Tomas and I cleared our plates, Catherine returned. She took our empty plates and her half-full one into the kitchen.

'Can I help?' I asked.

'Don't worry, we have a dishwasher. Would either of you like some apple pie?'

'I'm full, thank you,' I said.

'You're skin and bones, Giz. Eat something. Grow some breasts.' Tomas laughed.

I stared at him, hating him, imagining my eyes were daggers. 'What the ...'

'Tomas!' Catherine shouted.

'What?' he asked.

'What? Ummm, could you be any more rude, you asshole? I don't even know where to start with how wrong that was,' I said.

'Hey! What did I do wrong now?'

'You don't talk about women's breasts,' Catherine said. 'Especially not your sister's and especially not when she's sat right next to you. What are you thinking?'

Tomas shrugged. 'I was just saying.' He looked grumpy as he took another sip of wine.

I stared at them both, helplessly. Why was it so difficult to communicate with either of them? I wished for some shared language that might unite us and make them understand. In the end I sighed sadly and shook my head in resignation. 'Well, don't,' I simply said.

Catherine shot me an apologetic smile. I took my wine glass and headed for a comfortable looking arm chair. Catherine put a bowl of apple pie and a jug of cream next to Tomas and walked across towards me. 'Coffee?' she asked.

'No, the wine's great, thanks. Don't let me stop you though. Oh, I'm sorry. Is it okay if I sit here and wait until you guys finish?'

'Of course,' she said and returned to the kitchen.

I watched my brother's back as he ate. Sometimes he could be so blind, so self-absorbed, especially where I was concerned.

When they finished their meal, Catherine and Tomas settled onto the sofa opposite me.

'Can I ask you something?' Catherine looked nervous. Fingers twitched beside her face.

'Sure,' I said, worried.

'What happened to your cheek? That bruise. It looks painful.'

'Ahhh,' I said. Two steps forward, one step back.

'Yeah, I noticed it too. Did some guy hit you?'

'Not exactly. Did you see anything about the Brixton uprising on the news?'

'Yeah. It was about evictions, right?'

'I was there. A pig whacked me with a shield. It's a bit sore still, but I'm healing.'

Catherine and Tomas sat in silence. Their mouths

opened and closed as if they were mimicking fish faces. I found their reaction amusing and had to stifle a laugh.

'It's nothing, honestly.'

'Were you arrested?' Catherine asked.

I shrugged. 'It was nothing.'

Tomas sighed. His face was full of disappointment. 'I'm feeling tired. Shall we turn in for the night?'

Catherine glanced at her watch. I could see by the clock on the wall it was only nine-thirty.

'Shall I set up some blankets for you on the couch?' Catherine asked. 'Or should we call a cab to take you home?'

Home? I thought of London for a moment - the friendly faces, the shared language, the smell of spirits and narcotics and the sounds of laughter and free love. My mind returned to my shadowy childhood abode. That was where she meant, wasn't it? 'I'm happy to stay here, if it's no bother.'

'Of course it isn't.' Catherine smiled and headed upstairs, returning a few minutes later with a duvet and pillow. 'I'm sorry we're such early sleepers. You know ... the baby and all? It can get tiring sometimes.'

Tomas stood up and kissed Catherine's cheek. 'Goodnight,' he said.

'Goodnight,' I replied and waved to them.

When their feet disappeared out of sight at the top of the stairs, I unfolded the duvet, switched off the light and settled down on the couch.

9

That night I dreamed of a stag, charging through a forest, darting, with fluid movements, around every tree. I chased it and kept it in my sights, but couldn't reach it. Suddenly, it stopped and I crashed into its warm and musky flanks. It reared up and its hind legs became its only legs, its forelegs were strong arms. It turned to face me and its muzzle changed into the face of the blue-eyed man. He kissed me before I could pull away. His lips were like knives. They tore at my skin, exposing all I was so desperate to hide.

10

(Bristol, England - 2001)

I struggled out of the bathroom, my arms full of what were once white bath towels and were now covered in blood.

My brother was shivering outside his bedroom door. His face was so pale and round that he looked like the full moon as he stared up at me from his seated position.

'Sit with her, Tommy,' I said, trying to give him my most reassuring smile. 'Try to keep her calm while I get cleaned up.'

He stared at me then slowly shook his head. I sighed. The bundle was getting heavy and I didn't know how much longer I could keep doing this. None of the other girls at school had to take care of their mothers and their big brothers. The limit of their responsibilities tended to be tidying their rooms once a week. Why me?

'Please ...' I begged.

As he stood up the smell of blood must have hit him full force and his white skin turned green. He ran, away from me and away from the bathroom, out of the apartment door, not waiting to close it behind him.

'At least let Nanny know what's happened,' I called after him, not certain whether he heard or cared what I'd said.

I tried to rearrange the bundle so I could shut the front door. I must have tightened my hold on the sodden cotton; blood oozed onto the skin of my right forearm. I swallowed hard and told my stomach to behave. Tears rolled down my face as I made my way towards the kitchen and dropped the towels into the large aluminium sink. I turned on the tap and water rose above the fabric, strings of pink swirling through the fluid.

I washed my arms, scrubbing them clean while Vivienne's wails became louder. Then grabbed fresh towels, dark ones this time, from the airing cupboard and returned to the bathroom.

Beside the bath, crouched Vivienne. The dressings I'd wrapped around her wrists had already reddened. I sat beside her and pressed clean towels over the dressings. She stopped crying and stared at me.

'It's okay, Mummy,' I assured her. 'Tom's gonna get Nanny.'

As I gently rocked her body back and forth she stared at my face. Her eyes were blank and I wasn't sure she knew who I was. I could sympathise, half the time I didn't feel like her seven year old daughter, either. I guess I had to grow up fast.

11

(Bristol, England - 2007)

I returned to the bus station with time to spare. Shivering, I cursed leaving without a jacket or any change of clothes. I pictured my personal effects, still strewn across my bed and growled, letting my hatred for my mother surface. I allowed it to grow for a few minutes before pushing it back into the box in the pit of my stomach, which I had crafted over the years to contain it. A tear pricked my eye and I brushed it away. I was thirteen; there was no place in my life for childish tears.

I stood under the square archway and watched dark clouds puff up their bodies in sympathy with the rapid growth I must now make. Knowing I was unlikely to return to this city, I felt the sting of guilt and regret. I never got the chance to say goodbye to Tomas.

On the coach, I sat alone. Fields and houses, lakes and factories, towns and cities whizzed past. The expected feelings of lightness and release did not come.

The coach arrived at Victoria at eight o'clock. The London sky looked empty, other than sickly yellow haloes cast by street lamps. With nowhere to go, I purchased a coffee in a paper cup from a vending machine and sat on a moulded plastic seat, planning to wait until daylight before exploring the capital.

I must have fallen asleep. Angry shouting woke me and I looked around, confused. At first I couldn't see the source of the noise then I spotted a group of men and a woman tussling at the other end of the building. I turned away and hoped they would leave me alone.

The sky looked black, beyond the confines of the shelter. No stars penetrated the gloom. I sighed and wrapped my arms tighter around my body, hoping this night would soon be over and my life could begin.

One of the rowdy men ran past me and through the exit. The woman and another man chased him, shouting. Their slurred voices made it impossible for my tired brain to translate their cries. I imagined he was a thief and they were attempting to catch him and bring him to justice. Or maybe they were running to grab him, hurt him, for something he had said or done that had caused some offence, just as Vivienne had chased me up the stairs to my bedroom door when I spoke out of turn and I would cower, behind the fragile wood barrier, until she stamped off, cursing the day I had been born.

I glanced over my shoulder and saw another two men, still standing at the spot from where the three had fled. One appeared to be nursing his arm while the other paced back and forth, clearly agitated. I hunched my back and tried to make myself as small as possible.

Eventually the two men sauntered past and out of the building. I heard the roar of a floor polishing machine. The sound became louder as the cleaner moved across the building towards my spot and the exit. Suddenly, the noise ceased.

'Are you okay?' a man asked.

I nodded, not making eye contact.

'Where do you live?' I heard footsteps as he approached.

I shook my head. My mind begged him to just leave me alone. A few more hours and I could leave this dump. I wouldn't be his problem, not unless he made me into one.

'How old are you?'

I looked at him. He must have been in his forties or fifties. His face was pock-marked, but his eyes and smile looked kind.

'Do you speak English?' he asked.

I glanced down at my brown hands and made fists in my lap.

'Look, you can't just stay here. Do you have anywhere to go?' he spoke slowly and carefully.

When he received no reply he told me to, 'Stay here,' and walked away towards a door, half way along the wall. He was probably going into an office to discuss me with his boss, or even more likely, phone the police. As he disappeared through the door I ran out of the bus station and into the early morning gloom.

The traffic was heavy. Headlights bounced over speed bumps and uneven surfaces. Black cabs, and small cars stopped and started as they inched along busy roads. I guessed it must be nearly morning. Perhaps people were already travelling to work.

With no idea of direction, I turned right, crossed the road and took a left at the next main junction. I wanted to put some distance between me and the cleaner so I walked quickly. My skin prickled with goose bumps, but at least the air was dry. I watched as bearded men in thick coats folded blankets and stood up from their doorway shelters.

Chains rattled and shutters groaned open in front of a yellow café door. I waited for a few moments, before heading inside.

'Good morning,' said the assistant as he stepped behind the counter, hung an apron around his neck and tied it at the waist. 'What can I get you?'

'Tea, please.'

'Milk?' he asked.

I nodded.

'Take a seat and I'll bring it across. You look cold. Don't worry, the heating's on. It'll soon warm up in here.'

I smiled, nodded and made my way to a grey table. I played with ketchup packets while I waited for my drink. It didn't take long.

'Eighty pence, please.'

I grabbed some coins from my pocket and counted out eighty pence. I passed it to him and his fingers brushed against mine. I dropped the money and recoiled from his touch. They clattered on the table and one fell onto the floor.

'Sorry,' he said, picking them up.

The steam rolling from the pale grey tea was welcoming. I eyed the man suspiciously as he returned to his place behind the counter. I wondered whether he had meant to touch me. Was he like the rest of them? Did he hope to charm the dark-eyed girl? Were women his own age not to his liking? I kept looking across, but he wasn't watching me. He busied himself cleaning between the customers who arrived for take-away teas and coffees.

When I finished my drink, I left without a word.

The sky looked lighter and, if possible, the traffic seemed heavier than ever. People in business suits hurried past. The air smelled of diesel, masked every few moments by a nasal assault of heady perfume. I walked to a junction and looked at the sign posts, feeling completely lost. A blonde woman stood in a doorway, smoking. She looked young, sixteen probably, and was wrapped in a wool coat covered in streaks of black grime. I watched her for a while as she put out one cigarette and lit another; her eyes followed the people who marched past and I wondered whether she was waiting for someone.

I wanted to approach her, but felt too shy. I just stood there, watching as the morning sun rose above the tall buildings and painted her hair orange. It looked the shade of my Nanny's before she died although Nanny's was from a bottle, not the blush of dawn, it made me feel safe and familiar all the same. I took a step toward her, paused, nodded to myself then strode along the pavement without hesitation.

'Hi.' My voice was a mere squeak. It was amazing she heard me at all.

She turned to face me and smiled. 'Hi.'

'I wondered ...'

'Yes ...'

'Do you have any idea where I can find a bed for tonight?'

Her eyes washed over me, head to toe then back up again. Her smile fell as she reached out and gently touched my arm. I stepped away and she blushed.

'I'm sorry,' she said. 'I didn't mean to frighten you.'

I shook my head and turned to walk away.

'Wait,' she said.

I blinked tears from my eyes and kept walking. I heard her behind me. Her breath sounded ragged, presumably from the cigarettes. 'Please wait,' she said. 'I promise I won't touch you again.'

I stopped. She walked past me and turned so we were face to face. 'I understand,' she said. 'And I know where you can get a bed for tonight and as many nights as you need. Give me half an hour and I'll take you there.'

I smiled. I wanted to say thank you, but the words wouldn't make the journey from my throat to my lips, so I simply nodded and followed her back to the doorway.

12

(2013, Bristol, England - 2013)

I heard movement and opened my eyes to see my brother standing above me, smiling.

'Good morning, Bro,' I said, squinting.

'Good morning, sleep well?'

'Like the dead.' I pushed myself to seating position and stretched my arms above me.

'Want breakfast?'

'What time is it?' I asked.

'Seven.'

'So early.'

'Well, I wanted to go to the hospital before work. That way I could drop you back at the house and catch up at the office this afternoon.'

'Sure thing. Just coffee and a cigarette for me though.'

'You'll need to smoke it outside,' he said.

'I remember.'

'I'll bring your coffee out into the garden, shall I?'

'You call that a garden?'

'Patio, then. Whatever. At least it isn't a bloody jungle.'

I nodded and shrugged. 'Okay, I deserved that. So have you forgiven me?'

'For what?'

'For whatever pissed you off so much last night you had to go to bed at half-nine.'

Tomas smiled. 'Yes, I forgive you. I sometimes forget, that's all.'

'That we're so unalike?'

'Yeah. I guess so.'

'Well, big brother. It's a cross we have to bear.'

I grabbed my tobacco and papers from my bag, rolled three cigarettes, stood up and made my way to the kitchen door then out into the garden.

The air was warm. I imagined it would get hot later. I coughed then lit my first cigarette. I was half way through it when Tomas emerged with a steaming mug of black coffee. 'Thank you.'

'No problem ... ummm, Crow. Bring it back when you're finished.'

I nodded and smiled. 'Thank you.'

Three cigarettes and two cups of coffee later, I agreed to go with Tomas to see Vivienne.

Vivienne was staying at Oakwood. It took us thirty minutes to reach the hospital. The green gates were flanked by a dark, Harrods-green sign and an elegant Georgian stone villa. A barrier blocked the entrance. Waiting in silence for the guard to approach the car, I avoided Tomas's eyes. A uniformed guard spoke to Tomas through the open window and raised the barrier.

Speed bump after speed bump tested the car's suspension, and I felt as though we were on the lamest fairground ride ever. We followed the driveway, searching for a parking space. In spite of the early hour, we almost reached the exit before finding one large enough to accommodate the Volvo.

The hospital, on this side, consisted of single storey red brick wards, separated from each other by grey-slab pathways. The blue sign to Vivienne's ward was easy to spot. The noble oak trees that lined the small courtyard did little to detract from the obvious signs of security: the barred windows of reinforced glass and the heavy doors. Tomas pushed a button to announce our arrival and a loud buzzer informed us the door was unlocked. I glanced at the camera as I passed beneath it.

Behind a reinforced window sat the receptionist in her crisp pink uniform. Her soles squeaked as she shuffled her feet under her desk. She smiled, but her eyes did not reflect the changing shape of her mouth. As I looked at the woman's joyless eyes I felt a violent shiver rush down my spine. We were buzzed through two more doorways, glazed this time, and onto the ward itself. We passed a room where four women sat, watching television. The programme was completely unfamiliar, but it looked like a cheap pulp-romance. After passing through two doors, which we unlocked by pressing a button, we entered a room with six metal beds. Unable to see Vivienne in any of them, I followed Tomas to the second bed on the right.

The bed was raised at the head end, suggesting the occupier was conscious and alert. There were no sheets, but two leather bracelets were attached, one on each side at wrist position. The straps hung open on either side of the slumbering woman. The woman's hair looked lank and the black was shot through with streaks of white. It rested in a parody of gentle waves on her narrow shoulders. Her skin had the colourless hue of the dead, appearing like a heroin addict, lying there, nodding off. The smell of urine was overpowering and my eyes stung as ammonia saturated them. Tomas approached the sleeping figure and touched her hand. The woman's grey eyes flickered open. There was no look of recognition in them.

'Hi Mum,' Tomas said, leaning close to the pale, waxy face. 'Giselle's come to see you.'

I watched as he beckoned me, transfixed and still unable to recognise Vivienne. With an irritated sigh Tomas stood up, grabbed my hand and pulled me closer to the bed.

'Hi.' My voice trembled as I waved my free hand at the unrecognisable woman. How could she have changed so completely in just six years? If this wasn't some cruel joke, if this really was Vivienne, where were her beauty, her strength and her fire?

'Is this Vivienne?' I whispered to Tomas. This woman's grey eyes looked small, watery and weak. She couldn't be our mother. He nodded and a tear gathered in his eye. Turning to face the shadow in the white nightgown, I spoke again.

'Vivienne? Mum ... I've come to see you.' There was no response. I stared at Tomas in frustration.

'Giselle?' a weak, female voice rasped.

I poured Vivienne a glass of water from a plastic, lidded jug beside the bed and passed it to her. The woman's weak hands couldn't grasp it, so I held it to her mouth, the poisonous mouth that had so often derided me, and tipped it so Vivienne could drink. Not seeming to notice her nightgown was soaked through, the woman's eyes tried to focus on my face.

'Giselle, is it you?'

I nodded. 'But it's Crow now.'

She didn't seem to hear. 'Thank God. I wanted to tell you something ... what did I want to say?'

'It doesn't matter. I'm okay.' My voice and hands shook.

The woman closed her eyes. I heard a gentle snore vibrate her nose and mouth. I looked at Tomas and handed him the glass of water. Tears gathered in my eyes. I shook my head.

He went to grab my hand again, but I ran across the ward and called to be let out. There were no buttons on this side of the doors. Each time I had to knock and call until someone arrived with keys.

I sprinted out into the fresh air of the courtyard. Sitting beneath an oak tree, with my back pressed firmly against the trunk, I reached for my cigarette tin then remembered where I was and thrust it back into the depths of my bag.

Tomas walked across the grass towards me.

'I had no idea. She looks so old,' I said, shaking my

head.

'The hospital's no good for her. They should let us take her home.'

'The accident ...' I said then let my words drift into silence.

He looked away at the redbrick walls of the ward.

'What really happened?'

'They say she's mad.' A perfectly spherical tear rolled down his cheek and dripped from his jaw.

I couldn't think of anything to say. Instead of saying something stupid, I chewed on my knuckle.

'She isn't crazy. Whatever the white-coats say, but they won't let her out.'

'I'm sorry,' I said.

'I hoped, you know. If she got to see you ...'

'Is she dying?'

'Of course not.'

'What then?'

His shoulders shuddered and I heard a few deep, strangled sobs escape before he cut them short. 'She tried to kill herself.'

'Again?'

He looked at me. His eyes flashed with fury. 'This time she was found.'

Tomas frowned at me then turned and walked away, towards the car. I followed him, jogging to keep up with his long strides. We didn't speak in the car. The CD player spurted out track after track of melodic metal tunes to fill the uncomfortable silence. I stared through the window at rows of houses gliding by. When we reached Vivienne's house Tomas was eager to leave. He could barely look at me. I asked when I'd see him again, but he just shrugged and looked at the steering wheel. One step forward, two steps back.

'Tomorrow?' I asked. 'Can you come here, to pick me up, or I could cook?'

He nodded and switched the engine back on.

'Call me!' I shouted as he drove away.

13

'Crow!'

The musical tones of her voice broke my reverie. I looked towards the house and saw her standing there. Her blonde dreadlocks were swept off her face and held behind a red scarf. Her ivory blouse clung to her chest and a huge floral skirt hung from her hips.

'Chrissie!' I squealed, running towards her. 'What are you doing here?'

'I got your note and thought you might need my support.'

'I really do.'

'Why didn't you say goodbye?'

'I didn't know how.'

'Well now you won't have to.' She smiled. 'So this is it?'

'Yes, this is it.'

'I expected something with towers and barred windows.'

'She didn't need those.' My laugh was brittle.

'So ... are you going to open the door, or are we camping out here?'

I sighed and fed the key into the lock, opening the door to Vivienne's house, seemed as painful as ever. The darkness was oppressive as it surged out from the hallway to embrace me.

When we stepped inside, Chrissie's excitement seemed inappropriate, almost farcical. I watched her skip and run about the hallway, behaving as if she was in a Famous Five adventure, bounding like a frisky puppy through doors I had not yet dared to open.

'Chrissie! For fuck's sake, calm down.'

'Sorry. This house is massive. Does your mum ... I mean ... Vivienne, live here alone?'

'Guess so; most of the time.'

'How does she afford it?' Chrissie span round, eyeing the large hallway open-mouthed.

'It was Nanny's.'

I looked around me, trying to see the scene through my friend's eyes. I remembered playing with Tomas, in this hallway, on rainy afternoons, wearing roller-skates or riding scooters, with dolls or toy cars. The memory hid from me; I could see the edges of it, but couldn't tease it open. My brain cramped with the effort, but the hall looked just as dark and menacing as before.

Chrissie wandered into the living room. 'Phoar, it smells a bit in here. It's amazing though. Crow, look, she's got loads of crystals, so many they make the light dance.'

'Have a good look round, Chrissie.' I sighed. 'I'll make us a brew.'

Without needing to be asked twice, she leapt up the staircase, taking two steps at a time. I listened to footsteps above me, again.

'Found my room,' Chrissie shouted down the stairs.

'I've never seen such a big bed.'

I headed upstairs. Chrissie was sitting at the end of Vivienne's divan, bouncing happily.

'Unless this is your room, of course. Is it, Crow?'

I shook my head. 'It's Vivienne's.'

'Do you think she'd mind?'

'Who cares?'

She rushed across to me, arms open. She stopped mid-flight and blushed. 'Sorry. I'm just excited.'

I smiled. 'At least one of us is. I've made some coffee. Wanna come down?'

'In a minute,' she answered.

After coffee, Chrissie searched Vivienne's room. She didn't tell me what she was looking for, but she amassed a pile of photos, letters and bank books she placed on the kitchen table where I sat, drinking another mug of coffee.

'There's plenty more. I thought you might wanna look through these first.'

'Why?' I asked her.

'Find a connection, maybe. You know, something to help you understand her, and move on?'

'Chrissie, Vivienne's psychotic and cruel and she doesn't love me. There is no connection.'

'I think you're wrong,' Chrissie patiently replied. 'At least about the love part, look at some of these letters.'

As Chrissie lifted the pile to pull out Vivienne's letters, a photo drifted across the table.

I stared at the image of the blond haired man. 'It's him.'

'Who?'

'The man from my dreams.' I grabbed the photo and turned it over, hoping to see a name.

The back of the photo was discoloured. It had been well-handled and the edges were covered in greasy brown marks, but it bore no name. I turned it over again to look at the picture. The same blue eyes stared out at me. His hair was long, blond and untidy and behind him, I saw a shop front and the name sign - Healing Ways.

'Healing Ways,' I murmured. 'I saw that shop on Clifton Road.'

'Hey, I read something about it in here too,' Chrissie said, rummaging through the pile of papers. 'Ah yes, looks like your ... like Vivienne was working for them. It's owned by a man called Clive Davies; an alternative therapies place, by the looks of it. Wanna check it out?'

I stared at the photo. The hair on the back of my neck stood on end. I had been dreaming about this face and these eyes for years. 'I don't know.'

'Come on. What have you got to lose, and it'll get you out of this place for a while.'

I nodded and tucked the photograph into my pocket. 'You're right.'

We set off. We walked at our usual brisk pace, marching rather than sauntering. Chrissie admired the looming Georgian houses.

'It's lovely here,' she said. 'Much quieter than London.'

'Yes.'

'Have you seen her, yet?'

'Who, Vivienne?' I bit my nails.

'Yes.'

'Tom took me to the hospital this morning. Except, it isn't a hospital, exactly. More a secure mental unit.'

'Oh ... How was she?'

'She didn't recognise me.'

'I'm sorry.'

'Don't be. I didn't recognise her either.'

'Why?'

I paused for a moment. 'She looked empty.'

Chrissie caught my eye. 'I don't understand.'

I felt Chrissie's fingers brush against my arm then she pulled her hand back quickly.

'I don't, either,' I said.

We rounded the corner onto Clifton Road. The sky was blue and the air was full of bird song. Heat reflected off the pavement. Healing Ways nestled discreetly between a hairdresser and a whole-foods grocer in the small, local shopping precinct. A bamboo chime sounded as we opened the glass front door. From behind the beaded curtain, emerged the bald man. A huge white smile contrasted beautifully with his deeply tanned skin and today he wore a bright blue satin shirt.

'Welcome,' he said, beaming. His camp voice sounded musical.

'Hi,' Chrissie answered. 'Are you Clive Davies?'

'In person,' he replied with exaggerated hand gestures.

'I don't think I know either of you ... beautiful ... women.'

Chrissie glanced at me and grimaced by way of an apology then picked up something from the counter. I shrugged.

'This is Crow ... I mean Giselle Nightingale.' Fumbling with a crystal rod, she threw a big smile at Clive. 'And I'm Chrissie.'

'Giselle ... Giselle Nightingale?' He put his hand against his heart. His eyes filled with moisture. 'Giselle, dahling!' He climbed over the counter and rushed towards me.

I backed away, nervously.

He didn't seem to notice my discomfort and grasped my hand. 'What an immense pleasure it is to finally meet you. Vivienne has told me so much about you. I feel I know you already.'

I pulled my hand away, shaking my head. 'Www what has she told you?' I stammered.

'Ah, so much. She's very proud.' He stared at my face. 'But, I suspect you favour your father.'

Chrissie moved towards us and stood by my side. 'You okay, Crow?'

I nodded and took a step back until I was half behind her. Clive's smile fell for a moment before he clasped his hands together and reignited his face with a bright beam.

'Can you tell us about Vivienne?' I asked.

'What do you want to know?' With an air of dramatics he brushed a tear from his eye. 'It's so sad. She's my dearest friend. How I love her. I could talk about her all day ... Giselle, sweetheart, are you okay?'

I shook my head. My head was spinning. 'Crow,' I croaked then shook my head again. 'Sorry. I just need some air; I'll be okay.' I squeezed myself between Chrissie's spine and a display of crystal balls and darted out of the door.

Outside, the air was still and hot. I sank to the ground and looked up at the blue sky; finding it too bright, I looked down again. The air shimmered. The heat created a haze above and around everything.

Chrissie called to me from the door and I asked her for a moment alone. I glanced around and my eyes settled on a high wall to my right. Above it, branches reached for the summer sky and I heard the soft chimes of bells. Shielding my eyes from the glaring sun, I strode, purposefully, towards the wall. Ribbons trailed listlessly from the tree branches; they drew me towards it. The smell of jasmine and sage enticed me closer and I tried to climb the wall, but couldn't find purchase.

The ugly concrete wall blocked my vision. Frustrated, I narrowed my eyes and stared at the pitted greyness. Whether by imagination or magic my determination seemed to temporarily alter the laws of physics. The concrete blocks faded, becoming like mist at first then when the mist cleared I saw through them as though they were glass. The man from my dreams, blonde-haired and shoeless, stood in the garden beyond with his blue eyes fixed on the tree as he tied an orange ribbon to one of its branches. He wore only a pair of grey jogging bottoms, and his chest was bare and pink. He was thin but not emaciated; I could see the hardness of his muscles across his chest and arms. His mouth moved, saying words I couldn't hear then, kneeling, he placed a pebble at the base of the tree.

The scene vanished and I was left touching the rough concrete wall. I tried again to climb it, but it was too high, too smooth and I felt weak with the heat. Unable to see an opening, I followed the wall around a corner, until I reached a dull red-brick council-house. I glared at it, willing myself to stride down the path and knock on the door. I tried to see the rooms behind the windows, but the panes reflected back golden sunshine and I could see nothing beyond. Chewing my little finger nail then scratching my neck, I stood there, staring until I realised I could not approach the house. Instead I returned to Clive's shop to retrieve Chrissie.

Chrissie and Clive were hunched over the counter together, laughing. Typical Chrissie, everyone felt good around her; even I managed to smile in the reflected glow of Chrissie's energy.

'Chrissie,' I called. 'I think I've found him.'

She looked across at me and smiled. 'Cool. Just let me say bye to Clive.'

I walked towards the counter. 'Did you ask him about the photo?'

'No. I'm sorry I forgot. Should I?'

'Photo?' Clive asked. He squinted at me and I wondered

whether he needed glasses.

'I will.' I pulled the creased image from my pocket.

'Do you recognise this man?'

He pulled the photo closer and laughed. 'Of course I do. That's Scott Albion, heart breaker and shaman.'

'Heart breaker?'

'Mine and your mother's, dahling.'

'Were they ... involved?' The word left a bad taste in my mouth.

'She wanted to be. Who wouldn't? He's gorgeous.' Giggling, Clive blushed and looked at the photo again. 'Chasing after him is what caused the poor dahling's breakdown, in my opinion.'

'Does he live near here?'

'Oh yes. You can see his garden wall from the front of the shop. If you go around the corner ...'

'Thank you.' I tugged on the photograph.

Clive looked concerned, but released it with a sympathetic half-smile. I grabbed Chrissie's arm and led her outside.

'I'm sorry,' Clive called behind us.

Chrissie turned and waved. 'Thank you. Have a great day.'

Outside, the heat was relentless. Unable to find shade, we tried to fan ourselves.

'It's way too hot for me.' Chrissie sighed. 'Let's just head for Vivienne's house.'

'No. I wanna knock on his door first.'

'Scott Albion's?'

I nodded and started walking towards the wall. I pointed at the tree. 'On the other side of this wall.'

Outside the red-brick house it felt even hotter. With a sideways glance at my friend, I rang the doorbell. We waited as minutes dragged like hours. Disappointed, we turned to leave then the door opened and, in the shaded hallway, there stood a tall, blond, young man - Scott Albion.

Spinning round to face him fully, I collapsed.

14

(Bristol, England - 2007)

'What the fuck happened to you?' Michael asked as he opened the door.

'Better not to ask.' I looked at the reefer in his hand. 'Roll me one of those.'

He nodded his mostly shaved head and led me inside. The room was full of sour mist. We sat on his bed as he rolled the joint for me. It was a small room, but it was his. No parents, no room mates, his sanctuary and he liked to share it with friends on Friday evenings. He saw me wrinkling my nose.

'Better not to ask,' he said, laughing.

Michael was a stoner, and he was also my best friend. He was the most gentle and natural guy I had ever met. Nothing seemed to phase him. His main, perhaps only, flaw was a distinct lack of personal hygiene. Thankfully today he had decided to bathe and his *The Specials* t-shirt seemed almost clean with just a hint of old yellow stains beneath his arms.

He put his fingers up to the bruise around my eye and whistled. 'Crow ... why are you always so angry. Chill, chérie.'

'I wasn't fighting.' I stood up and pulled a book from his

shelf. 'New?'

He nodded as I stroked the cover. It spoke to me. 'What's it about?'

'Freedom,' he replied. 'Another way to live, man.'

'It was Mum.'

'Huh?'

'I told her she should keep her boyfriends on a leash.'

'She still doin' that shit?'

'I guess it's her addiction, like this is yours.'

'Bah, this ain't no addiction. I'm just unfurling. It's easy to get wound too tight.'

I smiled. 'Can I borrow it?'

'Borrow what, chérie?'

'The book.' I grinned. Sometimes Michael was a genius, but at others, he struggled to keep up with my most basic trains of thought.

'Sure, after I've finished with it.'

I placed it back on the shelf. 'Got any beer?'

'Nah, man. Shit, Crow, can't you settle? You're stressing me out.'

'Sorry. So who else is coming tonight?'

'The usual: Emma, Nick, Abbie ... maybe Chris.'

They were all a few years older than me. Some had jobs and others were students while Michael was between jobs. He always seemed to have enough to get by though and he never charged us for the weed we smoked there. He was a good guy.

'Put some music on, chérie. It might help you relax.'

I wandered over to his hi-fi. Above and around it the shelves were jam-packed with CDs of various genres. I didn't know half of them. I fingered a few spines then pressed play on the sound system. Massive Attack burst through the speakers. Michael nodded approvingly. I didn't have the heart to tell him it was his choice, not mine.

'You don't have to put up with it, you know,' he said.

'It's fine,' I answered, thinking he was talking about the music.

'You are a good girl.'

'I'm not a girl,' I answered, pouting.

'What are you then?'

'Dunno, but not that – what are my choices?'

'Infinite. You can stay here while you think about it, chérie.'

'I can't do that, Michael. Do you have any idea how much trouble you'd be in if a thirteen-year-old was found hiding out in your flat?'

He shrugged. 'Do you have any idea how many shits I give?'

'Thanks, but one of us has to be sensible. If I run I'd better go far away. London, maybe.'

'Tough there in the big smoke. Bad people ready to prey on young ... minds.'

'Bad people at my house too.'

He nodded, frowning. 'And she won't listen?'

'Nah.'

'What about your big brother? What's his name?'

'Tom. He can't see it. I guess they don't bother him. Wrong equipment.'

Michael snorted. 'You even told him?'

I blushed and shifted uncomfortably on the bed. 'What good would it do?'

15

(Bristol, England - 2013)

A cool breeze washed over my forehead and I opened my eyes. In the half-light, I saw two familiar faces smiling down at me. I wondered whether I was dreaming. The man's face soothed me and I drifted happily between the reality of lying on a lumpy sofa in a darkened room and another place, equally real, beneath the boughs of an oak tree, surrounded by fallen leaves of gold and red.

'You fainted.' The warm voice of Scott penetrated my consciousness. 'How do you feel?'

'Fine.' I struggled to sit up, but felt light-headed and heavy-bodied.

His hand hovered an inch from my skin. He smelled of earth and soap, with a gentle base of musk. Feeling like a child in my nanny's arms, I sensed I was safe. In a fluid movement, he moved the air around me from my throat to the crown of my head. I pushed myself into a seated position.

'Drink this.' He passed me a frosty looking glass of water.

With a desperate thirst, I gulped down the cold liquid, hardly pausing for breath. I studied his face, memorising every detail from a small mole at the centre of his shaven chin to the laughter lines around each eye. 'Do I ... do I know you?'

His gentle laughter unsettled me. 'I must have one of those faces.'

'I'm sorry.'

He shook his head. 'Chrissie told me you guys live in London and you're here to see your mum.'

'Huh? How long was I out for?'

'About ten minutes,' Chrissie answered. 'Any longer and we might have called an ambulance.'

Scott rolled his eyes.

'Could I have some more water?' I asked.

Scott took the glass and left Chrissie and me alone in the room.

'He's lovely. If you want to hear all the romantic details, he picked you up in his manly arms and carried you over the threshold.' Chrissie giggled.

'Stop it. You know I'm not interested.'

'Right, course not. Me neither.'

Turning away from her, I noticed the details of the room. The wall opposite had an ugly, bronze-coloured electric fire at its centre. On either side and above this, the wall was covered with chunks of beige and grey rocks which jutted into the room with practised audacity. In small nooks, between some of the stones, nestled cute china unicorns in a myriad of pastel shades. The deep-piled carpet was red with an orange swirling pattern. I felt submerged in dizzyingly 70s kitsch. Wondering what sort of man could tolerate such a room, I lay back on the settee and closed my eyes. Claws pierced my combats and a weight pinned my legs. Startled, I watched as a large reddish-black cat rubbed itself on my shins, purring.

'Ahh, Kitty!' Chrissie stroked its nose.

'Mandala, don't bother our guests.' Scott strode through the door.

Mandala stared at me for a moment then leapt onto the floor. After a few circuits of possessive weaving, between and around Scott's legs, he jogged out of the room, tail held high.

'I'm sorry we disturbed you,' I said.

'Not at all. It's hot outside, maybe you were just dehydrated.'

'Yeah, probably, but what I meant was, just turning up like that.'

'Like what?'

I looked at Chrissie. She shrugged.

'Umm, well we met with Clive, at Healing Ways.'

He cocked his head to one side and sat on the sofa beside my legs. I watched him, silently until he nodded for me to continue.

'My mum had your photo. I'm Vivienne Nightingale's kid, Crow.'

I thought I caught the flush of pink in his cheeks, but he didn't answer.

'Did you know her?'

'Your mum?'

'Yeah, my mum, Vivienne.'

He nodded and sighed. 'How is she doing?'

'I don't think she's doing well at all. Why did she have your photo?'

'I don't know,' he answered. He glanced at a clock on the wall. 'Sorry, I have to cook ... before my mum gets home. If you want, you can come back tomorrow, but I don't know how much help I can be. Clive knows her better than I do.'

'Why don't you come to Vivienne's house tomorrow?' Chrissie asked.

Scott looked hesitant. 'I haven't been there since Vivienne ...'

'What did she do?' I asked.

'Nothing, not really. Guess I should go back, dispel some negative energy.' He paused. 'But I think I might struggle to get there until Monday.'

'Okay, Monday it is,' Chrissie said with an air of finality.

'I'm not sure we'll still be there,' I said. I thought of my backpack, everything packed ready to run. I didn't want to be anyone else's rock. I was a raging river - pushing, rushing.

'Of course we will. Come on Crow, big house, bigger mysteries. We can't leave yet.'

I looked at her and saw her face beneath a heavy boot. Didn't she realise I couldn't be squeezed like that? Movement was my medium, my life blood. No roots. No history. No voices in my head to be pushed away. Silently I told myself I could leave. I could grab my backpack and head ... anywhere. My choices were infinite. Yet standing still ... could that be a choice and if so was it a choice I could make? Two steps forward, one step back.

Chrissie kissed Scott's cheek as we left. I waved and Scott simply smiled. I followed her, placidly, my head bowed and full of turmoil. As we turned the corner Chrissie mouthed the word Mum in disbelief. I shrugged, thinking instead about how I could have dreamed of someone I had never met.

16

(London, England - 2013)

I had spent another night in a cell - disturbing the peace, this time. Apparently moving towards a police officer who is trying to crush your friend's skull with his boot can be deemed as intimidating behaviour, poor piggies.

The squat wasn't far away. I walked the distance even though I felt a sharp pain in my hip every time I climbed steps or stepped on or off the kerb. It was impossible to sleep in a police cell and I felt so tired and sore I had to stop every ten minutes to roll a cigarette.

When I reached the squat everyone was already awake. Chrissie had arrived there a few hours before. They cheered as I walked into the living room and I took a deep bow, wincing with the effort. Apparently, only Chrissie and I had been nicked; the rest had made it out of the affray without arrest. Mitch, Wendy and Si lifted their cans of beer and toasted our return. Matty and Harv disappeared to the kitchen and Chrissie waved weakly from the floor. I grabbed a can of warm beer and gulped it down while my eyelids grew heavier. Exhausted, I lay on the floor alongside Chrissie.

The seven of us had lived together in this dark, damp squat for a little over a year. We were soldiers, idealists and wastrels. It was the closest I'd come to living life as a freedom-fighter, like my father. Sometimes it felt important, but at others I would look at my friends, listen to their inane chatter and wonder whether we were less a bunch of revolutionaries and more a group of children playing at non-conformity. One step forward, two steps back.

Matty and Harv returned to the room and nodded off in the corner, surrounded by burnt silver foil and the sweet smell of death. It sounded as though Mitch was puking in the bathroom again and, from their grunts and groans, I guessed Wendy and Si were at it on the stairs.

I turned around to face Chrissie. She held a pen in her left hand and sucked on her knee with a glazed expression in her eyes. I watched her as she faded in and out, sucking then scribbling in her red notebook. Her long blonde hair was twisted into dreads and a kitsch scarf, with a pink kitten motif, pulled it back from her freckled face. I left her to her thoughts and stared at purple and green islands of bruises on the ocean of my skin. My cheek bone throbbed and I wondered whether the bone had chipped on impact.

Chrissie looked across and smiled. 'My hero.' She closed her notebook and put down her pen.

'I tried, but failed,' I replied.

'I saw the blow. That was cold, Crow.'

I nodded and my cheek throbbed even more.

'Thank you.'

I tried to grin, but the pain was unbearable. 'Ta nada.'

'Looks like you got another letter.' She reached behind her.

I tried to sit up, but failed. 'It'll be from Tom.'

'About Vivienne?'

'Probably. That seems to be his subject of choice these days.'

Chrissie sighed, passing me the envelope. 'Families.'

'Uh, huh.' I turned it over in my hand.

'Will you go?'

I shook my head. 'There's nothing there for me.'

'I know.' Chrissie's voice was soft.

Turning away, I put the unopened letter on the floor beside my head, feeling angry and powerless. First Mum then all these stupid bruises, the arrest and the sleepless night, none of it seemed fair. I wanted to rage, not at Chrissie, but at the world, which had let me down so badly.

'She's a slut-psycho-bitch!' I said suddenly, shocking myself. Did I really feel that way? What right did I have to judge her choices? My body shook. Concentrating on my breathing, I tried to calm myself. 'She hates me.'

I felt Chrissie's hand brush the stubble on my crown then quickly withdraw. 'You know, Crow. Maybe you need to go back ... discover what skeletons lurk behind the stage curtains.' She grabbed my shoulder.

I recoiled and stared at her.

She blushed and let go. 'Sorry.' She shook her head and frowned. 'You can run away from your family, but not from yourself. You'll take your pain wherever you go, until you face your demons.'

I shrugged. 'The only pain I feel is from the beating I got, flower. I know what happened and I'd rather stay far away.'

She snorted but didn't argue the point. Instead she picked up her notepad and pen again. I lay on my back staring at the yellow and black ceiling. This place was a dump.

17

(Bristol, England - 2013)

'Morning,' Chrissie called through the open door.

'Wa, what time is it?' I yawned.

'Eleven. I found some things I want to show you.'

'Huh?'

'Sorry, Crow. Come, have coffee, I'll tell you later.'

I sat up in bed. Flashes from my dream raced through my head. I tried to hold onto them, but only clutched at the edges of fragments. Scott again, or at least his eyes, and a bird soaring beyond his narrow shoulder, a black bird, a crow or a raven, perhaps. I looked for more, but couldn't find it. Squeezing my eyes shut, I sent the memories away and pulled myself out of bed.

I felt Chrissie's eagerness the moment I walked into the kitchen. I accepted the black coffee placed in front of me, rolled and lit a cigarette, and rubbed my eyes with the back of my hand. The coffee was too strong. It coated my tongue as I sipped it, but it helped me shake off a little of the tiredness I felt.

'What were you dreaming about?' Chrissie asked.

'A bird. I can't really remember.'

'You were shouting, "leave him alone."'

'Sorry, Chrissie. Did I wake you?'

She gripped my hand and squeezed. 'It's okay. I'm here for you, sweetie.'

I grimaced. 'What have you found?'

'A stack of your old drawings in Vivienne's desk. I've popped them on the dining table. Come and see.'

The papers were yellowed, creased and had fingerprints around their edges. Most of the pictures were portraits. Amongst the pile there were a few of Tomas; in all of them he was smiling. There were a selection of self-portraits and two of Vivienne – in one she looked beautiful, her dark hair draped around her shoulders and her mouth smiling benevolently; in the other she looked frightening, her mouth twisted, her hair wild and her eyes dark and cruel.

Rifling through them, I discarded the ones of myself and lingered over the two of my mother, remembering each face in turn and how swiftly one could change into the other. Chrissie picked up some of the discarded portraits.

'Have you looked at these?' Chrissie asked. 'There's a hand on your shoulder in three of the four drawings.'

I held out my hand to take them. Looking again I saw large fingers, resting on my shoulder. The nails were closely cropped. The hand looked strong, but it was impossible to tell whether it was holding me in place or encouraging me onwards. I shook my head. The drawings were mine, but I had no recollection of what the hand represented, or even whose hand it was.

'You don't remember?'

'No.'

'I've found loads of stuff: Vivienne's diaries 'n' letters. There's loads about her boyfriends; a little about you and Tomas, basic stuff though, school etcetera, you know.'

'Found anything more recent?'

'Not yet. They don't seem to be filed in any order. I'll get there. She's written loads. Can't imagine she stopped. One thing is weird.' Chrissie raised her eyebrows. 'Her handwriting keeps changing, like the diaries were written by more than one person.'

I pondered this silently while staring, unfocused, out of the window.

'Penny for 'em,' she said.

'Oh nothing.' I glanced back at the two drawings of Vivienne. More than one person, that was true enough. How many people though?

Chrissie gathered up the pictures, leaving the two of Vivienne in my hands. 'I'll keep looking, okay?'

'What are you looking for?' I asked.

'Answers.'

I turned and looked at her blankly then placed the two portraits back on the pile. 'What if there aren't any?'

She shrugged. 'Then maybe you can find peace another way.'

'Should I help? Read the diaries and stuff.'

Chrissie sighed. 'I dunno, Crow. It might be painful, you know? And anyway, if I'm completely honest, I love this stuff: researching people's histories. Honestly, I'm happy to do it.'

I nodded.

'You hungry, Crow? I'll make lunch. Beans on toast or toast and beans?'

I laughed, sarcastically. 'Got a problem with the larder? Then you can do the shopping today.'

She stuck her pierced tongue out at me and I giggled then I was left alone with my thoughts. Did the hand belong to Vivienne? No, it was too large and the nails too short. It frustrated me to find I had no answer.

After lunch, we visited the grocers together. Chrissie waved at Clive as we walked past Healing Ways, but we didn't wait to check if he saw us. On the way back, we walked through the park, smoking and watching children play and young women chat.

'Think you'll ever want that?' Chrissie asked.

'What kids? God no. You?'

She shrugged. 'Almost did once.' She brushed a tear away. 'Mitch and I ... well we've never discussed it and it's not something that will happen by accident for us, you know? S'pose being a good mum would mean settling down ... joining the rat race.' Sighing, she stared at the children. 'No, I can't see us managing that.'

'Hey, maybe you'll get published and have all the money and security you'll ever need.'

She snorted.

Back at the house, we unpacked the lentils, pulses, vegetables and rice. Chrissie started preparing food while I ran a bath. I selected a lavender and rosemary soak and added it to the steamy jet of water. The room filled with its intense scent, making me feel drowsy. The hot water made my legs prickle. Lifting my arms, I surveyed the dark red skin.

I caught the movement of a shadow in my peripheral vision. I turned, but there was nothing there. I lifted my knee and rubbed soap onto my leg.

Something pushed against my shoulder and, before I could react, I was forced under the water. Struggling, fighting for breath, I thrashed my arms and legs under the white foam. Bubbles fled from my lips. My throat burned as did my eyes. I tried to scream, but only released more bubbles. Then, as quickly as it began, the pressure was released. I sat up, gasping for air, looking around the empty bathroom then another heavy pressure, this time on my forehead and I was choking again, on the scalding liquid. My face blistered and my eyes were on fire. Through the searing whiteness, I saw a shape bend above me; its crazed laughter echoed around the bath tub, beating like a drum against my ears.

'Filthy, filthy.' The words were repeated again and again. The room filled with maniacal laughter.

I was drowning and I knew it. Everything went dark then something cold grabbed me and pulled me upwards. I saw the worried face of my mother before I flopped over the edge of the bath, coughing up water. As soon as I had enough strength I pulled myself out onto the bath mat and lay there shaking and coughing until I felt able to drag a towel down from the rail and wrap myself in its warm fibres. 'Mum?'

There was no reply. I pushed myself to my feet and peered over the rim of the bath. A shadow lurked beneath the surface of the water.

'Mum?' I asked again. The shadow became more defined and a teenage girl lay in the bath, not me, her skin was much paler, although her hair was black. 'Is that you Vivienne?'

Eyes snapped open, grey and frightened.

'What happened? Who did ...?'

The image of the teenage girl evaporated. I dropped my towel and submerged my arms into the water, but found nothing.

'Mum! Mum!' I yelled and tore at the chain to pull out the plug. My tears mingled with the draining water.

18

Chrissie looked up from the hob and caught my eye. I stood, shivering, in the kitchen doorway.

'Crow?' Chrissie stared at my naked body. 'You okay?'

I wrapped my arms around my chest and hips, realising she had never seen me naked before.

'I think somebody tried to drown Vivienne.'

'Drown Vivienne? When? She isn't here. She's ...'

'No.' I shook my head, squeezed my forehead between the palms of my hands and closed my eyes, tightly. 'It was a memory, a ghost or hallucination, maybe. I was drowning. I thought I was gonna die.'

'Oh my God!' Chrissie ran towards me.

I let her hug me, fighting the desire to recoil. Her clothes against my skin made me feel vulnerable. I regretted running to her without first strapping my ill-shapen form into its armour.

'Come on. Let's get you dressed. Tell me what happened.'

Supporting my weight, Chrissie led me to my room.

'Something ... pushing my head ... under water, but I knew ... I knew it was really Vivienne and ... it's not the first time. I saw Nanny in the garden too. Chrissie, what's happening to me? Why am I seeing these things?'

'I don't know. Everyone's seen ghosts, Crow. Just some

people don't like to admit it.'

'Or I'm a lunatic, like my mother.' I pulled bedclothes over my flesh, wanting to remove myself from her gaze. I needed clothing.

She touched my arm and I scowled at her fingers. If she noticed my discomfort she made no sign.

'You're not. You're strong. Really you are ... look.' She smiled, sympathetically. 'I'm here for you ... and Scott.'

'What about Scott?' I asked, shaking my arm free.

'You guys have chemistry.'

'Oh, for fuck's sake, Chrissie! Don't you know me at all?'

'Falling in love won't turn you into your mother.'

I growled at her. 'I thought you understood, Chrissie. Shit! You really think that's what it's about? You think I'm afraid I might become my mother!'

'Shhh, sweetheart. I love you.' Chrissie clasped my hand and lifted my fingers to her mouth.

Trembling, I pulled away. My eyes glistened. 'No,' I whispered.

'Close your eyes.'

'No.' My voice was louder this time, more assertive. 'I don't want this.'

'What do you want?'

'I don't know. To be left alone, maybe?'

'You're not an island, Crow.'

'No, I'm not an island. I'm a mountain.'

'Shit.' Chrissie's face turned pale. She stood up from my

bed and shook her head before running out of the door. 'Dinner.'

I lay there for a few moments, thinking. Why didn't Chrissie of all people understand? I'd told her enough times. Oh well, I thought. I guess I'll have to try and explain myself yet again. I sighed, it was exhausting being me. So many people took who they were for granted and anyone outside of that, like me, had a constant struggle against erasure. I got dressed and stumbled down the staircase, still shaking.

Chrissie stood by the stove, the lid of the stew pot in her hand. 'It's okay. Nothing's burned. Here ...' She held out a wooden spoon for me to taste.

I nodded appreciatively and made socially acceptable noises to show her I found it delicious. She grinned and filled two bowls.

The flavours of Chrissie's curry were intense. Spices danced on my tongue as I devoured bowlfuls of vegetable curry, pausing only to smile appreciatively. The room fell silent except for the sounds of eating. Chrissie seemed thoughtful and I was still trying to decide what words to use to explain how I felt, yet again. How sex and romance were things I had never craved. How I couldn't even accept the treachery of my body and its soft curves. How I was not and would never be a damsel in distress, waiting to be saved.

Mozart's Sonata in C, its beauty all but destroyed by the tinny chiming, broke the silence. Shaking myself free from my reverie, I peered through the kitchen door and into the shadowy hallway. It must have been Vivienne's doorbell. I wondered whether it would be Tomas or a door-to-door salesman. When I opened the door, I was greeted instead by Scott.

'Is it okay? I mean are you guys busy?'

I hovered by the door, confused. 'I thought ... Didn't you say Monday? ... Sorry, yeah ... I mean, sure - come in.'

'Hi Scott,' Chrissie called from the kitchen. 'I made curry. Want some?'

'No, thanks. I've eaten ... Is it a bad time? I brought wine.'

'It's never a bad time for wine,' I said. 'I'll find some glasses.'

I led Scott to the kitchen, and asked him to sit at the table. As he entered the room everything seemed brighter, colours more vivid and anything seemed possible. Scott confused my senses, feelings of security and excitement seemed to radiate from him and the air crackled with energy when he was close. Closing my eyes, I forced myself to look away from his face, hunting instead for three wine glasses. When I found them, they were too high to reach. I looked for a ladder and decided instead to use a chair. Without waiting to be asked, Scott arrived at my side. As he reached above me, I smelled his warm, musky scent. Seconds felt like hours until, exhaling, I moved away.

'Your mum okay without you?' Chrissie asked, breaking

the spell.

Scott grinned. He seemed to know he was being teased. 'She's fine. I just like to cook for her, you know, when she gets home from work. It's only fair. After all, living with Mum gives me freedom from financial worries.'

I nodded. 'Gainful employment isn't my cup of tea either. Even so I couldn't live with Vivienne.'

'I think I have some idea why,' Scott replied.

I felt defensive and my eyes prickled. 'Why? Tell me, if you know us so well.'

'Ah, but if I do, you'll pout and deny it. You need to see for yourself. I can help you do that ... if you want, but for tonight let's drink a bottle of wine and smoke a large spliff – the English equivalent of the peace-pipe.'

I felt my face redden. Scott seemed so sure of himself. I wanted to wipe that smile from his face. How dare he feel so clean, so blameless? If Clive was right, this strange, confusing, arrogant man was the reason for Vivienne's mental collapse. Weaving his spell, like a web, around everyone who met him. He shouldn't be so careless with people's emotions.

The desire to flee from him rose inside me. My arm shook as I tried to lift my wine glass. Claret spilled onto my hand. My skin felt sticky. The room seemed to crush against me, squeezing my head and chest. I couldn't breathe. Dropping the glass, I ran out of the kitchen. I heard it shatter and Chrissie's gasp.

I was lying on top of my bed when Chrissie rushed into

my bedroom.

'What just happened?' Chrissie asked.

I stared at the ceiling in silence.

'Why did you do that?'

'Do what?'

'Don't you know? We were drinking with Scott. You smashed your glass and ran up here. Don't you remember?'

I shook my head. 'I don't know.'

'It's okay.' Chrissie voice was soft and soothing. 'It's just been a hard couple of days. That's all.'

'It's more than that, Chrissie. I feel so fucking angry and I'm not even sure I know why. What if I do need to see for myself, like Scott said? Fuck it! I think something in this house is forcing me to see ... to remember ... but I'm scared. Parts of me don't want to remember. I want to forget, forget all of it, flee back to London if necessary.'

She stroked my cheek. Tears ran down my face. 'So London's your bolt hole?'

'I'm sorry,' I said between sobs. 'I don't know what I'm saying.'

She nodded. 'Why don't you speak to Scott? Maybe he can help.'

I shook my head and pushed my body to the edge of the mattress as far from her reach as I could. 'I don't need his help. I'll figure it out. I just need to be alone.'

'Don't be silly. Come back downstairs. Have another glass of wine, sweetie?'

'Nah.' I sighed, knowing it would be that easy for her.

Chrissie found socialising natural.

The way she spoke was the way she wrote, full of grace and humour. I stumbled behind, face hidden. *Please understand, Chrissie, for once, let me hide.* 'I'll read for a bit. Calm myself down.'

Chrissie's lips felt soft and cool as they brushed against my forehead. I forced a smile. When she left I grabbed a book from the well-stocked shelves. I pulled out a well-worn copy of The Unbearable Lightness of Being, and opened it at the first page.

As I reached page one hundred and sixteen, "What was important was the golden footprint, the magic footprint she had left on his life and no one could ever remove," Chrissie reappeared.

Her face looked flushed. I wondered whether Scott and Chrissie had been kissing. I grimaced. What a ridiculous thought. Chrissie was in love with Mitch and Scott wouldn't interest her in that way at all.

'Has he gone?' I asked.

'Yeah.' She let her body drop onto the bed beside me.

'What did he tell you?'

'He thinks your visions are spirits, his word - not mine, trying to get you to face your fears,' she said, blushing. 'He says he can help you – when you're ready.'

'That can't be all he said. You've been talking for hours.'

'Just chatting.'

'About Vivienne?'

'Not really ... Maybe a little. He said something about her trying to initiate herself – I think that was the word he used. He doesn't seem to think her breakdown had anything to do with him though.'

'Does he know she's in love with him?'

'Don't think so, Crow, but hey, do we really know that either? It was just something Clive said. I haven't read anything in her letters or diaries about him yet.'

'Would you look again, for me, tomorrow? Please? I need to know ... if he was ... involved.'

Chrissie frowned and shrugged.

'Don't ask me why,' I begged.

'Okay ... sure. Look, I better get to bed. If you're okay, of course. I really need some zees ... Hey, did you phone your brother?'

I blushed and closed the book. 'I forgot.'

She laughed softly and shook her head.

'I'll do it tomorrow,' I said, yawning. 'It's too late now. Sleep sounds good. G'night, Chrissie.'

'Goodnight, Crow. Sleep well.'

19

Sleep came swiftly. Dark, chilled water surrounded me. Above me I saw a circle of light. Below, giant snake-like reeds reached towards me. The teenage Vivienne, the one I had seen in the bath, swam ahead of me. Her long hair floated around her face like seaweed. She opened her mouth, as if to speak, and bright green bubbles escaped her lips. Scott's face looked down at us from a circle of light at the surface. His mouth opened and shut, like a drowning fish and, although I couldn't hear his words, he looked as though he was trying to tell me something important. Fearful, I dived deeper, into the shadowy depths, brushing past the reeds. Their knife-like edges sliced into my bare skin. Vivienne and Scott vanished, and I tried to rise but couldn't. Tugging and kicking at plants coiled around my ankles, I struggled to break free. Snakes weaved through the aquatic jungle, moving closer and closer. I sat up and gasped, dragging air into my lungs. Sweat chilled my skin as I pulled the duvet that bound my legs.

I rubbed my forehead, stretching the skin upwards with aggressive strokes. The light in the room had a grey pre-dawn softness to it. I paced to the window, clutching my tobacco tin, its rich smell refocused me. The flare of my lighter and the nicotine hit of my first inhalation reminded me of Scott, although I didn't understand why. I considered my dream. Its meaning should have seemed clear, but I fought it. I fought against vulnerability. I didn't want to open myself up, care about Vivienne or Scott. I feared being hurt again.

The hairs on the back of my neck prickled as I sensed someone was watching. I turned away from the window and looked around the room. No-one was there. Turning slowly, I peered out of the window and saw an old woman looking up at me, frowning.

'Nanny?'

I stared at the grey-haired woman, standing just outside the garden gate. The upturned face reminded me of my dead grandmother in the half-light. Afraid to break eye contact, I leaned out of the window. The figure appeared startled and scuttled away behind a neighbouring wall.

The door-chime woke me at ten. My head still full of the echoes of sleep, I lay in bed, listening to male and female voices chat in the hallway below. My room was warmed by the sunlight pushing its way through the curtains. Pulling myself up, I shook the stupor from my brain.

The kitchen door stood open. I heard Chrissie explain to Tomas and Catherine, how delicate I was; they shouldn't push me too hard. Furious, I strode across the hallway.

Tomas turned to face me. 'G'morning, Sis. Sleep well?'

'Sure,' I lied, not wishing to be cross-examined about

the night's events.

'We're going to the hospital again today. Would you like to come with?'

Chrissie passed me a cup of steaming black coffee and a rolled cigarette. I squeezed the roll-up between tight lips and leaned forward so Chrissie could light it. Everyone was watching me.

I inhaled then exhaled. 'Sure.'

20

Vivienne's soft, grey eyes opened as I approached the bed. I offered her a friendly smile that made my skin feel cold.

'Hello, Vivienne,' I whispered.

Tomas nudged my arm. 'Hi, Mum.' His bright smile lit up the room and Vivienne's eyes twinkled in response. 'How are you feeling today?'

'All the better for seeing you, my dear.' A dry cackle escaped her lips. She reached for a plastic beaker beside her bed.

Tomas leaned across me and passed it to her. I shrank back. He tapped my arm and nodded.

'It's okay.'

'Mum, Cathy and Melissa are here.'

'Little Missie. How is my beautiful granddaughter?'

'Getting bigger and brighter every day.'

Vivienne nodded. 'Of course she is. She's a Nightingale.' Vivienne stared at me. Her pupils grew and shrank as she tried to focus on my face. 'I'm sorry, dear. Who are you again?'

'Crow,' I croaked.

Another nudge from Tomas. 'It's Giz, Mum. Giselle.'

Her smile wavered and she nodded. 'You look different.'

'Yes,' I answered. 'I cut my hair.'

'Shaved it, more like. How are you? How long has it been?'

'Six years, Mum.'

Vivienne nodded again. I couldn't read any expression on her face. She turned to Tomas and grinned. 'So what about a cuddle with my granddaughter?'

Tomas passed the pink bundle of flesh bound in cream lace frills and navy velvet across to Vivienne's eager arms. She kissed the top of Melissa's head and breathed deeply. Melissa reached up and tugged her grandmother's nose.

'You are so pretty, Little Missie, and such dainty toes. You'll be a dancer like Nanny one day, won't you?'

I sighed, loudly. Vivienne lifted her eyes to my face. A chill ran through me as I waited for her anger to strike. I turned away and glanced at Tomas and Catherine. Catherine gripped Tomas's arm so tightly I saw red crescents rise across his flesh. Both of them watched woman and baby cuddling on the bed. I looked back at Vivienne. Her eyes belonged to Melissa as she kissed the baby's fingers. I wondered whether she had ever kissed mine.

'Here, Tomas dear. My arms are getting tired. Could you take her?'

'I will,' Catherine said, picking her way across the narrow space to Vivienne's bed and sweeping her daughter up in her arms. 'We'll get a cup of tea from the café. I think Melissa will be hungry soon. Come for us when you're finished, darling?' She kissed Tomas's cheek.

Tomas placed his hand on my shoulder. The feeling reminded me of my drawings and I suddenly felt claustrophobic. I sat down on the edge of the bed and he released his grip.

'Giz is here, Mum,' he said.

'I know, I know ... Ask her what she wants this time.'

Tears stung my eyes.

'You asked for her, remember?' Tomas stroked my cheek in what I assumed was supposed to be a comforting gesture, but made my skin crawl.

I felt more awkward than ever. 'This was a mistake.'

'Giselle ...' Vivienne reached across and placed her hand on mine. Her skin felt dry and thin.

I wondered why.

'Mum,' I said. I couldn't force any warmth into my voice.

'Oh, Giselle ... Thank God you've come. So you forgive me, darling? Tell me you forgive me.'

I shook my head. 'What?'

'I should have protected you, all of you. I'm sorry.'

'Mum?' My voice lost all strength. It reminded me of a cornered mouse, trying to calculate the cat's next move. 'Mum. What are you talking about?'

'You ran away, but now you're home.'

'It's been six years, Mum. I'm a grown-up now. My home is in London.'

'Don't be ridiculous, Giselle. You belong with your family - with me. I'll protect you this time. Keep you safe.

Do you forgive me? I only wanted to keep you safe.'

I backed away. 'Safe from what? Forgive you for what?' My voice sounded unnaturally shrill. Blood pounded in my ears. I struggled to catch my breath. I heard the soft pad of tennis shoes hurry towards me from behind.

'Is everything okay?' A female voice enquired.

'Nurse. It's my daughter. It's Giselle. She's come back to me.'

'That's wonderful, Vivienne. I knew she would.'

Vivienne grinned at me. Her teeth looked darker than I remembered. She reminded me of death. How old was she? She could only be forty-something at most, surely. I couldn't understand her transformation. It was as though the fairies had replaced my mother's shell with one that mirrored the evil within.

'I need a coffee, Tom. Which way is the café?'

He nodded. It was a kind nod and his half smile was full of sympathy. He mouthed the words "I'm sorry". 'If you go through these sets of doors and turn right at the main corridor, you'll see signs for it. Let Cathy know I'll be about ten minutes, okay?'

I stood up and he took my place on the bed. He wrapped his fingers around Vivienne's tiny hand.

'Okay then,' I said.

'Goodbye, Giselle,' Vivienne called. 'See you soon.'

It sounded like a threat, but logic told me I was being stupid. I ran away towards the café.

The nurse nodded to me as I hurried past.

Chrissie was waiting for me at Vivienne's house. I grabbed a cup of coffee and a pre-rolled cigarette from the counter. I considered searching for alcohol, but decided against it.

'I don't know what they want from me, Chrissie.'

She didn't answer, but simply hugged me. My spine stiffened with the contact then relaxed as I allowed myself to cry.

'None of it makes any sense. They're all mad.'

I felt her lips against my brow. I shivered, involuntarily and she pulled away.

'Sorry,' she said.

I shrugged. 'It isn't you.'

She nodded. 'I know, but I'm still sorry.'

'Everyone's sorry,' I sighed. 'Even her. And Tom, I just don't understand him at all. Does he want me here or not? He didn't even speak on the ride home. How am I supposed to know how he feels if he won't talk to me? It's like a fucking puzzle box, Chrissie. Really, it is!'

I walked away from her and peered out of the kitchen window. The glare of sunlight reflecting on the glass almost blinded me. Beyond it I saw a white shape. I stared, ignoring the sound of Chrissie's voice. The shape became defined and I saw a white haired lady hobbling through the garden.

'Nanny?' Without moving I found myself beside her.

'Hello, darling,' came the unexpected reply.

'What are you doing here?'

'I came to check on my garden. It's been so neglected recently.'

'Let me help you, Nanny.' I headed to the shed to grab a spade. When I returned Nanny had vanished, but I started weeding the garden anyway.

I felt Chrissie approach me. 'Whatcha up to, Crow?'

'Weeding,' I panted, digging the soil of the vegetable patch. 'Nanny was here. She doesn't like it when things get neglected.'

Chrissie's shadow stained the earth as she hovered behind me for a moment. Her silence didn't cover the sound of her thoughts whirling within the machinery of her brilliant mind. I knew she worried about me and I was glad when, instead of shooting her concerns at me like arrows of accusation, she grabbed a trowel and started work on a flower bed. Her expression revealed the thoughts still grinding together like cogs needing oil, but she kept them to herself.

'Wonderful weather!' Chrissie said. 'Just right for tending to the garden.'

I nodded. 'It's looking better, huh?'

'Definitely, but can I ask you something?'

'Sure,' I said.

'Why?'

My clouded eyes must have revealed my confusion.

'Why are we weeding?'

'I don't know. I guess I felt it was what Nanny would have wanted. Look, I've finished the veggie patch for now.

I'll grab the lawn-mower.'

As I pulled open the greyed wood door I noticed how different it seemed inside. The neat rows of tools and the red lawn-mower I saw earlier were missing and in their place were an ancient shiny-green giant of a mower and two kids' bicycles. Smiling nostalgically at my childhood bike with its bright, blue frame, I noticed a shadow move across the toys. I turned towards the movement and saw a grey man in a beige cardigan crouching in the corner, his hands held over his head as if he was trying to protect himself. The sharp sounds of his sobs filled the tiny space.

Another shadow grew behind him. I tried to warn him, but he didn't seem to hear.

'Granddad!' I cried, but the words were lost in time. The second shadow became more solid until, above my cowering grandfather, stood a young woman with black hair, pulled back into a long braid. Even though the woman faced away from me, I recognised her. It was Vivienne.

In her hand Vivienne held a spade. Lifting it, she screamed. 'You evil, twisted man. Leave us alone!'

Muscles tensed, she slammed the metal head of the spade downwards, hitting the man on the crown of his head.

He looked dazed for a moment then he howled. 'Please.'

My body shook. I searched my memory for traces of this scene and could find none. I touched my mother's shoulder and the figure spun around to face me. At first she looked demonic - red eyes burned at the centre of a grey void then

Vivienne's beautiful face established itself in the true glory of her late twenties. The face showed confusion. Vivienne took a step forward, towards me. I couldn't swallow. I couldn't breathe. I could only watch.

I looked from her to him, my grandfather, his hair stained with blood. I shook my head. Her eyes followed mine and her grip on the spade tightened.

'Don't hit him,' I yelled. My volume startled me. It seemed unreal, less real even than the scene before me.

Vivienne turned to face me again. The spade fell from her hands and clattered on the floor. I reached out to her. Her lips curled into a gentle smile, but her eyes glistened with tears. I opened my mouth, but before I could utter a sound she vanished.

The cobwebs, tools and red mower reasserted their presence around me. I stood there, eyes straining to penetrate the darkest shadows in the shed, but my grandfather and mother were no longer there. My legs felt weak and I let myself fall to my knees, panting, every breath an effort. Was that a memory? However hard I tried I was unable to find its root in my mind. Were they ghosts? Could a ghost have heard me? Anyway Vivienne was alive, albeit scarcely, and even if ghosts were real, surely you could only see ghosts of dead people. I stared into a void. Pain brought me back when I slapped my cheek.

I retreated from the shadows to the sunshine. My face must have frightened Chrissie, she wrapped an arm around my shoulders and helped me towards the sun-bleached garden bench.

I touched the crispy surface and sighed. 'I should probably stain this too.'

Chrissie held her cool palm against my forehead. 'What happened?'

'I dunno. Ghosts?' I described my vision to Chrissie.

'She turned towards you?'

I nodded.

'Does that mean she wasn't just a memory?'

'And she listened to me,' I laughed, sardonically. 'Vivienne never listened.'

'Weird.' Chrissie shook her head, at a loss for words.

We stared at each other as though the answers we sought might be read on each other's skin. Chrissie chuckled, breaking the tension. Her mirth was infectious and we both began laughing hysterically, uncontrollably. Deep bellows of unrestrained laughter bubbled up out of us until our sides ached and we started to weep.

'So, do you think I'm crazy yet?' I asked.

She laughed harder. 'Fraid not.'

I shook my head. 'Why are we laughing?'

'I don't know, Crow! Look, let's clear this up and have a rest. My body aches and my head is spinning.'

We left our tools where they lay. I couldn't bear to open the door to the shed and she didn't seem any less reluctant. Still giggling, we wandered back inside the house, holding on to each other for support. I lowered myself onto a kitchen chair and used my hand to fan my face.

Chrissie suggested we pool our funds together and pop out for a pint. I agreed, eagerly, anything to spend some time away from the house. I showered and dressed quickly, another t-shirt over a chest wrapped in bandages and the same pair of combats I had worn for a week already and we were out of the house by six o'clock.

One woman and, well umm, me, drinking ale in a suburban pub, seemed to generate a magnetic pull. Men approached us incessantly, in pairs, like a strange and unwelcome parody of Noah's Ark. After repeating increasingly less gentle rejections a dozen times or more, we decided to give up and leave. A powder-blue sky with salmon-edged clouds hung above us.

Chrissie's hand moved to my elbow and I heard her sigh.

'What is it?' I asked.

'Oh, nothing,' she replied, moving her hand away.

As I opened the door to the dark, old house I realised I didn't feel afraid. Chrissie crossed the hallway ahead of me and settled at the kitchen table. She opened her well-thumbed notebook and started writing. I decided to prepare a simple dinner. We ate without discussing the garden shed, Vivienne or the unwanted male attention. In fact we said very little. The gentle evening evaporated, silently, into night, and another day ended.

21

On Sunday morning, I woke up late. Chrissie, singing in the shower, made me smile as I passed the bathroom door.

Her voice was deep and melodious and the revolutionary lyrics warmed me. It reminded me of home - my real home, if I had such a thing. I descended the stairs, nodding at the pictures of my mother. I smirked, wondering how Vivienne would cope with Chrissie's energy, excitement and defiant non-conformity. For some reason the idea whirled around inside my head and tickled my ribs, making me laugh out loud. I imagined the portraits were frowning at my mirth, but that only made me laugh harder.

Still wheezing and spluttering, trying to expel the laugh caught in my throat, I sat at the kitchen table. The kettle filled the corner of the kitchen with steam. I made myself a cup of black coffee and held it in one hand. In the other I fiddled with a hand-rolled cigarette as I considered the strange events of the previous days. I still believed I knew Scott from sometime and some place, but I couldn't remember where. I refused to believe my dreams of the blue eyed man were a spooky coincidence. The ghosts or memories, or whatever they really were, troubled me more. My mother as a teenager, that couldn't be a memory, but I'd spent the past decade denying the existence of ghosts. I just couldn't throw those convictions away so lightly.

There must be some rational explanation, but I was damned if I knew what it was. When Chrissie came into the kitchen, her skin pink and gleaming, I made her a coffee.

'What's your take?' I asked her as she took her first sip.

'Huh?'

'On ghosts and shit ... what do you think I've been seeing?'

'Dunno. Stress, imagination, memories or maybe your mum and you have some weird psychic connection?'

'Do you believe that?'

'Dunno.'

I shrugged and sighed. 'Whatcha gonna do today, Chriskins?'

She grinned at me. 'Chriskins?'

I poked my tongue out at her and chuckled.

'I'd like to keep looking through Viv's diaries and stuff. Is that okay with you?'

'Sure. What shall I do?'

'Are you asking me or wondering aloud?'

I shrugged. 'Everything here makes me crazy. Mind if I pop out?'

'Not at all. We could do with more food. No tins of baked beans though, okay?'

I nodded and finished my coffee. 'See you soon.'

I wandered around shopping aisles aimlessly. I felt lethargic, listless almost, as though I hadn't slept properly in weeks. I put bags of lentils and vegetables in a basket and breathed in the aroma of freshly baked bread. My thoughts wouldn't settle, they jumped from Scott and his bright blue eyes and quick, but gentle smile to Vivienne, first grey and frail on her hospital bed then strong, dark and foreboding, towering over granddad in the garden shed and, finally, terrified and powerless, drowning beneath the water of her bathtub. It was a puzzle I should be able to solve if only I had a few more pieces.

Back at Vivienne's house, I rushed around the kitchen hurriedly putting things away then ran up the grand staircase. Chrissie was sat cross-legged in the centre of Vivienne's bed, surrounded by papers.

'Can I help?' I asked, biting my lip.

'Of course,' Chrissie answered, beaming. 'Come with me.'

She took me to the dining room. The walnut table was covered with papers and notebooks.

'Wow,' I whispered, wandering around the table, touching leather bound notebooks and waxy sheets of paper. 'There is so much stuff. Which ones haven't been read yet?'

Chrissie grinned and swept her arms outwards in an arc over the table. 'None of them.'

'There's so many.'

'Ah, research.' Chrissie sighed. 'There's nothing better. Well, almost nothing.' She grinned.

'Start with these.' Chrissie passed me a small bundle of official-looking papers. 'See what you can find.'

'Are you heading back upstairs?' I asked.

She shook her head and took a seat opposite me, behind a pile of journals and account ledgers. We sat for hours, at either end of the table, huddled over the dark wood. Bundle after bundle of papers and letters were looked through and discarded.

'Look Chrissie!' I jumped up and waved a piece of paper above my head. 'I've found Vivienne's birth certificate. Nanny's name was Patricia Nightingale. Vivienne was adopted. Now that crazy story she used to tell me is starting to make sense.'

'Story?'

'Yeah, Nanny used to tell me about a Ballerina and a Revolutionary. There was always a part I didn't understand. Now I think I do.'

I let Chrissie take the birth certificate from my hand and gazed at the next official looking document on my pile. It was another birth certificate. My jaw dropped open.

'What is it?' Chrissie asked.

'I'm not sure. Let me look at her birth certificate again ... Oh shit! God, Chrissie, look at these dates!' I placed both certificates next to each other and pointed at the years of birth.'

Chrissie squinted then walked around the table and studied the documents over my shoulder.

She gasped. 'Your mum was only fifteen when she had your brother.'

My hands started to shake. "Filthy! Filthy!" The word echoed around my head. My heart started pounding. The shaking travelled up my arms and into my shoulders then my whole body shook. I struggled to breathe. 'I didn't know,' I whispered.

'Crow!' she shrieked. Her hand grasped a third birth certificate.

'No!' I gasped.

'A twin? Did you know you had a sister?'

I shook my head. 'Does Tom know he's a twin?'

I stared at the three documents. They looked genuine and I couldn't understand why fake birth certificates would be here in this house anyway, but none of it made sense, not Vivienne's age or the missing sister. Did she die?

'Where's my phone?' I stood up suddenly. Chrissie's jaw caught on my shoulder as I rose. 'I'm sorry. Are you okay?'

'I'm fine,' she answered, rubbing her chin.

I nodded and ran out of the room and upstairs to grab the phone from my bag. An answer machine clicked in when I dialled Tomas's number. I decided not to leave a message, but took my phone downstairs with me again in case he saw the missed call and rang back. Armed with more papers, Chrissie waited for me in the dining room.

'He wasn't there.'

She didn't seem to hear me. Her face was bright red. 'Your sister was adopted. I can't find any record of the biological father's name. Not yet anyway.'

'Fifteen,' I said, slowly. I thought again of the young Vivienne in the bathtub. 'Do you think?'

'What?' Chrissie shrugged.

'Vivienne, when she, I, whoever was being held under the water ... remember? I heard a voice. It kept saying "filthy, filthy". I reckon she was about fourteen then. Maybe this was why?'

'I s'pose your Nan wouldn't approve of her being a pregnant teen.'

'It couldn't be Nanny. She would never ... she was loving and gentle.' I shook my head, frowning.

Chrissie touched my arm. 'Your grandfather?'

'I dunno, maybe ... I'll try Tomas again.'

I still couldn't get hold of him. I sank into my chair, shivering. Chrissie looked at me with sympathy. 'I'm sorry,' she said.

I nodded. 'I wonder why they never told us. It doesn't make sense, does it, keeping one kid and getting the other adopted? Why would anyone do that?'

'Because he was a boy and she wasn't? It sounds stupid, but I've heard of weirder things. I wonder if your brother knows. Maybe they would have told you when you got older, but you left before they could?'

'Maybe,' I said, but I was certain Tomas didn't know.

I looked at the birth certificates again. The father's name was blank, I wondered whether Vivienne had ever told Tomas who his father was or whether he'd ever asked. At least, in that respect, I had the better deal. I knew who my father was, Enrique Herrera, a revolutionary from Bolivia. Vivienne had met him while she was touring with a ballet company in Latin America; their love had been explosive, but short lived, pulled apart by circumstance and bad timing. That was why she couldn't look at me, because she loved my father so deeply.

'Your birth certificate's here too, Crow. Giselle Antoinette Nightingale, born in Birmingham, United Kingdom on the 1st March 1994, mother Vivienne Nightingale and father Frederick Richardson.'

I stared at her. 'You what?'

She passed the document to me, frowning. 'What's wrong?'

I shook my head, staring at the name, willing it to change. 'Chrissie, any idea why the wrong name would be listed under my father's details? Is it normal when your dad's not a national or if he's a dissident?'

Without looking up, I felt her eyes bore holes into my skull. 'Ummm.'

'Yeah.' I sighed. 'Ummm, indeed.'

I folded the document and stuffed it into my pocket.

'I'm not sure you're supposed to fold them,' Chrissie said, weakly.

I shrugged. 'Fuck it! How do I research this shit? I want to know who my dad really was or is, and whether my sister's alive. Oh shit, Chrissie. The Ballerina and the Revolutionary ... what if it's all a lie? Who am I?'

Chrissie picked up the other certificates and placed them in a drawer she opened from the underside of the dining room table. 'We can keep looking through the rest of these, or you could go and ask your mother. The public records aren't likely to shed any more light than the certificates, I reckon.'

I sighed. 'Something tells me she isn't more likely to tell me the truth now than for the thirteen years we lived together.'

'I don't know. You were a child then, Crow.'

I shook my head. 'Skeletons ... what are they but the truth behind the pretty lies we tell each other ... Maybe she is ready to tell me ... but not because I'm older. It's because she's older. I was never a child, Chrissie. I never had the chance.'

I tried my brother's phone again and left a message on his answer machine. 'Hey big brother, we need to talk. Can you pop round after work?'

Chrissie stood behind me. 'What do you want to do, Crow?'

'I don't know. I – I, fuck it, Chrissie, why?'

'I don't know. Maybe it seemed easier?'

'Just the truth, that's all I wanted.' I felt the corners of my eyes burn with hot tears.

'I know.' She patted my shoulder, tentatively.

I frowned at her. 'Let's go home?'

'To London? I don't think that's a good idea, Crow.'

'It's gotta be better than staying here.'

'See what Tomas says and you might as well ask Vivienne. What have you got to lose, really?'

I laughed, sardonically. 'The last few threads of my

sanity.'

22

(London, England - 2007)

The girl wouldn't speak to me as I waited with her in the doorway. She acted as though I was invisible, a ghost perhaps, and focused on the adults in suits and fine wool coats, striding past.

With a soft voice and an even softer manner, she regularly stepped forward and asked for help. Her movements were tiny, completely non-threatening and full of a gentle humility and grace. The people who did stop, more than half of those she approached, would smile sadly and press a coin into her hand. She thanked them with such openness and raw gratitude they seemed to continue on their journeys with a lighter step, proud to have helped someone in need. It was a strange symbiosis, but it seemed to work.

After an hour, she turned her blue eyes to me. 'That'll do,' she said. 'We can eat now.'

I nodded and walked beside her to a grungy looking café where she purchased two pastries and passed one to me. 'I'm Roxie. What's your name?'

I paused for a moment then smiled. 'Crow.'

'Pleased to meet you, Crow. Did you just arrive?'

'Yeah, I took the bus ...'

'Don't tell me where you came from. It's better that way. Most people will be able to tell by your accent anyway, but from now on you're a Londoner, like me, okay?'

'Okay,' I said, spitting out crumbs as I spoke. 'Sorry.'

She grinned. 'Street kids don't need good manners. Come on. I'll show you where I live. It's okay. A bit cold sometimes, but we've got plenty of blankets and the people are kind. No one will ... bother you.'

No one to bother me? That sounded luxurious. The cold I could handle, but ... my skin crawled for a moment before I regained control. 'Thanks.'

'No problem. Rule number one - we always help each other.'

'Are there other rules?'

'Don't get arrested is a good one.' She laughed and while I wasn't sure I understood the joke I laughed with her. Her humour was compelling, and I wanted to wrap it around myself, to shield me from the terrors beyond.

Her home was a third storey apartment in a run-down tenement building in the East End. We ducked under lines of washing hanging across a narrow walkway come balcony. I imagined sun worshipping out here in the summer until my nostrils caught a whiff of something revolting and I quickly reconsidered.

'What's that smell?' I whispered, not wanting to offend our neighbours.

Roxie shrugged. 'Piss probably.'

I wasn't convinced. I'd smelled urine before, but never anything as pungent and malodorous as this stench.

'Here we are,' she said, pushing down the handle on a non-descript aluminium framed door.

I picked my way between piles of rubbish across a threadbare carpet and followed her through a curtained doorway on the left. The floor was covered in blankets and sleeping bags.

'How many live here?'

'It changes. There's about twenty kids here at the minute. The girls share this room and the boys share the one across the hall. There's six adults too. They have a room at the back. I'll show you the kitchen and the bathroom. We've hooked up the electrics so we even have hot water a lot of the time.'

'Is it noisy?'

'Sure, but hell it's a roof, right? I hope you weren't expecting the Ritz.'

I blushed. 'Of course not. How long have you lived here?'

'Oh just a few weeks in this place. We have to shift around a bit, you know, but I've been with a lot of the same people for almost a year. It's a good group. It's safe.'

As we stepped back into the hall I almost collided with a tall white man with light brown hair. 'Hi Roxie. Who's this?'

'Matty, this is Crow. Crow, this is Matty. Are you heading to work?'

'Yup.' He rubbed his eyes. 'Hi, Crow. Welcome to the Palace of Dreams.'

I laughed and curtseyed. He grabbed his stomach and almost collapsed in a fit of giggles.

'You're okay, kid. You'll fit in fine.'

I pulled a face.

'Where's Max?' Roxie asked. 'I managed to get thirty squid for the pot today.'

'She's in the kitchen. I'll see you guys later, okay?'

'Bye, Matty,' Roxie said.

I waved as he left and he offered me a quick salute. I felt my cheeks warm as I blushed fiercely.

Roxie nudged me. 'He's awesome. Come on, let's meet Max.'

Max was the most beautiful woman I had ever seen. She must have been close to six foot tall. Her skin was chocolate brown and her head was shaved. Thick eyelashes framed eyes that glistened like gold. When she spoke, her voice was like syrup, rich, sweet and melodious. I wanted to be her.

Roxie passed handfuls of coins to Max who was sat on a sparklingly clean kitchen counter with her ankles crossed.

'T'ank you, Roxie. We feast like kings, now, hah? Who's this you bringing 'ome, mtoto?'

'Max, this is Crow. Crow, Max.'

'Like a bird, hah?'

I nodded.

'You flew de nest, sweet mtoto?'

I smiled, shyly.

'Well 'tis okay now, ya hear. Roxie, she look affer you. She look affer everyone. De mama kuku.'

Roxie puffed out her chest with pride.

Max rubbed her forehead and sighed. I looked to Roxie and she nodded.

'See you later, Max,' she said.

Max waved as Roxie gave me the rest of the guided tour, a tiny bathroom with no window. Unlike the kitchen it had not been recently scrubbed. I decided I'd adopt the room and pay for my keep with a cleaning brush. 'Can I stay?'

'For as long as you want,' Roxie said.

23

(Bristol, England - 2013)

I wandered out of the dining room and into the kitchen. Chrissie joined me. She sat in silence, unable to find any words to console me. I appreciated the company anyway.

'Shall we go out?' she asked after I finished a second cigarette.

'Where?'

'Anywhere. Just out.'

'Why not? Let me go and take a piss first.'

'No problem, Crow. I'll just wash up a bit while I wait.'

'You're too good. You'd make someone a lovely wife ...'

'Fuck off!'

I giggled as I walked out of the room. I mounted the stairs slowly, my head full of questions. They swirled around me like a dense fog, making it hard to navigate. As I stepped onto the landing I heard a voice.

'Gramps, Gramps.'

My stomach felt like lead. I breathed deeply trying to shut out the sound. Not again. I shook my head and tried to walk away, but the voice dragged me back. The sound was coming from the attic. I peered up the shadow filled staircase. The door at its apex stood ajar. I stood at the bottom, straining my ears, wondering whether my imagination was playing tricks on me until I heard it again. Shaking, I climbed the steep, narrow stairs, my heart shuddering with every fall of my feet onto the treads, thud, thud, thud. Memories flooded into me as I felt the stairs getting steeper, or rather my legs shrinking.

'No! Not again,' I whispered in a voice too low to be heard, but I couldn't stop climbing.

When I reached the top I pushed the door fully open and looked into the attic room. At its centre I saw a boy, a youth, no older than thirteen. His dark brown hair curled slightly out at the ends. His feet shuffled then he started to turn around. In mere seconds I would be able to see his face. I felt my throat constrict as though a hand was squeezing my windpipe. I tried to turn away, avoid his gaze, but I couldn't move, I couldn't even cover my eyes. I saw the tip on his nose and the cleft of his chin then his hazel eyes stared at me; they were full of fear and confusion.

'Gramps?' he said again, looking at me for an answer.

'What is it, Tommy? What's wrong?'

He pointed to his right, to something beyond my field of vision. I swallowed painfully as I took a final step into the attic.

A large figure stood in the corner of the room, his head almost touching the ceiling. No, he wasn't standing, he was swaying. A rope stretched above him, fastened to the roof.

'Grampy,' I called, rushing towards him then, as I saw his face, I screamed.

Wrapping my arms around me for comfort, I fell to the floor, remembering every detail, the bloated face, the bulging eyes, the horror of it. Vivienne had rushed up the stairs and taken each of us under her arms and ushered us away before phoning the police. She left in a police van and one of my friends' mums looked after us. We were never told what had happened. Grampy was simply there one day and then he wasn't and eventually the memory had become a shadow like a forgotten nightmare. If there had been a funeral, I didn't go. I never got to say goodbye. Life returned to normal and the horror, the bloated face and the bulging eyes, seemed like a dream, until I forgot it completely. Now I remembered again and it was time to grieve.

I remembered his huge hands. He always gave us sweets and told us stories in hushed whispers so no one would overhear, sitting in a battered armchair, reading or smiling. I couldn't remember him ever frowning or angry, but I recalled being afraid of him sometimes. Maybe they were scary stories.

'Crow, are you up there?' Chrissie yelled from the landing.

'Sorry. I'll come down.' I stood up, slowly, my legs shaking and wiped the tears from my face with dusty hands, leaving dark streaks down both cheeks.

'You're filthy.'

Filthy, filthy! 'What?'

'Your face is covered in dirt, Crow. What happened? Are you okay?'

I shook my head and lurched towards the bathroom, the word "filthy" echoing around my brain. My reflection looked as though I was in full camo-gear. I imagined myself by my father's side, winding our way through trees or jungle, guerrillas and outlaws, then I wondered whether that was really my father or just another lie. *Who am I? I'm filthy.* I washed my hands and face. The water gurgled around me as I leant, nose mere inches from the plughole. When I glanced back in the mirror I jumped, startled by the reflection of my friend looking over my shoulder, frowning.

'What happened?' Chrissie touched my shoulder.

I shuddered, too many memories beating against my skull, demanding to be set free.

'Grampy hung himself in the attic. I just saw him.'

Chrissie's frown deepened. Our reflections made eye contact. Her wide eyes stared through mine and into my soul. 'Hanged himself? Why?'

'Don't know.' Abruptly, I turned away from the mirror and walked out of the bathroom, leaving my friend behind.

I expected Chrissie to follow me and I sat at the kitchen table and waited. When she didn't appear, I rolled and lit a cigarette. It seemed like ages passed before Chrissie entered the kitchen and sat down. She looked pale and frightened.

'Nanny died when I was ten,' I explained between puffs.

'That was when we moved here.'

'Was your grampy living here too?'

'Yeah, Vivienne said we needed to take care of him.' I paused, twisting a hoop in my ear.

Chrissie waited for a moment then spoke. 'How was he?'

'He used to give us sweets ... He'd always sit in his huge, green chair ... We didn't see him that much I guess. I remember now, he always smelt funny. Gin, I think.'

'Why do you think he killed himself?'

I leaned forwards across the table, pressing my fists into my cheeks. My shoulders and torso swayed forwards and back. The rocking motion felt comforting, familiar. I realised I hadn't answered Chrissie's question and sat up straight to look at her and recall what she had asked. *Ahh yes, why did he kill himself?* I rubbed my forehead roughly upwards, stretching the skin above my eyes, trying to retrieve the memory. It felt ironic, considering the times I had pushed memories like this one away. I needn't have worried; the memory wasn't really there, only the shadow of it. 'Maybe he just couldn't stand living with Vivienne anymore. Maybe it was because he missed Nanny.'

'Do you remember when it happened?'

'Not really. I think he died pretty soon after we moved in, but it's all a blur. Maybe his death certificate will be here somewhere?'

I headed into the dining room and looked at the mountains of paperwork. Rifling aimlessly through the piles of paper, I created chaos across the table, searching without direction. Chrissie pulled me back and held me tight in her arms, rocking gently and cooing like a mother settling her upset child. My sobs were guttural, deep and uncontrolled. Rolling my head around, I started to wail. Pain radiated from me, the force of it physical. Waves of sound and energy bounced around me, crashing against the walls of the room like waves against a ship's hull. I wanted to cut through the water. It felt too deep, like I was drowning.

Chrissie clung to me as my body shook violently. Together we sank to the floor and Chrissie's mouth found my lips, wet and slippery with tears and mucus. Her kiss silenced me. Hair brushed against my throat, the smell of patchouli oil and fresh sweat covered me. Opening my eyes, I saw Chrissie's blurred cheek and soft ear.

'No!' I screamed, pushing Chrissie away.

'What?'

'We can't do this. I don't want this.' One step forward, two steps back.

Chrissie backed away, hiding her scarlet face with her hands. She scrambled to her feet and stumbled out of the door. I watched her leave, my head spinning with a thousand feelings and sat dumb. I sniffed my sweaty palms and realised I smelled of Chrissie. Closing my eyes, I felt my friend's hands again, stroking my skin, wanting me, needing me. My stomach somersaulted and I felt queasy, empty and alone. I squeezed my eyes shut and saw Grandfather's purple face, staring at me through milky eyes. It was too much, too vivid. I focused on the doorway, drinking in reality, the here and now, Chrissie stood before me, her face awash with tears.

'I'm sorry,' she said.

I could not answer. Instead I crouched silently, watching my friend's face.

'Mitch and me, we've been having problems.' Her explanation pained me.

I shrugged, the old cliché "she doesn't understand me" rose from my stomach as I tried to think of words to say, to erase the embarrassment and shame and repair the friendship, but I could find none. Chrissie knelt in front of me, offering a cigarette and a timid smile. I accepted the cigarette and left the smile unreturned.

'It's just that ... you need me, Crow, and I guess, at some

level, I need that. Mitch doesn't need me, she never did. I'm sorry. I really am. It wasn't the time or the place. I've made a terrible mistake ...'

We looked at each other; Chrissie's eyes seemed desperate, searching them I sighed.

'I don't need you, Chrissie. Having you here has been great 'n' all, but I don't need you. Don't look to me to complete you. I'm not that person.'

Chrissie cocked her head and wrinkled her nose. I turned away from her. My crouched position offered me an unobstructed view of the underside of the dining table. I saw forester's marks on the unfinished wood, rough knots and childhood graffiti and there, just visible, I could also see a tightly folded piece of paper stuck to the bottom of the table. I felt Chrissie's stare and forced myself to stay still rather than crawl straight over to the folded note, unwilling to investigate until Chrissie's scene was over, but I couldn't drag my attention away from the paper. I didn't hear what Chrissie told me and only noticed her absence when the room had been empty for some time.

The room felt cooler now I was alone. I crawled under the table. The piece of paper was wedged firm under a support. Gripping it with my fingertips, I gently wiggled its corner, trying to work it free. The edge started to fray and the paper threatened to tear. Letting go, I crawled further under the table and studied the support, trying to see whether there was a safer way to release the paper. There was no paper protruding from the other side. As I scrambled out from under the table, I knocked my head on the wood and sat for a moment until the dizziness subsided. I lifted the edge of the table top, but I couldn't reach the paper from that position. *Chrissie.* She was in the kitchen, holding a cigarette in one hand and lifting a bottle of bourbon to her lips with the other.

'I'm sorry,' I offered.

'Me too. You're right.'

'What you gonna do?'

'About Mitch? I dunno. Probably carry on as normal. I don't want to be alone.'

I slid onto the chair, next to my friend and hugged her. 'You sound like Vivienne.'

'Do I? People do things for all sorts of reasons.' Chrissie shrugged and looked away. 'I've done things ... No-one's perfect. But we all want to be loved.'

'I don't.' Even as I said the words I wondered whether they were true.

'Yes, you do. You just don't believe anyone does love you, but you're wrong, so wrong.'

I stood up. 'I need your help with something - the table.'

'Huh?'

'Something's stuck. I need you to lift the table so I can get at it.'

'Okay.'

Chrissie lifted the table top while I worked the paper loose. When, at last, I had it in the palm of my hand I stared at it reverently, hardly daring to breathe.

'What is it?' Chrissie asked.

The folded paper was only an inch wide by less than two inches long, folded so tightly that it felt like a tiny paper box. Hooking my finger under the first layer, I pulled it back. The closely-packed fibres tried to cling to each other and with every movement they threatened to tear.

Chrissie bent down to look under the table, but I was as aware of my friend as I might have been of a fly buzzing against a window pane, trying to get in. Licking my lips, I pulled back another layer and another. The paper guarded its secret until the very last fold was opened outwards. Across and down the page, in tiny yet elegant, black-inked script, two words were written over and over again. "Help me, help me, help me," was the whispered plea. I stared at the message, knowing it was not an accidental discovery. The message was meant for me. I focused on the tiny letters. Who needed my help? Folding the paper once, I passed it to Chrissie who took it eagerly. I watched her read it, shocked to see her face crumple and a flood of unsuppressed tears fall from her tightly shuttered eyes. I was unable to help, not knowing whether I should touch her arm or hug her while feeling unable to do either.

At last Chrissie passed the paper back and wiped her cheeks with both hands. Her bloodshot eyes stared at my face as if she wanted to say something, share some secret, but she didn't say anything and I did not to ask. Minutes passed in silence, as I turned the paper over and over in the palm of my hand and Chrissie stared at the floor, absorbed in her misery.

'It could have been me,' she said without warning. 'Remember when we met, how lost I was? Someone here was hurt, just like I was. Someone had their childhood stolen away.'

My mouth felt dry. I balled my hands into fists, crumpling the paper, concentrating on my breath - in out, in out. I sucked in air through my nostrils and blew it out through my mouth as goose-bumps prickled my legs and arms. I didn't know how to respond. Not only did I know that someone, probably Vivienne, had suffered deep and lasting wounds here in this house, I also felt a burden of responsibility towards Chrissie to help her make sense of everything. If I managed to put things right for Vivienne and Chrissie could I also heal myself?

'Tell me ... what happened to you?'

'My stepfather happened. I couldn't stand it, the way he looked at me, the way he ... I left when I was twelve. Younger than you ... I ... No ... Not yet ...'

'When you want to talk, I'll listen, Chrissie,' I said. 'Always.'

She smiled and mouthed the words, "thank you", then sank to the floor. I left her alone in the room, embraced by her sorrow. I switched on the kettle and placed my mobile phone on the kitchen table. Between the hissing of the kettle and Chrissie's distress I couldn't think. I closed the kitchen door against the sound of sobbing and picked up my phone.

'Tomas Nightingale,' my brother's confident voice announced.

'Hi, Bro.' As I spoke I twisted the hoops in my right ear. My breath felt ragged.

'Giz,' he said. 'I mean, Crow.'

I strained to understand the tone of his voice. Was it loving, excited to hear from me, or cold and distant?

'I've found some stuff. I think you need to see it.'

Tomas didn't answer.

'Did you know you have a twin, another sister?'

'W-w-w-hat?'

I bit my lip, forcing back my tears. 'Did you know?'

'What the f ...?' I heard the mouthpiece being muffled and urgent whispering. 'Look, Giz, I'm in work. What do you mean? What are you talking about?'

'Can you come over? I've got so much to tell you.'

'Look Giz, I'm sorry. I think I made a mistake letting you stay there.'

'What do you mean a mistake? What's going on? You didn't let me stay here, you forced me ... Come over, Tom. This is important, to you as well as me ... unless you don't want to hear anything about your precious mummy, is that it? Or ... what, do you think I'm crazy, as mad as her? No, you're jealous, that's it isn't it. You wanna be here, lookin' through her stuff, sniffin' her panties.' I knew I should stop, but I couldn't. Pent up rage exploded into the mobile handset, I didn't mean a word of it, I had no idea where the words were coming from, but they kept flowing. By the time I stopped for breath I realised the line was dead and my brother had hung up. 'Shit!' I growled. My tears flowed freely and I stood there sobbing wildly, an echo of the sounds nudging through the hallway.

25

(London, England - 2008)

Living with Roxie and the others was fun. I felt like part of a large and, more or less, loving family. There were arguments, of course, but bad feelings rarely lingered and people said what they meant then got over it or moved on. There wasn't the need to read between the lines of every conversation, every glance or movement of the body. I felt, at last, that I understood what was happening around me.

The adults were great fun, Matty in particular. When he wasn't working he would take interest in us all. Roxie and I followed him everywhere we could, to protests, meetings and even to the library. I think we both needed the respect and kindness he offered. Roxie was right. The people in that flat were good people. Nobody undressed me with their eyes and no one called me darling or gorgeous. I was another member of the team, no more and no less. I cleaned and when I needed money I begged or sold drawings. I was both useful and appreciated. I hoped it would last forever.

Then, one day, Max came home in tears. Her brother had been shot by police; they claimed he had a gun, but she insisted that was nonsense. We could feel the anger in the air around us. Our rage had a focus, those murdering bastards in black uniforms. There was only one way to get past this. We would have to make them pay.

When we arrived at the police station, me, Roxie, Matty, Max, Drago, Krim and Frank, we joined the edge of a large crowd. Some of the women wailed loudly. Some people were singing, but the atmosphere was tense, explosive. Without an apology and an explanation things would go bad. I could feel it. I realised the thought excited me.

Officers in Kevlar vests stepped outside the building. Murmurs travelled in waves, back and forth within the crowd. One of the police, the pigs as Matty called them, was making a flapping motion with his hands. I thought he looked ridiculous. He said something I couldn't hear above the other voices.

'What's he saying?'

'They want us to leave,' Matty explained.

'We aren't, are we?'

Matty chuckled and patted my head. 'No, we aren't going to leave, my little revolutionary.'

I grinned with pride and felt twelve feet tall.

More pigs swarmed out of the building. They waved their truncheons, menacingly. From the back of the crowd it resembled a pantomime or a Punch and Judy show. The crowd didn't move and I couldn't see what the police could do about it other than speak to the mothers, the sisters, the brothers, the fathers, the shopkeepers and the concerned neighbours. Suddenly, I was jolted backwards and fell onto my ass with a bump.

'Hey!' Max shouted and lifted me to my feet.

Bodies were rushing backwards, the crowd expanding outwards. I smelled panic and heard screams, screams of pain and of fury. Glass smashed. Voices were raised in anger and defiance.

'Come on,' Max said and grabbed my arm, trying to pull me away from the crowd. Matty was pushing forward. I tried to shake my arm from her grip and follow him. I wanted to help, but more than that I wanted to understand what was happening.

Bodies exploded outwards from the central point, pushing, rushing past us. I moved closer to Max, so she could shield me with her bulk. I started coughing and realised others were coughing too.

Over a megaphone a voice shouted, 'Disperse.'

From the right another magnified voice yelled, 'This is a peaceful process. We only want the truth.'

Max yanked my arm and I stumbled back. We stood in front of a shop door as young men swarmed around us. Some had scarves tied around their faces, others peered through the shadows of hooded sweatshirts. The sound of glass smashing echoed through the street. I felt afraid yet exhilarated. I couldn't see Matty or the others any more. It was just Max and me, sheltered under the awning of a newsagent shop, when a car exploded, a black cloud filled the sky and I screamed.

26

(Bristol, England - 2013)

Chrissie wasn't there when I went down to breakfast the next morning. The kitchen seemed too quiet, like the feeling you get when your ears pop. Trying to compensate, I knocked cups together and tapped my feet on the stone floor as I boiled water for coffee and rolled cigarettes at the kitchen table. By three o'clock I wondered whether Chrissie had left the house before I awoke. I crept upstairs and stood outside Vivienne's bedroom, now Chrissie's room. Images of my mother fucking any number or manner of men, sliced through my mind and my arm jolted back from the door handle. After standing outside the room panting, I went back downstairs.

Steam enveloped me as I poured water over coffee granules. The smell was calming and with a mug of coffee in one hand and a lit cigarette in the other, I grabbed a few moments of peace before facing whatever waited in Vivienne's room. I kept looking at the clock. Time had never seemed important before. If I had to be somewhere, a rally or protest or even a party, someone would remind me. I noticed a calendar attached to the back of the kitchen door and wandered over to it. It still displayed February. Notes were scribbled all over the page, plans Mother had made. It was probably February when Tomas first wrote about Vivienne's breakdown. Four months or more had passed since then. During that time I was only vaguely aware of this family; my friends in London were my life. Now I found myself, once again, stuck in this insane asylum, never knowing what might happen next, except this time Vivienne was not my gaoler, but a fellow inmate. I wondered whether this was how Vivienne had felt, whether the same ghosts had haunted her and how she had coped. Any better than me?

I unhooked the calendar, looking for a moment at the ballet dancers in the photograph, so serene yet so sad, their beautiful costumes masking the pain of each movement. I folded back the pages until I reached June. I wondered what day it was and guessed it was Monday and the latter half of the month. In the space under the 21st of June was scribbled Tomas's birthday. I wondered whether I had missed it, or whether it would be soon. I remembered making arrangements to be somewhere, Scott's place. Perhaps that was today? I scribbled a note for Chrissie, grabbed my rucksack and headed out of the house.

The day was hot again. Scott led me into the garden and poured a glass of minted water. I saw the tree near the wall, exactly as I had that first day when the bricks became glass.

'What a beautiful tree. What do all the ribbons mean?'

'They're offerings. If I ask for something I give something back. It's a very old oak. Full of power. Touch it.'

We wandered down the garden path and stood in front of the wide trunk. Scott's slim hand extended towards it. I watched him, searching his expression for any trace of mockery, but found none. My palms tingled in expectation. The wide branches were full of leaves and ribbons. I reached out to touch its rough bark. It felt cool in spite of the sunshine, shaded by its leafy canopy. Scott smiled in approval and I pressed my cheek against the dragon-scales bark and felt a soft, slow heartbeat, so slow I could hardly distinguish when it began or ended, nevertheless I was convinced I could hear it. Pressing my whole body against the tree, I slow danced with nature. Tears washed my face. Beneath the salty wetness I was beaming.

'Beautiful isn't it?' Scott said. 'I'm glad you feel it too.'

I moved away from the tree, unsteady on my legs. 'I've never heard anything like that before.'

'All of nature has a rhythm, a heartbeat if you like. With trees it's simply slower. Rocks are slower still, but they are just as alive as you and me.'

My face twitched involuntarily in a smirk then I nodded in earnest. His words echoed through the cells of my body, whispering the wisdom of his beliefs. I wondered whether he was mad, but dismissed the thought as lazy. I always wondered whether people were mad, like some strange defence mechanism against things I didn't wish to understand or accept. Of course, if Chrissie, or anyone, asked me later how I could feel something and know the opposite to be true, I would never have been able to explain it yet at that moment both truths felt comfortable juxtaposing within me.

'Are you hungry,' he asked.

'Thanks, food would be great.' I lit a cigarette then apologised, fanning the smoke away.

Scott shook his head. 'It's fine, go ahead.'

As Scott disappeared inside the house I sat on a carved wooden chair. The warm orange wood glowed with the patina of use. I stretched my feet out in front of me and reached over with my free hand to remove my boots and socks. The breeze tickled between my wrinkled toes as I fell asleep.

I awoke to the sound of cutlery and crockery chiming against each other. The simple lunch of steamed vegetables and rice was perfect. The vegetables were full of flavour and probably home-grown. I complimented him on the food and guzzled two glasses of water. Finished, I sat silently, full of questions and thoughts, but unable to decide where to start. I wanted to tell him about the ghosts, my mother and my newly discovered sister. I also wanted to ask him more about the tree and about what he took from it before he tied each ribbon. Finally, I wanted to share with him my confusion about Chrissie and Tomas, but I couldn't frame the first sentence.

He remained silent and together we sat in the garden, smelling the herbs and flowers, sharing each other's time and space but not each other's thoughts.

When a woman joined us I found myself unsure as to

whether she was real or just another ghost.

'Mum,' Scott said. 'This is Crow.'

'Crow!' The woman hurried over and took my hand. 'Vivienne's kid. Wow, it's good to finally meet yer. How's it goin' over at the Nigh'ingale place? Scott just don't shut up about yer.'

'Would you like some tea, Mum?'

'Ooo lovely. Ta, dear.' The woman settled into the wooden chair next to me and smiled awkwardly. 'Ahh, that's perfect. I loves the hot weather, don't yer? Course we won't never wanna get back off our asses.'

I smiled and looked out over the garden, nodding. I felt the woman's eyes on me, but was loath to face her and invite any form of conversation. She continued talking anyway. 'The Nigh'ingale.'

'Huh?' I replied.

She sniggered. It was a rich and dirty laugh. 'That's what we used to call yer ma. Never met anyone as lush as Vivienne. Like a movie star. Bet she was a devil t'live with though ...'

I nodded. 'She's in a secure mental unit now.'

'Noooo!' She gasped. 'Why?'

I shook my head and blushed. 'I don't know.'

She patted my hand. Her smile looked both sympathetic and confused. 'Oh, by the way I'm Dorothy, but call me Dot or Dottie if you like. Most people think I'm dotty these days ... Oh sorry. That was ...' A harsh cackle bent her in two for a moment and she punched her chest. 'Just can't seem to shake this summer cold.'

'Did you know Vivienne? When she was a girl, I mean.'

'Not well, she's a decade younger than me. Everyone knew of 'er, though. She were just that kinda girl, if you know what I mean. Such a pretty face. She were always doin' stuff: school plays and the like. Me younger sister woulda known 'er better, of course. She always wore a smile, Viv I means, but I could tell she weren't too 'appy. All airs and graces, mind you and too finely polished for the likes of us council estate kids. She got into this fancy bally school in Londin and we only saw her in the holidays affer that.'

'Did she have any friends here? People she'd talk too.'

'Well there's that there Clive at the New Age shop. He'd be her best friend, been thick as thieves for years. Scott knows Clive.'

I nodded. 'I've met him. He seems ...'

'Loud, camp ... but his heart's in the right place.'

Dorothy's shoulders rose and fell with each breath. When Scott arrived with the tea I saw a complete change in the woman. She sat straighter, her eyes sparkled and her face widened into a smile. 'Thank you, me lover,' she said, taking the mug of steaming liquid and sniffing it. 'Gert lush after a long, hard day.'

'How was work, Mum?

'Same ole same ole,' she said dismissively.

'What do you do, Dottie?' I asked.

'Nurse.'

Dorothy sipped her tea and relaxed into the chair. Scott passed me a black coffee and sat, cross legged, on the grass. I sighed as I felt my eyelids grow heavy again. I thought of Chrissie and my heart raced, my shoulders shook and I stared at the blades of grass, trying to control the adrenaline rush.

'Look, sorry. I'd better run. Chrissie might be worried.'

'You can use our phone,' Dorothy offered.

'Thanks, but I'd better go.'

'Okay then. Come back for tea. Scott's a great cook, though I may be biased. How's about Thursday?'

'I, I, I don't know.'

'What's wrong?' Dorothy asked, staring at me.

I shook my head. 'Nothing.' I grinned. 'I'm crap at making arrangements to do stuff.'

She laughed and nodded.

'I'll walk you to the door,' Scott said.

'Thank you.' I stood up, smiled at Dorothy and glanced at the tree. Its branches seemed to open out as if expecting a hug. 'Actually, you know what? Thursday would be great,' I said, still facing the tree.

'Do you want to bring Chrissie?' Scott asked.

It took a moment for me to answer. Did I want to bring Chrissie? Chrissie would take the focus off me – always the centre of attention and some time away from ... all that would be a relief. Time to think. 'No ... thank you,' I said. My eyes met his and he seemed to understand.

27

The moment I woke up it dawned on me Tuesday was going to be an awful day, and I was tempted to spend it in bed. It had been awkward, coming home to Chrissie. She had a haunted look in her eyes and kept walking away when I tried to speak to her. I decided it would be best to stay out of my friend's way as much as possible, give her time to process whatever mix of emotions she was feeling.

I grabbed my book and flicked listlessly through the pages. Outside my door, I heard a soft movement, Chrissie. I pushed my body deeper into my mattress and started to read.

Hunger and nicotine cravings gnawed at me, calling me to rise from the bed and by half-eleven I knew I needed to feed them both. The corridor was empty when I opened my bedroom door. Tiptoeing downstairs I heard papers rustling and headed towards the dining room. Chrissie stood beside the table, shedding tears and pulling apart Vivienne's diaries and letters, throwing scraps into a black bin bag.

'Stop it!' I ran towards Chrissie and span her around. 'We need those.'

She shook her head. Her eyes were rimmed with crimson, and she looked as though she hadn't slept in weeks. 'No we don't. They're just bad memories. Let them go.'

I hugged her and it felt like the most natural thing in the world. 'I'm sorry.'

Her body shuddered and I felt my shoulder grow wet with her tears. Clinging to her I cried without restraint.

'Let's go home,' Chrissie said.

I shook my head, still holding her tightly. 'You were right. I have to stay, but maybe you should, Chrissie. Go home and sort things out with Mitch while I stay here.'

'You want rid of me?' Her eyes shone with tears.

'No. Of course not. It's just ... I know it's not easy ... to be here. You should be with your lover, not trying to take care of me. I don't need to be taken care of, but I think ... perhaps ... right now ... you might.'

Chrissie dropped the bundle of letters and hugged me back.

Together we gathered the torn and crumpled papers, flattening each one carefully and matching fragments. Restoring the documents, this evidence of my mother's life, felt cathartic. With every piece stuck back in place I felt more complete. I glanced up and saw Chrissie smiling apologetically. "It's okay," I mouthed and returned to my labour. It consumed me, this act of putting things back together, mending rather than destroying. I was unaware of the passage of time, but when I looked towards the doorway again Chrissie had gone.

At eight o'clock, when Chrissie called me to dinner, I was still surrounded by ripped sheets and balls of paper.

We sat down to our last shared meal in this city and ate silently, each of us absorbed in our individual thoughts and hopes. When the food had been consumed I cleared the table. I didn't hear Chrissie leave the room. Her footsteps and movements had taken on a ghostlike hush as if they were already somewhere beyond the limits of my perception. Only when the plates were all clean and draining next to the sink did I turn and find the kitchen empty.

I didn't try to find her. I embraced the solitude. Lying in bed, I thought about the day's events: my rejection of Chrissie and her deep, inexplicable sadness. The sound of creaking stairs roused me from my thoughts. Relaxing again, I smiled at the melody of the old house – ghosts or water pipes. The bedroom was dark, but flashes inside my mind kept me awake. After a while I gave up on the idea of slumber and turned on the lamp. Soft light flooded the room, illuminating a small, twisted figure at the end of my bed.

'Nanny?'

'Hurry child.' Nanny's ghost pointed towards the door.

'What's wrong?' I jumped out of bed and followed the spectre. The glowing figure glided towards the attic door and waited at the foot of the steps, watching me. Her eyes fell from my face to my feet as I shook my head. My rejection made her appear crestfallen and my heart ached to make it better, apologise, but I was afraid to see my grandfather again. I did not want to climb those terrible stairs. Chrissie, the word hissed in my mind as Nanny pointed up the stairs, her eyes imploring me to action. I raced up the attic stairs, two at a time and reached the top just as my friend kicked the chair from under her.

'No,' I screamed.

Chrissie jerked at the end of a rope. The manic movements turned her around until she faced me, her face ashen. I ran across the creaking floorboards and held her legs while using my foot to right the fallen chair. I heard her sobs, loud and unrestrained. I cried too, soaking her pyjama bottoms. Moving up her body I loosened the noose, and Chrissie collapsed in my arms. I lowered her awkwardly to the floor. Rocking her shivering body in my arms, I looked up at the egg-shaped loop in the rope, a featureless face mocking me, still jolting with vicious laughter.

I stroked Chrissie's hair until I felt her body relax. Without thinking I found myself humming a tune Nanny used to sing to me. I felt the old woman beside me, taking care of both of us. My love for her filled my soul and I wished she had been my mother instead of Vivienne. I might have turned out very differently under her loving guidance.

I pulled Chrissie to her feet and, supporting her weight, guided her back down the stairs. In the dark Vivienne's bed looked even larger than normal. I led Chrissie towards it. Its turned back covers looked like a gaping mouth ready to swallow us both. As the back of Chrissie's head fell gently onto the pillow she fixed her eyes on me.

'Don't leave me alone,' she pleaded.

'Shh, it's okay. I'll stay with you.' I slipped under the covers beside her. The heat choked me, but I stayed, hand resting on my friend's shoulder as she fell into a troubled sleep.

Memories flooded my own mind as I lay in bed, awake. I remembered the times Vivienne claimed Nanny had told her something, like the time I left home all those years before. A heavy realisation settled inside me, either Vivienne hadn't been hallucinating, or I was just as crazy as my mother. The usual panic did not rise within me at this thought. That hallucination, if indeed that was what it had been, saved my friend's life. I figured I could live with such visions.

28

I woke in my mother's bed with my arms wrapped around Chrissie. I slipped out from under the covers to fetch my knife. At the attic door I stood, heart pounding, sweat pouring down my face, wondering what I might see. I pushed the door open, climbed the stairs and stepped into the empty attic. The noose still hung from the rafters, an empty space waiting to be filled. Cutting through the rope was hard work but the knife was sharp and I was strong. As the rope fell to the floor I breathed a sigh of relief, gathered up the remnants and threw them behind some boxes. One of the boxes was slightly open and a hard backed book poked out between the flaps. I leaned across and pulled out a diary, opening the box I found a dozen or more diaries inside, resting on top of a pile of fur coats. The softness of the fur as it brushed my hand made me feel strange. The last time I touched dead fur mother had been wearing it. The sensation made me sad, angry and happy all at once. I gathered the diaries in my arms and left.

I stuffed the diaries into my bottom drawer before checking on my friend. Chrissie was still sleeping soundly, her forehead wrinkled with some unknown dream. I decided to make coffee before she awoke. The aroma of the two steaming cups filled the bedroom when I returned to

Chrissie's side and I placed one on the table next to Chrissie and nursed the other cup, entranced by my friend's sleeping face. It was impossible to believe this peaceful woman had tried to kill herself less than eight hours before. Why had she done it? Asleep she looked confident, better able to face the world than I had ever felt. It made me wonder for a moment why I had never been tempted to commit suicide, what spark had kept me going through all the pain and rejection?

Vivienne had tried many times: pills usually, but sometimes slicing her wrists. Covered in vomit or blood mother would scream for help then the ambulance would come and Vivienne would get better again. Her near-deaths were a theme throughout my childhood and while other girls were learning about their periods, I'd be cleaning Vivienne's arterial blood off our bathroom floor.

I rubbed Chrissie's shoulder, gently, to wake her. Her eyes were swollen and looked unfocused and distant when she opened them. I shuddered. Now the peace of her sleep had been broken, Chrissie's turmoil was apparent.

'Do you wanna talk 'bout it?' I asked.

Chrissie shook her head slowly and carefully as if each movement was carefully choreographed and could only be achieved with complete concentration.

'What do you want to do, now?' I asked, afraid I would be left to decide for her. I didn't want to make that call; how could I decide whether Chrissie was a danger to herself?

She closed her eyes.

'You can't give up, Chrissie,' I said. 'People need you. Mitch needs you ... so do I.'

'I'm sorry,' Chrissie whispered in a voice so quiet I had to strain to hear it.

'No need. It's an odd house. It fucks with your head. I know that. Did you see someone or something? Or was it my fault? Is it because I pushed you away? Look, I was just angry yesterday. I still love you. You gotta get past this. Go back to London. Live even if you feel like giving up.'

'I'm so ashamed.' Chrissie covered her face with her hands. Deep and thick sobs pushed their way through her fingers.

I held her in my arms and kissed her cheek. Her smile looked thin, but her eyes seemed to focus on me at last. 'You'll be okay.'

Chrissie nodded. 'I suppose I'm a big disappointment to you.'

I shook my head, but Chrissie frowned and carried on.

'You came here in search of your mum and I don't know what I thought, but I was wrong. You're strong, Crow. Stronger than me. Will you keep looking? Can you forgive Vivienne?'

'Yes.'

'Will you go and see her again?'

'Yes.'

'When?'

I sighed. 'That's the question, isn't it? Days have passed

and I've seen no one. Well except you of course ... you and ghosts. I reckon I've been here for what ... a week, is that right? And I've seen Mum twice in that time. And what about Tomas? Has he been hiding from me? Have I been hiding from Vivienne? No, no, not from her, from me I reckon. I've been hiding from myself. One step forward, two steps back. You know what it's like ... or maybe you don't. Growing up you hear all these stories: fairy tales and legends, except mine were about us, about our family, and I thought they were the truth. Yet I'm still here ... figuring I can learn all about her from these second hand stories, but I know less than I thought I did when I arrived. Mum's life is a confused blur, full of children, ghosts, violence. It's the house, Chrissie or at least part of it is. It's full of memories, buried and repressed. You need to leave here. You need to go home and I need to find myself.'

'Will you stay here alone?' Chrissie asked, worried.

'Don't worry about me.'

'I, I don't know what to do or where to go,' Chrissie said. 'What would you do?'

I searched my thoughts for the right answer. It was the first time I had been asked for advice and I wanted to get it right. What would I do? Return to the squat, find my family, start afresh somewhere new or stay and help? 'Go back to Mitch. I'll be home soon.'

Chrissie picked up her cup and took a sip, her movements slow and thoughtful. At last she nodded. 'Okay. Will you come back?'

'Great,' I said, although I wasn't sure my voice was convincing. 'And yes ... of course I will. I can't walk away from all the fun. Umm, can you wait here a minute? I'm gonna phone Tom.'

Tomas's phone rang three times. 'Hello.' The voice was female, Catherine.

'Hi Cathy, it's Crow.'

The line was silent for a moment. 'Oh hi, how are you? I'm afraid Tomas isn't here,'

Catherine's voice sounded saccharine. When I tried to visualise her I saw a smile forcibly held on her face. 'Giz ...'

'Crow.' My grip on the telephone tightened.

'Sorry, yeah Crow.'

'What, Cathy. Is something wrong?'

'It's just ... no it doesn't matter ...'

'Please, what? Tell me.'

'He isn't jealous.'

I shuddered, unable to understand her words. 'Why is he so angry with me?' I asked. The phone shook in my hand, my knuckles tense and white.

'He's trying to protect your mum. It's what he does. He doesn't mean to hurt everyone else around him. It's just the way it works out.'

I gulped. realising I hadn't considered how Catherine was affected by all this. Did she feel jealous too? I wondered whether I should ask her, but it felt too intrusive. Safer to stay on the subject of Vivienne. 'Protect her?

Protect her from what, from me, from the past? Cathy I don't understand. I want to understand.'

'Yeah. Well it is what it is. Look, forget I said anything. We'll see you tomorrow - Wednesday, right?' That smile again, I could hear it stretching across Catherine's cheeks.

'Of course. Hey is it Tom's birthday?'

Catherine laughed. 'Yes it is. We're making a cake. Oh, does your friend want to come too?'

'No, she's heading back to London. You want me to bring anything?'

'Don't go to any bother,' Catherine said. 'Just bring a smile and leave the drama behind.'

I gulped, feeling insulted: *the drama?* The phone clicked dead and I walked back to the bedroom in a daze. Chrissie looked up. I smiled to show all was well and joined her on the bed. *Leave the drama behind* – the words kept echoing through my mind. 'Cathy just told me to "leave the drama behind",' I said, not really speaking to Chrissie, but sounding the words out to see how they felt.

'The cheek of her,' Chrissie said. 'I hope you swore at her.'

'I didn't. I didn't say anything. I didn't know what to say.'

'Ignore her, Crow. You're not dramatic. You're perfectly well balanced and charming and, and, and completely normal.' She grinned.

I returned her smile. As we stared at each other, the tension started to slip away.

'I'm glad you're going to see Mitch,' I said.

Chrissie nodded. She opened her mouth to say something then seemed to think better of it.

I raised my eyebrows and she blushed under my scrutiny. 'My relationship with Mitch has gone to shit so I guess I've been trying to take care of you instead. Except, well you know how that worked out.' Her eyes looked haunted.

'Come down to the kitchen. Let me roll you a cigarette. It'll all be okay, I promise.'

'It's okay, I kinda, I think I wanna be alone for a while.'

I stood up. My face must have reflected my concern and Chrissie waved her hand, dismissively. 'No I'm not going to do anything stupid. It's a relief, to be honest. Yes a relief. I'll be okay.'

I watched as Chrissie shuffled about under the quilt. The boundless energy she had brought with her, just a few days before, seemed like a half-forgotten dream. It was the house. It had to be. The bricks were a black hole that swallowed happiness and left its occupants empty and afraid.

I wandered downstairs, wondering what to give Tomas for his birthday. I decided I'd do what I did best, paint a picture for him, but of what?

29

Footsteps fell heavily on carpeted treads. The darkness of my room swallowed me as the sounds came closer. The door creaked and the padding of leather approached my bed. A hand stroked my hair, a big hand with rough fingers. I pushed my face deeper into my pillow, pretending to be asleep. Cold breath tickled my neck and my nostrils recoiled from a scent that reminded me of cleaning fluid. I tensed as fingers coiled in my hair. No longer feigning slumber, I struggled to free myself. The grip on my hair strengthened and tugged at my scalp. The pain made me cry.

'Shush little petal,' rasped a familiar voice. A man, someone I knew. 'Don't fuss, it's our little secret.'

Gritting my teeth, I pulled harder against my captor.

His fingers clung to my hair, willing me to stay. What hair? I had been shaving my head for over five years. Was I dreaming or was this another ghost? This wasn't real, the pain was a phantom, like the aching of a severed limb - severed time. No one held me back, no one except myself and yet the fingers kept tugging. I felt my roots tearing from my follicles.

I slapped the palm of my hand against my crown. The pressure vanished and my hair was as short as ever. I turned to check, but there was no-one behind me. Perhaps my captor fled as I freed myself from his greedy grasp?

My heart pounded and I pulled the covers over my head. *It isn't real. No one can hurt me, not anymore.* Deep inside me I realised how wrong I was. The pain was always there, waiting to be acknowledged. Running away didn't make me free and pretending didn't make me forget. What had happened to me as a child remained in my marrow. I might not recall the details, but I understood the powerlessness and the overwhelming fear all too well.

As I pushed myself up from the bed Chrissie opened my bedroom door. She held her bag in her hand and was smiling. I saw no trace of fear or indecision in her eyes.

'When do you leave?' I asked, rubbing the back of my head.

'Will you be okay?' It looked as though Chrissie was trying to straighten her lips, to a more sympathetic expression rather than the happiness, relief and sense of purpose she obviously felt.

'Of course.'

'Then today, right now, before I lose the nerve. Wish me luck.'

I gave her all my best wishes although I felt she wouldn't need them. She just needed to put some distance between herself and this toxic house. It was a relief to say goodbye. The thought of nights spent worrying about the suicidal thoughts of another was too much to bear. I fled that demon, years before. Chrissie kissed me goodbye. I waved until I could no longer see her blonde dreads. The house seemed unnaturally quiet and the diaries in my drawer beckoned to me. As I opened my door a blast of cold air pushed me back. I shook my head and retreated, conceding the battle temporarily. The diaries would wait. I had no desire for a round two with the ghosts. Instead I gathered what I needed, checked the bus timetable and headed towards the hospital and Vivienne.

30

The ward was quiet. Perhaps, the inmates weren't expecting company? The television seemed hushed and the faces gazing intently at its shadow-play were silent. I tiptoed past beds, not wishing to disturb the serenity and sat next to Vivienne. My mother was fast asleep, snoring softly as her chest rose and fell with each breath. It seemed unreal to me, almost impossible to believe this was her. She looked twice her age. Her once poisonous, lips now quivered with shallow breaths and those powerful, defiant eyes were shrouded by tissue-thin skin that looked as though it might tear with the slightest force. Watching her, my feelings of animosity for this old nemesis became confused with feelings of pity and a soft, but heavy weight in my stomach. My hardened heart felt tender and I wondered, *is this love?*

The warm air in the ward soothed me and made me feel sleepy too. I closed my eyes for a moment. When I opened them again Vivienne was watching me. The older woman smiled warmly.

'Giselle, you came,' Vivienne said, holding her hands out towards me.

I hesitated, unable to remember my lines. This show of motherly affection was alien to me. Vivienne frowned, confused, then smiled again, but a softer, less eager smile. She patted the bed. 'Please come and sit next to me.'

I did as I was asked and remembered how it had always been that way. 'How are you feeling?'

'Good, good. I'm so glad you're here.'

'I came before. Don't you remember?'

Confusion darkened Vivienne's face and I wished I hadn't asked the question. She looked towards the doorway.

'Are they with you?' she asked.

'Who?'

'Tomas, Cathy, the baby.'

I turned and followed my mother's gaze towards the door. The phantom of my absent brother mocked me from the shadows.

'No.'

'Good,' Vivienne said.

I stared at her face, trying to figure out whether I'd heard her correctly.

'Cathy and I don't get on,' Vivienne explained. 'She's probably pissed off I'm not dead. Watch out for that one. She's all smiles until she bites.'

'It's Tommy's birthday today,' I said, changing the subject.

Vivienne's wrinkled face looked at the withered hands in her lap. She silently rubbed her knuckles for a moment. 'Are you staying with them?'

'No, I'm at the house.'

'You are?' Vivienne looked surprised. I nodded. 'Watch out for the ghosts. Sometimes ...'

'I know,' I replied quickly, looking around the room, hoping no one heard. I leaned towards her and spoke in a low voice. 'One tried to ... drown me.' I sat back, anticipating Vivienne's scornful laugh.

'No, that was me,' she answered without a trace of humour. 'She tried to drown me.' Her clear grey eyes started to cloud and she shook her head as if trying to clear her mind. 'She never believed me. Never forgave me.'

'Why? Who?'

'Filthy,' Vivienne hissed, a chillingly accurate reproduction of the voice in the bathroom.

'Who said that to you, Mum? I heard it too. Were you pregnant?'

Vivienne didn't seem to hear. She stared at her hands again, grasping the knuckles, squeezing and twisting them between thumb and forefinger. 'Filthy ... secrets.'

'Shhh, Mum, it's okay' I looked around the room, but no-one had noticed her distress. 'Mum it's okay.'

I tried to pull her hands apart. As I touched her cold, thin fingers the narrow, almost skeletal face looked up at me again. Its grey eyes bore holes in my own and I felt her unspoken accusation.

'Mum, it's okay. It's me.'

'Giselle?'

I sighed and nodded. Two steps forward, one step back.

'I thought you were her. I made her hate me, but what else could I do? Too young. Too vulnerable. You understand, don't you?'

I nodded and squeezed her hand gently, afraid to break anything.

'Have you read the diaries?' she asked.

'Diaries? No.'

'In the attic. Read them and please ... tell Tomas I'm sorry.'

'Tommy loves you, Mum.'

'He might not ... when you tell him.' Her fingers worked frantically again, squeezing and twisting with such force I heard bones grind against each other.

'Tell him what?' I felt cold in spite of the ferocious heat of the ward.

Vivienne shook her head, eyes wet with tears. 'I wanted to see you, Giselle. I thought you wouldn't come. I know I hurt you. I never meant to ...'

Her hand felt insubstantial within my fingers. 'Mum, don't ... it's okay ... Look my life is great now. I'm living in London. I changed my name. It's Crow. I'm free see, like a crow. I don't hurt anymore.'

'Please, Crow ... my sweet, darling child. You always took care of me and I never told you ... I never said it. Please, let me finish. I need to say it now. I ... I just ... I hurt so bad, but I wanted ... better ... better for you, but ... in the end. I hurt you too. It's my fault. I'm so sorry. Please ... forgive me.'

'I forgive you, Mum.'

Vivienne smiled and pressed so gently it felt like a butterfly brushed against the back of my hand. 'Watch out for ghosts. My babies ... my beautiful babies.' She closed her eyes and a fat tear rolled down her sallow cheek. 'Don't go there ... dead ... killed them ... couldn't cope ... not again ... too many ... needed to ... car ... dead ... ghosts wouldn't let me ... Scott's stronger ... not like him ... rope ... lost ... mountains ... dancing ... dancing in the mountains. Ricky's there ... dancing ... no home, no family, only him, only us.'

I shuddered and let Vivienne's hand fall from my grasp. 'Mum? Mum, is Ricky my father? Who is he? Mountains? The stories Nanny told me - the ballerina, the revolutionary, are they true? Who is Ricky?'

Vivienne's chin drooped onto her chest, her vision unfocused or else she was looking at something I couldn't see. She didn't answer my questions. My desperate pleas went unheard. Perhaps it didn't matter; maybe I wasn't supposed to know. Two steps forward, one step back. I just wanted to understand whether my life, Tomas' life, Mother's life had simply been a web of lies.

'I'm so tired. Tell Tomas I'm sorry. Tell him Happy Birthday. Read the diaries ...'

'Bitch!' The yell echoed around the room followed by a cracking sound.

Plimsolls squeaked as a nurse sprinted towards a bed behind me. I turned around and saw a woman, not much older than myself, staggering around holding her face, her fingers red with blood. The door opened and more nurses, male and female hurried to the scene.

I looked at my mother. Her expression hadn't changed. It was as though the violence hadn't phased her at all, either that or her mind was somewhere else entirely.

'Mum.' I said. There was no response. I wiped a tear from Vivienne's cheek. 'Tell me about my father. Tell me about my sister.' If she heard me, she chose to ignore the questions. 'It's her birthday too, isn't it? Does Tommy know?' She closed her paper thin eyelids. The movements of her eyes, beneath mottled skin, suggested she was already dreaming. I held her hand, knowing she was far away from me. 'I'll come back, Mum. I'll read the diaries and I'll come back soon.'

It was late when I returned to the house. Shadows clawed at me as I walked towards the kitchen. I checked the clock, twenty minutes before Tomas was due to arrive. I placed his present on the kitchen table and looked at it. The charcoal drawing showed the three of us: Tomas, Vivienne and me, shoulder to shoulder. Tomas and Vivienne in the bloom of youth and me looking worried and tired, head shaven, genderless, just as I appeared in the mirror; although I looked taller in the drawing, my face on the same level as Vivienne's and only slightly lower than my brother's. In the image it seemed as though I was the parent and they were my children. Would he like it? Maybe I should've hunted around the house for an alcoholic gift instead? No, he had always appreciated my art; he would like it. I wondered whether I should take the birth certificates as well and give him the second gift of a twin.

No, Cathy had said 'No drama.' I solemnly promised not to mention any of my discoveries tonight unless asked.

Time raced past and Tomas arrived after only one coffee and cigarette. I greeted him with a smile, which he returned. My relief was palpable and I flung my arms around his neck and reached up to plant a kiss on his cheek in a motion so naturally affectionate it surprised me as much as it did him.

'Happy Birthday, Bro.'

His smile was warm and open. I held it in my mind and studied it, turning it this way and that. My artist's eye saw love in the smile and was satisfied. I held up my forefinger to ask him to wait a moment then rushed back to the kitchen for his present. Holding it out to him, face down, I shivered. What if he hated it? But he didn't hate it. He took the drawing and studied it. His smile returned and his eyes looked moist. He nodded.

'It's beautiful, Giz ... Sorry, I mean, Crow. Thank you. You know it isn't fair to just change your name and expect others to remember, don't you?' He embraced me, squeezing so hard I struggled for breath for the few seconds before he set me free.

I felt like I should apologise, but I wasn't certain why. Was I unfair expecting others to change how they saw me? I didn't think so, but maybe he was right. Maybe to him I would always be Giselle, his little sister. I wondered whether I could accept that and decided to try. I loved feeling like we were family again, close and loving, sharing his joy. Two steps forward, one step back. My thoughts flitted across to the withered blossom of his anger before, but I pushed the memory away, placing it with other memories I preferred not to study. I rationalised it was a perfectly reasonable change in mood and his anger had been legitimate; I had provoked it and now I had been forgiven again.

Cathy was all smiles when we arrived. She embodied the perfect hostess and the dinner party was her domain. Even so, her smiles seemed thin and fragile like a cracked mask and her make-up too carefully applied - war paint.

'Food won't be long,' she said.

The evening was different from the last meal we had eaten together and I struggled to plot my coordinates with any certainty. Cathy seemed angry and hardly communicated while Tomas seemed nervous, talking so quickly I was barely able to keep up. I ate the roasted vegetables and the salted potatoes, but left the steak Cathy had, giving her the benefit of my doubt, absent-mindedly placed on my plate. The blood from the partially-cooked meat created a wall of inedible food, but I chose not to complain – *no drama, right?*

After the plates were cleared Cathy returned with a huge chocolate cake. Light from the twenty-three candles danced in front of her face. She wasn't beautiful like Vivienne had been, but there was something magnificent about her, an ease of movement and a gracefulness that Tomas obviously adored. He looked towards her and I imagined his thoughts before shying away.

After devouring a huge slice of cake Tomas rubbed his stomach and moved towards the armchair. I followed him. The plates and dishes were cleared away by Cathy. My desire to share the task of cleaning up was outweighed by my wish to speak to my brother alone. I leaned towards him from my place on the sofa in what might have looked like a conspiratorial stance to the casual observer, but no one was watching us and when Tomas looked at me even he seemed unfocused, hardly present.

'I saw Mum today,' I told him.

His interest was spiked and he leaned towards me. His face flushed, he held his stomach and grimaced.

'Too much cake?'

He nodded and moved backwards to a more comfortable position. 'You did? How is she?'

'She seems fine. We had a good chat. She's kinder than I remembered. Tom, I can't believe I've hated her for so long. I must have missed so much.'

'I told you so,' Tomas answered, delighting in the words.

'Now there's a birthday present for you, eh? Reconciliation.'

We both smiled and I leaned closer still until my knees skimmed his.

'She says to say sorry.'

Tomas's confusion was apparent and he shrugged his shoulders.

'Oh and she said Happy Birthday too.'

The tension fell from Tomas's face and shoulders. 'Ah, she needn't have worried. I didn't expect a gift. Where's she gonna buy it anyway? I should have called to see her though.' He checked his watch. 'I guess it's too late now.'

'I don't think she meant that. Look Bro ...' I chewed my lip, feeling guilty, but the truth was desperate to reach out. No drama, Cathy had said, but was this drama? I hoped not. I was sharing a moment given to me by a loving parent. There was no harm in telling him. 'There's some diaries. She ... she hid them in the attic. She wants me to read them. I'm, well I guess I'm kinda nervous. It can't be good huh, if she's apologising for them already. Would you read them with me?'

Tomas crinkled his face, the same look he'd used when pondering a question when we were children together. He sat silently for a moment, staring in my general direction but without focus again. 'You know I love Mum.'

He paused and I nodded.

'Well I've always loved her. I guess neither of us had a father. Mum was it. She was ... is everything. I know you two had your differences. I even understand why you didn't get on. But, but, God I wish I could explain this better.'

'You're doing fine, Bro. Keep going.'

'It's gonna sound, odd, creepy even. I know that, but hear me out, okay. I guess, when it comes down to it, Mum is ... well she's sort of the model by which I judge all women ... Yeah, yeah, I know ... Freudian much. But you see ... How do I say this?' He leaned forward again, looking uncomfortable then took a deep breath and stared into my eyes. Moisture gathered in his eyelashes. 'You see ... no one, not you, not even Cathy has ever measured up to her.'

He glanced at the doorway. I followed his gaze, no one was there. I nodded for him to continue even though what he was saying was painful to hear.

'If I read the diaries and I discover Mum isn't perfect ... No that's not it ... that's wrong, I know she isn't perfect and I know she's made some pretty bad choices in her life ... But, if I read them and find out who I think she is ... well maybe it's a lie, what then? I'm not sure I could cope. I really don't think I could. Not now and maybe never. I love her, Giz. I love her so much and she's dying in hospital. She's a caged bird and she can't even spread her wings.'

I reached for his hand. He sniffed and pulled back, moulding his spine against the chair. His hands were fists that he shook and bounced against his lap. I smiled at him, hoping he would be helped by my acceptance, knowing I wanted his, but he felt too distant to reach. If I couldn't reach him, my own brother, what was I doing with my life? One step forward, two steps back.

'It's getting late,' he said.

It wasn't, but I could empathise with his tiredness and wish for solitude. 'Will you take me home?'

'I've been drinking. How about a taxi?'

I nodded and accepted the ten pound note he passed across the void.

31

I kept my eyes on the garden path as I approached the dark house. The silence was thick with menace as I stood in the hallway. I raced upstairs, clinging to my echoing footsteps, leaving the lights switched off, knowing an electric bulb or two wouldn't stop them. Inside my room, I breathed deeply. The stink of stale sweat, wafting from the sheets, filled my nostrils and the sour smell comforted me, told me I belonged.

I switched on the light to remove my boots. The bed looked like a harbour, jutting into an unforgiving ocean. I swam to it and it welcomed me. My eyes darted back and forth between the well-thumbed novel and a drawer filled with secrets. I picked up The Unbearable Lightness of Being and started to read, but that night the sense of Kundera's words eluded me, dancing in front of my eyes, just out of reach. I put the book back and reached for the drawer and the diaries. I took four journals and placed them on top of the divan. Looking at the first page of each, I established they were from very different times. The first diary had been started just under a year ago, but the others stretched back in time, one to when Vivienne must have been a teenager. I held them in my hands and the weight of the knowledge inside them pinned me to the bed. Here lay

Vivienne's story and perhaps mine as well. Contained within these four volumes were all the mysteries of this house and my mother's life. I wanted to know, yet was afraid to read them. Unlike Tomas, I had never placed Vivienne on a pedestal. There was no gilded image to be tarnished with new knowledge. I wanted to understand all that had happened to her and to me, but the power of that knowledge intimidated me. I wondered whether there were things I should not know, but today, in the hospital, Vivienne begged me to read them, demanded it. But where to start: at the end or the beginning? The beginning terrified me, within those years the pregnancy and the near drowning would lay in wait. I was certain of it. The end then, if it wasn't too confused to understand.

After replacing the three earlier diaries in my drawer, I opened the last. Foetus-shaped, curled up in the womb of my bed, with one hand holding the book and my cheek resting on my pillow, I began to read. 19th September 2012, I wondered what I was doing that day. With no diary, or permanent record of my movements, each day blurred into the next until they became a homogeneous mass of rebellion and self-hatred. But what of Vivienne, what happened to her on that day - the day she started a new diary?

Unlike those of the novel these words did not elude me, they entered me. Reading, I heard my mother's voice; not the pitiful voice of the woman glued to a hospital bed. This voice was full of energy and vitality, a strong voice that beckoned to me from nine months before. As I absorbed the thoughts and words on each page, the silent house filled with creaks and moans; phantom footsteps echoed across the landing, pacing restlessly, showing their distress. The door handle rattled. I slammed the diary shut and squeezed the palms of each hand against my ears. When I released the pressure the room remained empty and the rattling had stopped. I found my place and read some more.

"More discussions, more deliberations and more stalling. I grow impatient while he tries to hold me back. These swaddling myths I use to suppress my more destructive memories also hamper my determination to seek enlightenment. Would it be, as he claims, folly to immerse myself in the persistent feelings of an omnipresent violence inextricably linked to my individual sexual morality?

"He offers me knowledge and adventure, seeking answers that may of themselves prove revolutionary, a oneness without the physical hindering the psychic victory I seek, and a reconstruction of self; the courage to harmonise with the elemental, searching for a revival of that inner mother in those receptive Northern lands. He argues that in the process of guiding me towards enlightenment we must move slowly, organising each stage according to my increasing efforts, but cautions against too early a step from the old regime to the new. He advises me that ghosts still dwell within my fundamental being and it is better to defend than attack.

"I disagree, arguing for a psychic assault on the

metaphysical, purging ancient history from all compartments of that other, the physical self and seeking new freedom through death and subsequent revival. Yet, when I try to touch his essence, he scurries from me and without sex I am powerless, fragile. Is this, in fact, his purpose and if so what is the end goal? I worry he wishes only to stifle when I seek release, release from guilt and responsibility, and an understanding of the child as a product, packaged in the raw materials of upbringing. When the package is torn the individual leaks and this is the normal process of growth, a growth that swallows all obstacles, utilising mankind for the inner journey of self-determination."

I looked up from the elegant scrawls. Although the language Vivienne had used was ambiguous, the meaning behind her words seemed clear to me. My mother desperately wanted to be free of her past. It was a desire I understood and shared. I wondered who "he" was. Was she writing about Scott, Clive or some other man? So far I had no clues to this person's identity. I felt determined to read on, take what I could from the phrases she used and discard those things that were unclear, knowing I could ask her about them when I next visited her in the hospital.

I licked the tip of my finger and turned to the next page. The handwriting was different from before, simpler, smaller and neater. It was a new entry on a new day, this time the 25th September. She missed six days of entries, perhaps nothing happened during that time, or perhaps she fell ill, laconic or manic and feverish. I remembered all those moods clearly from my childhood and the speed with which she could switch from one to another. Yet again I realised how unusual my childhood had been, an atypical upbringing to say the least.

"Pride is a terrible and pointless thing. It separates us and turns privilege into something earned and admired, makes us forget others may work just as hard and never achieve our success. I was proud of two things: my beauty and how gracefully I danced. At least I worked hard at the latter, but the former was simply chance, an accident of genetics and perhaps the reason he made me his victim, or so I once thought. Looking back, I suspect he was just a filthy pervert.

"It's his birthday today. I'll remember but never celebrate, no flowers to lay on his grave. If I could face going I might gift him a heavy globule of spittle or some tears of regret that I wasn't quick enough to ensure I was his last victim."

I stared at the page, the tiny handwriting and the concentrated pain it contained. Someone hurt my mother. They hurt her badly. I shook with fierce anger, wishing I could have protected her, but I was too young, or perhaps not even born, and I didn't know. A lump filled my throat, and I shut the diary, too afraid to turn the page, afraid to see what else Vivienne had suffered, and the ever changing writing that reflected her perpetually altering personality. As a child she'd made me dizzy just watching her swing back and forth between excitement and sadness. There seemed to be no balance, no mid-point, only elation or desperation. If I read on would I find out why? Was I ready to face such a revelation? A creak outside my door and the book fell from my hands, thudding onto the floor. I didn't follow the sound. I had no wish to leave the relative sanctuary of my room and face what waited beyond.

32

The doorbell rang, waking me. I looked around the pitch black room, wondering whether I had dreamt the sound then it rang again. I pulled on my clothes and hurried down the stairs.

There was no chain on the door and no spy hole and I had no idea who could be calling this time of night.

'Who is it?' I shouted.

The reply was muffled, but definitely my brother's voice.

I reached for the door. I heard his sorrow and felt it too. As I pulled the door open Tomas shouldered his way into the hallway. His face was red and wet, his hair unbrushed. As I stared at him he shook his head. With a hollow chest I enveloped him with my arms.

'Is she?' I asked.

Tomas nodded.

'I'm so sorry,' I said and I was, sorry for Tomas's loss and my own. Realising any chance I ever had of a loving relationship with either of my parents had evaporated. I was alone, an orphan and so was my brother.

In spite of my emptiness I did not cry. Nothing had changed, not for me. I had always been alone. But the house around me wailed with grief. It had lost its plaything.

Vivienne would be missed. Sounds of sorrow whirled about me as I remembered Vivienne, the ballerina. I held Tomas tighter and breathed deeply; his tears washed my shoulder. We were two children, hiding in the dark, both wishing for a parent who would never return. In the past this would have been different parents, Tomas had always wanted his mummy, me my absentee daddy, but now our thoughts combined, directed together towards the void, the space left by Vivienne's stage exit right.

'Will you come to the hospital?' he asked at last, wiping his eyes roughly with his sleeve.

'Of course,' I said. 'I'll get my things.'

Melissa was gently snoring in her car seat and Catherine stared blankly ahead, not acknowledging my arrival. I smiled at the peaceful baby.

I guess I'd been lucky; I had never seen a dead body before although I had witnessed much violence. Vivienne looked as though she was sleeping, her face peaceful, no sorrow, no regrets. I imagined her with her lover in the wild Bolivian mountains, reunited after all those years.

'She's with Dad now,' Tomas said.

I wondered which one. The phantom lover I painted in my head wasn't a blood relation to Tomas, in fact his father had never been discussed, neither had our sister. Perhaps he shared my father that night, and the story wheel turned a full circle, the ballerina and the revolutionary together again.

33

Walking towards Scott's house, I remembered what Cathy said over breakfast. 'So I guess you'll be going back to London now?'

In that one question, or was it a statement, Cathy had left a second wound in my chest. What would I do? I could go back. My reason for coming to Bristol had been to see my mother and appease my brother. The first task had been more than accomplished. I had gained a new understanding of Vivienne and sympathy for what she'd endured. Was Tomas appeased? I had no idea; sometimes it felt as though he was sorry I had come back at all. His mother, the beacon he had held aloft all these years, had died, appeased perhaps, happy no. What next? I supposed I would need to move out of the house when ownership passed to my brother. I would leave with regret, however, without learning the secrets Vivienne had been so eager for me to read. I could take the diaries with me, hide them from him. He had said he wouldn't read them. But what of Scott? Yes, what of him? I shook my head. Perhaps my dreams were a mystery I could never solve, in fact perhaps everything was.

Tears filled my eyes as I realised I loved my mother. Loved her in spite of all the beatings and the name callings, in spite of the damage I carried with me all these years.

When I saw Vivienne in that hospital bed I had felt love. I loved Tomas too, even if he was choosing his wife and family above me, even if he refused to hear what Vivienne wanted, so desperately, to tell him; I still loved him. Did I also love Scott? No, Scott was different; loving him would mean having some sort of sexuality, wouldn't it? I remembered brushing past Scott's warm body in the kitchen and my mind skipped to other potential lovers who were never lovers and how I had cast each moment aside before it could mature, including Chrissie and those microseconds of passion I had felt for her. No, not passion, something else - romantic longing perhaps?

'I'm sorry I'm late,' I said as Scott opened the door. 'You won't believe the day I've had.' I smiled then felt guilty about smiling. As I hovered at the doorway, focusing on Scott's kind face, I felt unable to fix an appropriate expression to my own. He smiled at me, his eyes suddenly warm and wise, and invited me inside.

'Would you like a drink?' he asked.

'Scotch.' I laughed and shook my head. The laugh kept bubbling in my chest and I felt frightened of losing control of myself. I gripped his arm to steady my body and felt grounded. The threat of hysteria ebbed away. 'Just kidding, um, water, please.'

I followed him into the kitchen and sat down. 'My mum died today.'

He dropped the glass in the sink, but it did not break. He turned and looked at me, gentle sadness in his soft eyes and creased face. 'Are you okay?'

I nodded. The movement of my head spread to my shoulders and back, and the tears I had held at bay started to fall. Choking laughs escaped with my sorrow. Scott knelt in front of me and steadied my shoulders with his embrace. Once again, the hysteria subsided as I concentrated on his blue eyes, so deep and intense. In his eyes I imagined lazy days spent on a Mediterranean beach. I willed my body to be still in spite of my ragged breath and stared into his eyes. He didn't seem to mind, returning my greedy stare with a steady gaze.

'I'm sorry,' he said eventually.

'What for?'

'Your loss,' he said. 'Vivienne was a ... she was a ... an impressive woman.'

I held my hand in front of my mouth stifling nervous giggles that started to bubble inside me. They forced their way through as hiccups of amusement. 'Impressive?' I shook my head, slowly, controlling every muscle so I wouldn't lose myself in involuntary shaking again and looked at his baffled expression. 'Do you know she was in love with you?' Anger replaced my amusement and my hands balled into fists as I ground my teeth. 'She died because of you, didn't she? What did you do to her?'

Scott's hands moved from my shoulders to my cheeks. He held me firmly in his soft touch. I tried to look away, but realised I was unable to move my face. I looked downwards, momentarily, but felt even less comfortable staring at his crotch. I closed my eyes then opened them again wider than ever, feeling closed eyes were too submissive to communicate my defiance.

'Well?' I asked again.

'I knew she was in love with me.' His voice was a whisper and I had to strain to grasp the meaning of the words that crept towards my ears across the soft cloud of his breath. I wondered whether I was dreaming and whether this cushion of words had been sent to carry me away from the pain. 'I never encouraged her, and I didn't love her back. But I admired her strength. She asked for my help and I tried to help her, but she ran on ahead. When she failed, she ran straight into the bonnet of a car.'

'I don't understand,' I whispered.

'She wanted to be free. That house was filled with ghosts and terrors ... she told me. She wanted me to heal her, but before we really started she changed direction and wanted to be me. I warned her, what I do would take time and needed a healthy mind, but she wouldn't listen.'

I listened and as I did pictures formed in my mind - my mother, foolish girl, rushing from one thought to another in a whirlwind of madness. I nodded to show Scott I understood, but he remained on his knees before me, holding my face; so I asked him to continue.

'Well, maybe she wanted to fail, I don't know, but she tried to initiate herself. It's intense stuff, Crow. Only strong minds can get through the trials.'

There was no pride or arrogance in his words, only

simple explanation. Where his words led I tried to follow, but they were misty, obscure and I found myself lost in a labyrinth. Frustration built inside me as I saw how his use of language concealed the truth rather than revealing it. It reminded me of the diaries and my frustration grew into an intense heat.

Through gritted teeth, I growled at him. 'What the fuck are you talking about, Scott?'

He released his hold and stared at me in shock. His natural calm wavered against the onslaught of my anger. 'Your mum felt she should be a shaman. She took psychedelics and buried herself in her garden. She wanted to visit the spirit world.'

'Buried herself?'

'It's what the ancient shamans used to do. I guess she read it somewhere. Perhaps she lost her mind.'

'There wasn't much left to lose,' I told him.

Scott nodded. 'When she clawed her way out of the hole, who knows how much later, she grabbed her spade and ran into the road. A car hit her then ricocheted into a wall. A fourteen year old passenger died – a girl.'

'That's why they locked her up?' I asked. I wondered why Tomas had never told me this story.

'They did a psych assessment. But ... she ... she also told them she'd killed before.'

'Who?' I asked.

'I'm sorry, I don't know. Maybe they'll have a record at the hospital.'

Scott's arms hung limply at his sides. Having broken eye contact, he stared at my feet. My legs did not quite touch the floor and swung to and fro under his gaze. For reasons I could not fathom I felt suddenly ashamed and held them still.

'What do you know about the ghosts?' I asked.

'She didn't say much really. Just that she was afraid, but it feels like a house full of painful memories,' he told my boots.

I looked at the crown of his head and the dreadlocks starting to form at the roots of his matted blond hair. Rage and a strange, unwelcome, desire bubbled inside me. I wanted to stretch out my leg and use it to push his face up then I wanted to slam my heel into his mouth. My feet started swinging again. 'I see them too.' I waited for a reaction, but he hardly moved. He looked serene like the statue of a saint, folded neatly into a posture of prayer or supplication. He wasn't praying though. 'Stop looking at my damn feet! What's wrong with you, Scott? You seem ... fuck I don't know - spaced out. You're supposed to be consoling me, not the other fucking way around. Explain it to me. Why am I seeing ghosts?'

'I'm sorry, I guess I'm ... shocked. Your mum, I dunno, but for some reason I thought she'd outlive us all. The ghosts though, I don't know why you see the ghosts Crow, don't you?'

At last he looked at my face. I felt like crumpling under the weight of his sad eyes and I wished he'd look at my boots again, but didn't voice the request. 'I think they're trying to show me something. I've seen my Nanny, but ... then again, that might have just been my memory. I saw Vivienne beat up my granddad in the shed and Granddad hanging from a noose in the attic. And I've felt, god I've felt some weird and frightening things. I know why she was scared. I'm scared too, but what can I do?' I nibbled the tip of my thumb, tearing back thin strips of skin with my teeth. Scott reached for my hand to stop me, but I pulled it away from him, violently. 'What should I do?'

'I can bless the space. I should have done it before. I was going to the other night, but you ran away. I could sweep it clean. I'll do it tomorrow if you want.'

'Will it work?' I asked. 'I don't mean to diss you, but ...'

'It will work, but it might not solve everything. How's Chrissie doing there? Does she see them too?'

'She's gone.' I looked at him, wondering what he was thinking about. I counted seconds of silence then broke it myself. 'She missed her girlfriend.'

'I understand,' he said.

It felt like a lie.

He tried to embrace me again. I wondered whether he expected me to cry again. I didn't. My tear ducts had dried up over the past twenty years, my grief barren and only extreme rage or desperate sorrow could moisten them. I pushed him away, feeling confused. His closeness made me feel safe, but his touch threw me off kilter.

'So you're alone again?'

I looked at him askew. I had never been anything but alone. Why would he ask such a question? 'I like being alone, but I'd like to be alone without ghosts watching my every move.'

'Ghosts aren't like that. They're memories. They can't see you.'

'Believe me, these fucking can. They interact with me ... speak to me.'

'Sounds like hallucinations.'

'Fuck off!'

'Huh?'

'I'm not schizophrenic,' I shouted then wondered whether I was trying to convince him or myself.

'No you're not.' He nodded and touched my cheek.

'So why would I have hallucinations?'

'Perhaps you've connected to the dream world. Maybe you need to travel with these ghosts and learn what they want to teach you. Do you have many unanswered questions?'

'Oh yes ... thousands.'

'Would you like me to guide you?'

'Like you guided Vivienne?'

He blushed. 'No. I told you, she did that alone. I had no part in it and would never suggest you follow in her footsteps, but this is a landscape you can traverse. You will return changed, but stronger, when you accept the truth.'

'Okay,' I answered. 'Yes. I'd like you to guide me.' It felt like a big deal, accepting his help.

Everything I did, I always felt I did alone, but doing things alone put Vivienne into hospital and Scott seemed to know more about what was happening than I did. Strangely, I felt lighter as though some burden had been lifted from my shoulders and was now shared between the two of us. I smiled.

We sat, like statues, searching for a conversation light enough to allow us to skim across the deep waters beneath. As if struck by inspiration Scott rose to his feet like a Jack in the box.

'Lunch?' he asked.

I smiled again, wider this time, eager to communicate my appreciation. The perfect answer - feed the animals and keep the cages to their minds locked for a while longer.

34

After lunch we sat in silence again with steaming cups of green tea clutched in our hands. My body felt weird, as if by indulging one animal need others were nudging me to get my attention. I thought of Vivienne - that would be her answer - a quickie to restore balance. An alien heat burned between my legs and I wondered if I needed to pee, knowing this couldn't be desire. I never felt desire, only unease and bewilderment when the thought of sex flitted through my mind, flirting with my senses was something I ought to try one day. As always, I pushed and squeezed the thoughts away before they could take hold and make me nauseous, but they refused to leave, settling there, spreading fingers outwards, making my stomach tingle and my bound breasts strain against the swaddling bands beneath my shirt. I sipped my tea, focusing only on the taste and warmth. When I looked up at Scott's face, he had turned away and was staring out of the kitchen window. My eyes traced the curve of his ear beneath his hair and saw the light flutter of his pulse in his throat. Closing them, I breathed deeply and took another sip of tea.

'How's Madala? I've not seen him today,' I said, trying to break the tension.

'Hmm, sorry I was thinking. He's good thanks. Probably out hunting.'

He turned towards me and I felt his body ache as if he

fought a desire to touch my face. He looked down at his cup then back into my eyes. My thoughts betrayed me and I imagined him doing it, reaching out to stroke my cheek, brushing his lips against my mouth. I trembled and realised I wanted to be in his power. I wanted to shirk all responsibility for a minute, an hour, a day, a year, or perhaps forever. He held back, perhaps as frightened and confused as me. I realised if he did caress me I wouldn't resist, or at least would try not to push him away, try to stay calm and in the moment. I didn't want to resist. In fact I wanted to be unable to resist. If I could do this, things would be clear again and we'd stop bumping into each other like dodgem cars at a fairground. We could move on.

I saw a question form on his lips and wondered what he wanted to say. 'What is it?'

He looked confused and embarrassed.

'Penny for 'em.'

'You don't have a path,' he said.

My eyes widened and all the strange tingling, burning sensations fled from my body. 'What?'

'Sorry,' he said. 'I didn't mean to insult you.'

'I have no idea what you're talking about. If it was an insult it missed its target.'

'Your life, all those things, terrible things, you went through in your childhood, they're all here.' He moved his hands around my face and shoulders, inches away from my body. 'Your aura.'

'Okay.' I scowled at him.

'Everything has led you here: back to Bristol, to your mother and that house.'

I nodded and felt my scowl dissolve.

'But there is no path away from the house. I've tried to see one, but it hasn't formed yet. I'm, I'm worried about you.'

He looked at me. Did he think I would end up like my mother - alone and insane or dead? I knew that wouldn't happen. I would return to London, to my friends and the cause, my fight for justice, peace, equality, but first I wanted to read those diaries and take my journey through the dream world. I wanted to understand my past before I faced my future.

'Maybe you shouldn't go back there,' he said. 'At least not until I've smudged it for you.' He seemed to sense my question before I asked it. 'Cleansed it,' he added by way of an explanation.

'I have things there I need to do,' I told him. 'Anyway, where else would I stay? Here?'

He looked away.

I grunted and fidgeted, awkwardly shifting my weight in the chair. My body felt heavy and cumbersome. 'Maybe we should get one thing straight. I don't want to have sex with you any more than you want to have sex with me.'

He looked at me and smiled. 'You think I don't want to have sex with you?' A laugh stirred in his throat. 'I'm celibate. I don't ... it's because I'm a shaman. I've been celibate for years. So long I can hardly remember any other way. It helps the magic, but don't think it's easy around you. I've loved you in dreams, before the first time we met. I thought that was understood.'

In dreams?

'You too? You were there? I fucking knew it.' My cheeks glowed with warmth at his words and I felt free, knowing I could love him and be unafraid. He could be my brother or my friend, but he would never be my lover. I could be myself, laugh wildly and let my body move the way it wanted to move - without fear and with only the faintest kernel of sadness.

He noticed the change in me, stood up and stepped backwards to give me space. Filling it, I unfurled like a fern reaching from the shadows towards sunlight. Stretching and moving around the kitchen, I felt light on my feet. I wanted to dance and spin, for a moment, in an awkward pirouette then grinned at Scott. Never before had I revealed this side of myself, not to him, not to anyone - the child and the prepubescent - full of love, pure, whole, sexless love.

I talked without a break, checking every now and again I still held his attention. He sat cross-legged on the cool vinyl, his chin resting on his arched fingers and watched me, silently. His eyes wide open, he saw me now, really saw me. To be seen for the first time felt exhilarating and I told him about my life as a child, how my concern for my mother had later become hate and resentment, how I had felt trapped and controlled and how I had escaped to London. I told him about each of my London friends in loving detail, making their faults into virtues then I described Tomas's obsession with our mother and his increasingly dramatic letters as he pleaded with me to come back to Bristol. I detailed my arrival and my meetings with each ghost in turn, starting with my shameful mother. I even told him about my dreams: the stag, him and the woods. He looked as though he wanted to ask about the dream, but I couldn't stop talking and cut him short before his words were articulated. I explained about Chrissie and about our mixed up feelings for each other that led to her leaving for London, and I told him how powerless I felt sometimes, a problem for my adult self, but my child self comfortably acknowledged the feeling and was able to accept it. I described the discovered birth certificate and my unknown sister, the way Tomas would not listen when I tried to tell him about both and my sense of wonder at the possibility of another sibling. I didn't know if she was alive or dead and I desperately wanted to meet her. Finally, I told him about the last time I saw my mother and those words of love expressed on what was to be her death bed, her insistence I read her diaries and my fear about what I might find inside them. Vivienne knew Tomas would not be able to handle the truth inside those pages, but would I be any stronger?

At the end of my fast-paced soliloquy I paused for breath. Scott was still watching me, entranced and unmoving. Was he expecting more? There was no more? Or was there? I smiled, so wide I thought the pressure might split my cheeks. 'So here we are: the shaman and the anarchist, two unfashionable souls who find something precious in each other to love. I love you too, Scott. I can admit it now that I'm no longer running away from you.'

He stood up and stretched out his body. As I watched him the sexless child shrank back to make way for the woman, but our choice had been made and accepted. I left him with a chaste kiss. He asked me not to go back to the house, but I insisted it was where I had to be.

The diary lay open on my bed. I picked it up and started to read. "I knew something was wrong even before I opened the front door. I shouldn't have left them with him, but they are so young. Much younger than I had been and I thought they should be safe. As I walked into the drawing room I saw him in his usual spot. His head tipped back and licking his lips. The sight of him made me shudder - the leery, old wolf.

"I heard the children sobbing. They were hiding under the dining table - my old spot. They wouldn't tell me what happened, but as I walked towards him I saw his hand still lingering in his lap.

"I know what I have to do. I will protect them."

I heard footsteps in the attic, something heavy being dragged across the floor, and the chink of glass hitting the boards. It's not real, I told myself, but it was real - a memory replayed, not understood then, but fully realised now. Oh mummy!

It was after midnight, but I ran to him anyway. I wondered whether I locked the front door - fuck it, I wasn't going back. The diaries in my backpack weighed me down. Perhaps I should burn them, but I decided to take some time to think about it first. The streets were quiet, incessant drizzle keeping marauders in their homes and those few bodies who were leaving the late-night lock-ins slouched quietly towards home, heads bowed. I ran, unimpeded by any other living person.

Scott looked sleepy as he led me to the kitchen and offered me tea. I asked for somewhere to sleep and he showed me his room.

'I'll sleep on the couch,' he said.

I realised that wasn't what I wanted. Not tonight. Not with this dark memory curled up inside my soul. I wrapped my arms around him, pinning his arms to his sides. I couldn't reach his mouth, the difference in our heights too great, but stretching up I kissed his shoulders and throat. For a moment he remained still: frozen into the statue of gatekeeper then he bent over and fixed his lips to mine and I managed to lose myself for a few blissful moments before teeth clashed together and he pinched my nipple too eagerly while fighting with the fly of my trousers. I moved in a daze and before I realised what was happening we were on the bed. I wrapped my legs around him and he filled my emptiness at last for a few brief moments until it was over and I sat up, feeling soiled and ashamed. He gathered his robe, staring at the floor while I lay back on the bed and turned away from him. I listened to his forlorn footsteps as they receded from me.

When I was certain I was alone, I grabbed my knife from my bag and pricked my thighs with its point, sucking breath between clenched teeth. Blood slipped and slid between my thighs, but my wounds stung less than my pride. Eventually I fell asleep. The stag visited my dreams, but I threw stones at it to chase it away.

That morning, I lay awake listening to Dorothy and Scott's movements around the house. Hearing the dull blah, blah, blah of an edge of conversation, I assumed I was the subject at hand. I didn't want to get up; getting out of bed would involve seeing them. I just lay there, cursing my choices. Why had I forced myself on Scott? I knew his reasons for celibacy; he had explained them to me quite clearly, so what right did I have to make him break them? I had raped him or as good as. I felt ashamed, torn between a need to apologise and a need to escape. I reached for the knife again, but my hand wavered above the backpack as I wondered whether I could, should face this in a different way and talk to him. My stomach rebelled as fear and nausea gripped me.

There was a hesitant knocking at the bedroom door. I remained silent, hoping to be left alone, but the door inched open and Dorothy's face peeped around the edge. I watched through the veil of my eyelashes as the woman frowned and closed the door again and I was left alone with my shame and self-pity. I grabbed my knife and started cutting.

One step forward, two steps back.

35

Even after carving the pain from my skin, I still prickled and couldn't lie still. I knew I shouldn't be there. I had tainted the place, tainted Scott. I was more like my mother than I'd realised. Panicking, I decided to creep out and wondered where I should go. The idea of returning to the house frightened me, but at the same time it held an aura of inevitability. I was sure Tomas wouldn't let me stay with him and I doubted I'd feel more comfortable there anyway. The small amount of money he had given me had almost run out. Soon I would need money for food and how would I make the trip home. Would Tomas drive me back to London? Did I want to return to the squat? I wasn't certain of anything, least of all that, so I decided to return to Vivienne's house. I thought again about the diaries stuffed in my backpack and crammed in my bedside cabinet, plus the many more scattered around the house like skeletal leaves, a dead memory of things past. After reading about my granddad, and how that made me feel I didn't feel ready to read further.

Vivienne killed her father or forced him to commit suicide, because he abused me and Tomas. She'd found me under the table, her table, the one where I found her note. She had wanted to be his last victim, that meant he had abused her too. He had stolen her innocence and done the same to her children. I couldn't remember it, but I knew it was true. I considered burning the records – the diaries and the birth certificates alike. What good could come from knowing more? But I was afraid, not only of never knowing peace, but also of letting Vivienne down. If I burned them all, these buried memories, would I be consumed by the same fire?

Anyway, I couldn't burn them, not without first knowing what had happened to my sister.

I gathered my things and tiptoed out of the house. If Scott heard me leave he did not challenge me. The air outside was full of mist and chill air bit at my face, a shock after the recent hot summer weather. I lit a cigarette.

The hallway was full of unsettled energy, welcoming me back. The air seemed to sniff me, trying to explore me, know my secrets and understand the change in me. I met it with a defiant stare and strode to the kitchen. Realising I hadn't drunk coffee for over twenty-four hours, I made myself a cup and guzzled it greedily, enjoying the scratch of roughly-ground grains in my throat. I made another and sat cradling it, smoking. The house might have been frightening, but I belonged there. Its memories were mine, mine and my mother's, and to move on I needed to face them all, even the diaries. I opened my bag and touched one of the cool covers then withdrew my hand, leaving it there, waiting. I needed sleep first.

My bare feet crushed moss in the shadow-filled forest. Movement ahead – a stag darting between the trees, I did not follow it. The stag held no secrets for me to explore, not today. Its coat looked tarnished and its eyes never met mine. I touched the bark of a tree instead. The wood felt like skin and I jumped back, shaking my hand as if it had burned me. I knew I must not touch the old, rotten flesh. I knew it was wrong, but it bent towards me, closer and closer, crowding me, jeering at me, until I turned and fled.

The ringing of the borrowed mobile-phone woke me.

'Hullo,'

'Hi Giz, it's Tom. We're just trying to sort out the funeral and the reading of the will. The will's gonna be read today so we can know Mum's wishes. Do you wanna come?'

He was still calling me Giz. The idea of correcting him yet again felt too exhausting to contemplate. 'No thanks,' I said, sinking into the pillow.

'Are you sure? Look maybe you should be there. You're in her house after all. You need to know what's gonna happen.'

'Why can't you tell me later?'

I heard him shuffling the phone in his hands. His breath grew quiet, muffled then he was back again, whispering. 'We may have conflicting interests, Sis. Cathy wants to sell the house.'

I nodded. The news did not surprise me. 'I don't see why it'll make any difference if I'm there. I won't leave here, not until I'm finished. But, it's okay, Bro. It shouldn't take long. Then I'll be on my way home and all this will be yours.'

'Are you sure?'

'Yes, I'm sure.'

I hung up and got out of bed. If I planned to stay in Bristol longer I'd need to do some shopping. I checked my money and found only a couple of pounds. I would need to start earning soon. If Cathy wanted me out it was unlikely Tomas would keep paying me to stay. There were a few art supplies in my bag so I could go back to painting tourist's portraits or I could just sell some things; after all it would be far quicker to rifle through Vivienne's jewellery, one or two things should raise enough to tide me over and they were mine anyway, really.

Vivienne's room looked empty as if it knew all that had happened and had given up waiting for its mistress to return. Hunting for a jewellery box, I opened wardrobes full of beautiful clothing; almost all of it was purple or black. I found my mother's ballet shoes, sniffed them and held the soft leather against my cheek. Nanny's story of the ballerina and the revolutionary filled my head with images of Vivienne dancing for the queens and kings she had described. How beautiful and graceful she must have looked. I start to cry. Cradling the slippers, I rocked to and fro and gulped back wails before they could escape, wails full of regret and sorrow. Mummy was gone and I could never get any closer to her. I tried the ballet shoes on and laughed. My feet were tiny inside them and I felt like a child again, wearing my mother's footwear, expecting to be punished if discovered. Lifting my feet, I left the shoes on the floor and continued searching for jewellery. I opened the lid of a puce-coloured leather box and a prima ballerina sprang into life, pirouetting in the mirror. Swan Lake chimed as I dug through the jumble of gold and silver. No rings, they would be missed. Not that pendant either, it was her favourite. I found a watch, a Cartier that looked as though it might be made of gold. Perfect. I grabbed tissues from a frilly box and wrapped it carefully before sliding it into my backpack. Now all I needed to do was find a jeweller.

'And you say it was your mother's.' The jeweller's face glowed in the reflected beauty of the watch, kindly yet suspicious.

I nodded. 'It was a present, but now I need money more.'

He looked me up and down. 'It's a nice watch, but the market is slow at the moment. I could only offer you one hundred pounds.'

I knew I could get more. His kindly face looked sly after all, but I accepted the exchange.

Food bought I made my way back to the house. Scott was waiting outside the front door.

'Do you ever wear shoes?' I asked him. 'What are you doing here?'

'I brought my box of tricks, to clean the house ... Remember?'

I brushed past him to unlock the door. 'Yes, yes, of course. Come in.'

I led him into the kitchen and switched the kettle on. 'Tea?'

'What kinds have you got?'

'Tetley,' I answered. 'Or coffee.'

'Just hot water, please.' He opened his box of tricks that was really a bag and brought out a large bundle of twigs tied with string that reminded me of a mauled bridal bouquet.

I brought his water and my coffee to the table and lit a cigarette. 'What's that?'

'Herbs. We burn them to cleanse the house.'

'Okay. How long will it take?'

'An hour maybe. It's a big place.'

I shrugged. 'True.'

I passed my lighter to him and he set light to one end of the bundle. The smoke was pungent and it made me cough. He blew gently on the flames until they dulled into gentle embers. The smoke grew thicker. He took a sip from his mug and stood up. As he walked around the room, leaving trails of smoke in his wake, he whispered words that sounded random to me. A few of them made sense, but not many.

He left the kitchen and wafted into the hallway. I stayed behind and opened the door to the garden. The air stung my eyes and I wanted to breathe something that didn't stink of burning sage.

The sun shone through gaps between low white clouds. I realised I hadn't been in the garden since Chrissie had left for London. We had tended to this garden together, tried to grow new life, sowing seeds in the earth. It seemed pointless now Vivienne was dead. I heard laughter and scanned the perimeter wall, looking for visiting ghosts or lost children and found neither. I wondered whether I was making a mistake. I had learned so much from the spirits in this house, most of it painful, all of it important. Most important of all I had learned to forgive my mother.

I stepped inside again and listened for Scott's footsteps. I heard him above me as I entered the dining room. He must have been in my room, purging it of bad memories and toxic energy. I felt sceptical and wondered how a few whispered words and some herbs could change anything, but the dining room did seem brighter, lighter and less oppressive than before. If nothing else, perhaps the scent would clear my head.

He moved from my room and I followed the sound of his footsteps across the hallway. He was in Vivienne's room now. I could hear him through the kitchen ceiling, treading lightly.

I returned to my coffee. It had cooled a little, but was still drinkable. I imagined the soft squeak of his soles against floorboards were my mother's. That she was gliding about her room as graceful as ever, getting ready for a night of entertaining some infatuated gentleman. That was all she ever seemed to do, when she was not flirting with death, she was always dancing or making love. I swallowed an uncomfortable lump in my throat and realised I had envied her, both for her beauty and the ease with which she spoke to people, enchanting them. She had been a lot to live up to, my brother's perfect woman, deeply flawed though she was. She was also impossibly magnificent.

I heard the stairs creak and realised Scott was returning. When he reached the table again he stubbed out the herbs in a pewter bowl. 'That's the smudging done.'

'What now?'

'I guess that's up to you. The house has been purified. If you really want to journey into the dream world you can do so today.'

I stared at him.

'You've decided not to?'

I shrugged. 'I haven't thought about it, not really. I thought after ... you know ... well I didn't expect to see you again. Look Scott ... I'm sorry. What I did ... what I did to you ... that was wrong.'

He smiled at me and nodded. 'I forgive you.'

I sighed and tried to communicate my gratitude through my eyes. We were silent for a moment as the ache of understanding was salved. 'So, no more ghosts?'

'They should quieten down for a while at least, but we'll need to keep cleansing the place. I can teach you how.'

'I doubt I can stay.'

'Why?'

'My brother and his wife want to sell the house.'

'Will you go back to London?'

'Probably.'

'That's a shame. Just when I was getting used to having you around.'

I smiled and placed the palm of my right hand over the back of his left. 'Thank you.'

He nodded and picked up his mug. 'We can chat about it another day.'

Excitement burned my chest. 'I want to.'

'Yes?'

'Yes. I want to take that journey. I don't want to leave without answering certain ... questions.'

'Great. I'll set things up in the living room. Come in when you're ready, Crow.'

I smoked another cigarette before I followed him. My heartbeat quickened. I didn't know what I was about to do and the adrenaline rushing through my body cautioned me against stupidity. I didn't listen.

'What are you trying to find out in the dream world?' he asked.

'Why I am the way I am. I feel like a piece of me is missing. Perhaps it's my mother.'

'Perfect, we'll start there. I'll guide you. You can go as slowly or as quickly as you wish. There are no rules except those you set for yourself. I'll get you to sit or lie here and I'll count slowly, from one to ten. Feel yourself relax. I'll describe a tranquil place and you should imagine yourself walking there, along a path through woodland, until you reach a clearing. You'll enter a sacred space. You'll know it when you're there,' he told me. 'It's a safe place to start your journey, or you can stay there a while: plant a tree, build a house or just sit and think. When you're ready to move on, you'll see a pathway ahead. Follow it. Keep walking until you meet your spirit guide. Greet it warmly, it is an old friend. The love you show it will make your time there more special and more useful. The guide will appear in the form of an animal. Tell your spirit guide what you seek. It'll lead you to a gateway. Some gateways lead downwards, these can look like caves or lakes. Others lead upwards: ladders or mountains to climb. You will need to journey upwards to find your fragment. When you see it you will know, but it might be well hidden and it might take you many journeys to find it.

'I'll call you back when it's time to return. I'll count backwards from ten then you'll wake up. If you want to come back before I start counting go to your sacred space. From there you should be able to return yourself. If not you'll be safe and comfortable until I call you.'

'Can a sacred space be a mountain range?' I asked.

'Usually it's a woodland clearing or a cave, but I guess it could be anywhere.'

'What's yours?'

'Discover your own. Then we can talk about mine,' he answered.

'So what do I do first?' I chewed my knuckles wondering whether I could do this and how crazy I was for even trying.

'You need to visit your sacred space. Make it yours. You shouldn't start any journey until you have somewhere familiar to come back to.'

'Did you tell Vivienne this?'

He sighed. His brow furrowed and he looked at his hands.

My heart lurched to fill the space between us. He looked sad and exhausted. I felt sorry for him and chastised myself for picking at that wound again. 'I'm sorry, I didn't mean ... I'm sure she found her space and was happy there.'

Scott shook his head, took a deep breath in and sat on the floor with his legs crossed in the lotus position. I knew there was no way I would be able to get my body moulded into those painful looking knots and hoped it wouldn't be necessary.

'If you're ready,' Scott said, motioning to the mat between us.

'Not yet,' I answered. 'Physical needs before spiritual ones. Loo and a cig, then I'll do it.'

He smiled and touched my cheek. The physical contact was unexpected and made me shiver.

'I'll wait here for you. I'll smudge the air again.'

As I returned to the room, he asked me for the last time, 'Are you sure you wouldn't prefer to do this at mine?'

'No, I lost my soul here and here's where I'll find it.'

He shrugged. 'That's not how it works.'

'It is for me. Call it symbolic.' I sat on the rug, crossed

my legs like a school kid and rested my hands on my thighs, palms facing skyward. 'Okay, how do I do this?'

'Breathe deeply and count to ten. Concentrate only on your breathing and the numbers. Each number should be one breath.'

He was only a few feet away: my magic mirror, my guide.

I nodded. 'Eyes open or closed?'

'Closed is probably easier.'

I shut my eyes and breathed in deeply through my nostrils.

'When you reach ten you should visualise a place in which you feel safe. It can be a real place or one from your imagination. Look around you. Hear the sound of the birds above you, feel the grass, moss, sand or rock beneath your feet, feel the breeze on your skin. You will see a path below your toes. If you follow it will you will reach your sacred spot - the place you can visit whenever you wish.' His voice faded and he faded with it.

My shoulders and upper arms were pinned into place between the torsos of friends. Ahead, a line of police shields blocked the street. Chants of defiance filled my ears and I joined them, filling the air with hot breath and strong language. Grinning, I slipped my arms through those of my comrades, Chrissie and Matty. Together we pushed forward as the bodies became a wave of solidarity pouring onto the barren shore. Police turned and ran from our mass of people power. I kissed Chrissie on the mouth and exhaled loudly.

'What the fuck? Right on!'

I turned and stretched my body, ready to sprint towards our goal. With a wide smile that threatened to tear my cheeks, I stepped into a woodland clearing. I spun around, bewildered and looked at the circle of silver birch trees that had replaced the crowd. Birds were singing, but their bodies were hidden by the leaves. Springy moss cushioned my steps. It felt cool and tickled between my toes. The air was fragrant and the sweet scent of lavender and honey calmed me. Laughing, I flapped my arms like wings and danced around the circle, brushing the bark of the trees with my fingertips. Something was missing and the scene did not feel quite right to me. I faced the centre of the clearing and imagined planting an acorn then watched as a mighty oak filled the void. Now it was perfect and I stood there, silently admiring it for a while.

I felt I was being tugged towards the circle of trees and spotted a gap between two of the birches. The trees stood so pale it reminded me of a lucky gap between two front teeth. Between them I could see a path covered in golden pine needles. I knew this was where my journey would start and followed the pathway without any reservation. The trees along this avenue were evergreens. Scots pine and spruce trees stood tall and proud on either side. Crumbly earth spotted with clumps of grass and pine needles stretched out in front of me and behind. The pattern reminded me of a giraffe's tall neck.

I walked and walked, but my view never changed. The

woodland looked labyrinthine and I began to worry I would never reach my gateway. I closed my eyes and tried to remember Scott's instructions. I needed to find a spirit guide – that was it. My eyes scanned shadows and I saw movement between the trees. The creature showed itself and stepped towards me; its head was the same height as my own, but crowned with silver antlers: my stag. Of course! All tension flowed from my body into the earth. I had always known which animal it would be. I reached out my hand and the stag's soft nose nuzzled against my palm. Stroking its cheek, I saw wisdom in the gentle brown eyes. I smoothed the velvety hair of its throat, then hugged and kissed its warm shoulders, telling my spirit guide I was pleased to meet him. I explained my mission and told him I needed to reach the gateway. The beautiful head nodded in acknowledgement. I smiled at the perfection around me and felt confident any journey I made here would be successful.

The sound of a voice cut through the avenue of trees. 'Ten.'

'I'm sorry, I haven't got ...' I turned around and sprinted back towards the clearing. I could hear the stag running beside me.

'Nine.'

'Long but I'll come back.'

'Eight.'

'Soon, I promise, I'll.'

'Seven.'

'Meet you here, I'll.'

'Six.'

'Look for you.'

'Five.'

'Goodbye.'

My eyes flicked open and I found myself back in Vivienne's living room. Scott sat cross-legged in front of me, smiling.

'How was it?' he asked.

'Not long enough, but amazing. Where is it?'

'The dream world, but it's as real as this one.'

'I felt it. I want to go back,' I told him.

'You can go back any time you want, but I'm asking you to wait. Let us do this together, at least at first, please.'

I nodded. 'When?'

'Tomorrow,' he promised.

Tomorrow seemed too far away, but I agreed. I offered him a drink, but he told me he had another appointment, made his apologies and left, but not before promising to return the following day at eleven.

Twenty hours stretched out in front of me like a desert highway, its shape distorted in the heat haze. Exhilaration from my psychic journey still made me shiver and I wiped sweat from the back of my neck. I realised how much I missed the stand-offs between police and comrades, the state and the people. No other feeling came close. It was as though everything else was hibernation and I only truly came alive when fighting for my beliefs, my rights and those of others. It was a drug to me and I felt the sting of withdraw. I wondered how to fill this soulless day and considered returning to Vivienne's diaries, but I wouldn't read more about my granddad, I couldn't. Perhaps I could uncover a written account of my mother's experiences of shamanism and see how closely they echoed my own, or I could check whether I could find any mention of my sister.

I opened my bag and felt inside. The house seemed empty without Scott there and the air was quiet as if the building was holding its breath. I hoped Scott's smudging worked and the spirits were calm. I pulled out the books and placed them on the grimy kitchen table. I hadn't realised before how dirty the kitchen had become. I hastily returned the books to the backpack, not wanted to soil them, and searched for a cloth. This was not a squat; it was a home. A saying replayed in my head as I dampened a dishcloth. "You can take the anarchist out of the squat, but you can't take the squat out of the anarchist." I decided it was time I challenged that thought - squatting was necessary sometimes, a means to an end, but not a style I wanted to emulate always. By the time I had finished cleaning, the kitchen sparkled in the late afternoon sunlight.

After the quick reward of lungs-full of nicotine, I claimed the vacuum cleaner from a cupboard and started work in the living room. When I had finished the ground floor it was evening and I felt exhausted. My muscles burned, but a sense of calm settled over me, not unlike the sensations I experienced after a large protest or a riot. I smiled, content at last.

Before I could settle I heard my stomach grumble. I grabbed food and shovelled it into my mouth. The window was no longer able to capture natural light, so I sat in the growing gloom, contemplating. I no longer felt afraid. A profound sense of calm assured me I had almost reached the end of my journey. I wondered about Tomas and Vivienne's will and what might happen, but the question held no fear and didn't keep my interest for long. I considered phoning my brother, but decided to wait until morning, opting for an early night instead. As I rambled up the stairs my eyes wandered over pictures of my mother. They no longer judged me. I could almost hear Vivienne cheer me onward, desperate for me to win this race.

The physical exertion of housework had made me sticky with sweat and I wanted to bathe. The house seemed peaceful; there were no creaks or groans, no sign of anything otherworldly so I decided to take the chance and ran some hot water and oils into the tub. The smell reminded me of the woodland I had visited in my trance and I had to force myself to keep my eyes open as I soaked my aching limbs in the warm water. Nothing attacked me as I lay there resting and my confidence grew. I felt certain Scott's smudging had done the trick and cleared the place of all its bad memories at least for tonight.

As I walked naked from the bathroom to my bedroom I felt no invisible eyes upon me, watching me, waiting to strike. Shapes no longer lurked in every shadow. Without dressing, I settled into bed and read until my eyes could no longer resist their tug-of-war game with slumber.

In my dream, I walked through the forest, one of my hands draped over the shoulder of my stag, feeling its taut muscles shift as it moved. I had no idea where we were headed, but it didn't matter as the stag led the way. Gaps between the trees widened and the canopy opened to welcome the soft blue sky as we journeyed closer to its edge. Beyond the limits of bark and leaves I saw a purple mountain. As we left the woodland behind, the stag held back. I looked at its face, confused, but its eyes urged me to continue onward. At the base of the mountain a deep pool of green water reflected a snowy summit. I dipped a toe into warm water and looked at the welcoming pool then the menacing mountain before diving downwards.

36

I woke refreshed, stretched my limbs and sat up. My body jolted back as if I had stuck wet fingers into an electrical socket. In the dawn light I saw a dark shape, someone sitting at the end of my bed.

'Mum?' I asked.

The black haired figure started to turn around slowly and a pale ear poked between thick locks then the tip of a delicate nose and dark eyelashes were revealed. I held my breath and the face stopped turning.

'No,' I whispered.

As if answering my dismissal, the figure vanished. My body ached and I reached toward the space the phantom had occupied. No sense of the interloper remained and I felt both relieved and disappointed. I cursed my haste in telling it to go. Reluctantly, I picked up my clothes to get dressed and realised how badly they stank. I couldn't remember the last time I had washed them, not even my underwear. I bundled them up and walked naked into the kitchen. After studying the washing machine for a few minutes, I used a setting I hoped was right. Mesmerised by the tumbling laundry, I sat watching the porthole with a hot drink and cigarette. I glanced at the time - seven o'clock, plenty of time for my washing to dry. The morning sun warmed my skin as clothes pegs and wet linen weighed down my arms.

I stood surrounded by the high walls and hedges that cut the garden off from the rest of the world. Even so, I felt eyes studying my flesh and glanced nervously around the garden. I hurried inside. My uncovered skin made me feel vulnerable so I raked through Vivienne's wardrobe and chose a black cotton blouse and a gypsy style skirt. The skirt had probably been mid-calf length on Vivienne, but brushed the floor as I walked around the bedroom. Catching a glimpse in the mirror, I laughed. My bald head paired with such a feminine outfit looked comical and I felt as though I was wearing drag, but it was better than being naked.

Eight o'clock - would Tomas be awake yet? He wouldn't phone me this early of course and I felt too nervous to dial his number. My growing interest in the contents of my mother's will disturbed me and I wondered why I should care. I decided to force myself to wait until he contacted me. If he didn't call today I would phone tomorrow and ask about the funeral arrangements and the will.

Only three hours until Scott was due to arrive and I could hardly wait to visit my dream world again. Of course I could try to go there alone, Scott told me it was possible, but he also asked me to wait. For once, I felt like doing as I was asked.

My larder was full, the ground floor of the house was clean and my washing hanging on the line; I had fulfilled every household duty I could imagine. Strangely, these things felt like huge achievements and my mind reached for other things I might do as well. My hollow pride made me uncomfortable, none of it really meant anything I argued to myself, fearing I might lose focus on what was actually important. In London ... well at this time of day, I would probably still be sleeping but, when I woke up, what would I be doing? Most days I'd sketch tourists' portraits for coins, but I didn't need the money now and there was plenty left to sell when the watch fund ran out. In London, if a protest was planned I would, of course, join my comrades-in-arms. I felt ashamed I hadn't yet approached political movements in Bristol. The city was famous for its anarchist movement. How could I become so easily distracted? I realised there wouldn't be enough time before Scott arrived, but I promised myself I would search out the local activists if I planned to stay longer in this city; I needed the violent reality of a struggle to ground me. It felt too quiet, surreal almost, without the shouting of slogans, the standing arm-in-arm and the throwing of missiles at hostile targets. I needed friends, needed to be useful. Loneliness washed over me, I had nothing but ghosts to keep me company in this big, old house.

Eight-fifteen – time crawled by and I decided to sketch the garden and included, in the picture, my Nanny digging the vegetable patch and me as a child beside her, playing with worms. I became absorbed in my work. Smudges of graphite darkened my skin as thoroughly as they marked the paper.

The doorbell broke my reverie at eleven-fifteen. I hid my drawing in a cupboard and went to greet Scott, pushing the awkward memory of that humiliating night aside. The beauty of my dream world was all I needed from him. He returned my smile and stepped inside, pulling his heavy bag after him. I led him into the living room and we spread out the mat together.

'How do you smudge?' I asked.

'I'm just burning some sage. The smoke cleanses the room. Did it work? Was it peaceful?'

'I think so.' The smoke hung heavily in the air, but as it dispelled the room did feel more welcoming.

'They're still here,' I said.

An arcing movement of his head informed me he didn't understand.

'The ghosts, they're still here, but they're behaving themselves at the moment.'

He nodded. 'Maybe they always will be. Maybe you're not ready to let them go. That's okay though. It really is - the ancient tribes co-existed with their dead ancestors and learned from them.'

'Were they ever drowned by them?' I asked.

'Probably not,' he conceded. 'Do you want them gone?'

'To be honest I don't know.'

I sat on the mat and crossed my legs, placing my hands, palms up, on my thighs while Scott lit candles around me. I started counting. When I opened my eyes I was in my woodland grove. An oak tree stretched its limbs towards the blue sky above. Its pale bark felt warm to my touch as I embraced it and felt its ancient power course through my body.

Faster this time, I moved onwards. My stag joined me at the start of the path. I stroked its neck and kissed its nose then we walked together towards the mountain.

'I have to go up,' I said. 'I have things I need to find. I cannot play in the water. Not today.'

The stag nodded with movements so graceful they made me cry. I let warm saline wash my cheeks, feeling no shame. The lake and mountain came into view. The mountain was so high its apex was hidden by clouds. The sides looked sheer and slippery, too difficult to climb. The stag wandered around its base and I followed the animal until, at the far side of the mountain, I found foot and hand holds perfect for my height. Thanking my guide, I started to ascend into the chill air. I did not shiver, but instead, gripping the rock-face tightly, I climbed neither looking down nor up. I inched my way higher until my face was surrounded by cloud and water droplets tickled my skin. I kept concentrating on the foot and hand holds, knowing I was almost there.

My eyes rose above clouds that seemed to make a plateau solid enough to walk across. The mountain reached further up, but I was convinced these clouds would support my weight. Heart beating fast, I let go of the mountain with one trembling hand and reached across. My fingers did not sink into the cloud so I climbed higher and tried again, with a foot this time. Solid whiteness beneath me, I took a deep breath and stepped off the mountain, half-expecting to plummet to the ground below. With each step I gained confidence and moved further from the peak, rationalising - of course I wouldn't fall through, this was my dream-self and I weighed nothing here. But the magic of it was beyond rationalisation and adrenaline rushed through me, making me giddy with excitement.

I wondered what I had come here to find. I had told Scott I felt incomplete, as though I had lost some essential part of myself within the walls of Vivienne's house. Perhaps I might find them here, those soul fragments or whatever they might be called? The perpetual whiteness was mind-bending and I searched for breaks in the monotony, however small. Finding one, at last, I walked towards it and found a ball of indigo energy, about the size of my head and perfectly spherical.

Energy crackled as I approached and it reminded me of a plasma ball I once saw in London but, around this sphere, twisted razor wire seemed to grow like ivy, organic and part of this place. I couldn't reach past the barbs to touch the ball, but I felt certain it was my soul, protected from the world by defences that would strip flesh from the bone of any transgressor. I circled around it to view the other side and found, near the top, a wide and jagged gash. The torn section was a painful looking crimson and I guessed this was the piece I had lost or had been stolen from me. I winced as I stared at it - so much pain. I could hardly bear it. My body shook and tears fell.

Scattered around the sphere, some laying inert on the cloud-floor and others suspended in the air, were things I recognised from my childhood: roller-skates and dolls, Nanny's gardening gloves, and my grandfather's chair. Wondering where I should look first, I pressed my temples, trying in vain to shut out the painful screams of my wounded soul, knowing this was not a dream; it was real and I wanted to leave, run far away. Within moments I was far away, back on the woodland path. Ahead of me stood my oak tree and I sensed the mountain scowl at me from far, far behind, frustrated by my fear and indecision. The stag stood beside me, licking tears from my cheeks.

'Shit.' I turned around, ready to head back towards the mountain, but the branches of the trees echoed with the sound of Scott's voice.

'Ten.'

'I saw it,' I told the stag. 'I found my soul.'

'Nine.'

'I'll come back tomorrow.'

'Eight.'

'Goodbye,' I called as the wood faded around me.

Scott sat on the rug in front of me. 'Are you okay? You were shaking. You seemed frightened.'

'I'm fine,' I said. 'I want to go back.'

'Tomorrow,' he promised.

'Do you have to rush off again?'

'No, not today. Why? Do you want me to stay?'

I breathed noisily through my nose, and looked at him. 'Look, I know the other night was a mistake. I'm sorry.'

He turned away, but not far enough to prevent me seeing the edge of his cheek flush. 'It takes two to ... Look it wasn't your fault. I just wish ...'

Poor Scott. Like Eve, I took the blame for what had happened onto my own shoulders without considering an alternative. 'Me too.'

When he turned towards me again he had managed to control the colour of his cheeks. I sat and watched him as he marched around the living room, shaking out his limbs. Maybe my stare made him feel uncomfortable because he kept glancing down at me then turning away again.

'I'm hungry,' he said, eventually.

I pushed myself to my feet. My muscles protested at the sudden movement and I felt much older than the caged animal before me.

'I'll make lunch,' I said, but really I wanted him to go so I could be alone with this feeling of fragility, let it roll about on my tongue and juggle it between my hands. I held open the fridge door, inhaled the odours of food then gathered together salad leaves and hummus and carried them across to the kitchen table.

'So tell me about these diaries,' Scott said through a mouth full of hummus.

I touched the skin beside my own lips to wipe away a mirrored smear on Scott's face, but he didn't notice. I shrugged, not bothering to tell him. 'I've only just started reading them, but from what I've seen so far they seem to cover the worst parts of Vivienne's life. I don't know whether I'll carry on. Some of it I ... well I don't wanna know. I guess I'm kinda scared what more I might find. And ...'

'What, Crow.' He stared at me, as if trying to read the answer in my eyes.

'And ... the ghosts; they move about when I'm reading the diaries. I can hear them outside my bedroom door.'

'Even now?'

'Yes. There's things in there ... darkness ... something happened to me, to Vivienne, to all of us. I think I know what it was, but at the same time I don't want to know. Would you want to know if your grandfather abused you?'

He shook his head. 'If you think they're important, do you want me to read them for you?'

I stopped chewing and stared into his blue eyes. Some of the entries would be about him. Would his eyes lose their sparkle if he read them? I shook my head, the diaries were for me; Vivienne asked me to read them and I would, as soon as I felt ready.

'You've got food ... here,' I told him, pointing.

Scott sniffed and wiped it away.

'Do you want to read them?' he asked me.

'I, I don't know,' I admitted. 'But, I do wanna know if there's anything about my sister in them.'

'Why don't you read them somewhere else, away from

the house, the park or maybe my garden? At least the ghosts shouldn't bother you there.'

'Good idea,' I said. 'Another problem solved by Doctor Scott.'

He narrowed his eyes and didn't reply. I smiled to show him I was being playful, but he didn't reciprocate. Bruised male pride, I wondered.

Everything had changed since the afternoon I shed my inhibitions and danced before him. I'd wanted unconditional, asexual love but, in my grief, I'd pushed for something else. Scott still supported me, but part of him was guarded. I wanted to reach beyond this barrier, like the time my mind had reached beyond his garden wall and watched him tie ribbons to his tree. I yearned to touch that vulnerable secret side, but knew I couldn't rush him. I needed to be patient, and respect his boundaries as he'd respected mine.

The mobile phone started chirruping from inside my backpack. Grabbing it, I looked at the number. 'Hi, Bro!'

A cold, female voice answered. 'He's not well. I thought you'd better know. The funeral's tomorrow. Two o'clock, Cadford.'

The line went dead before I could ask about my brother. I sat there, cradling the phone against my ear. Silence. The room spun out of focus, my ear burned and my muscles stiffened. I felt hands on my shoulders: gentle hands. One pulled the phone away from my ear, then after a pause, maybe to listen, placed it gently on the kitchen table. I stared at it then snatched up Catherine's phone and threw it at the wall. It shattered and fell to the floor in pieces.

Hands remained on my shoulders. I tried to shake them off, but their light yet insistent touch endured. Spinning around, I pulled back my fist and let it fly. It made contact with Scott's jaw and he stumbled back, cupping his chin with one hand while the other twitched by his side. I stared at him, defying the sting of accusation I sensed in his blue eyes.

'Crow.' Blood and spit dripped from his mouth. 'Crow, it's me: Scott.'

I didn't care who it was. The desire to hurt him, anyone, pushed me forward. I punched again. He caught my fist mid-swing then embraced me. I tried to pull away, grunting at him through bared teeth like a wild animal, but he held me firm. I stamped on his naked feet, but he didn't let go. Burrowing my face in Scott's t-shirt, I wept as my muscles lost their rigidity and I felt like jelly, unable to support my weight. Scott held me up, and I soaked him with my sorrow.

When I was empty of tears and my throat felt raw from crying, I looked up at the mess I had made of his face and stroked his cheek. 'I'm sorry,' I said. 'I'm so ashamed. I don't ... that's not ...' I let the sentence trail off. Finishing it would be a lie.

He looked at me and tried to smile, although the movement made him wince. He tried to answer, but spat blood in my face.

'Let's clean you up.' I fetched a glass of water for him and took him to the sink. As he rinsed blood from his mouth, I found an ice pack.

He sat at the table, holding the ice against his swelling chin.

'I'm sorry,' I said again.

He shrugged. 'I've done worse.'

I didn't believe him. My gentle Scott wouldn't hurt anyone. He probably meant he'd had worse. That I could believe.

Staring at me, he shook his head, slowly and deliberately. 'When I was a kid I pushed a girl under a car.'

I tried to absorb the information - he was a child, it was an accident, but he had said pushed. 'Why?' I asked.

'She was bullying me and I'd had enough. I'm not proud of it, but it happened. Everyone's anger gets out of control sometimes.'

'How old were you?'

'Thirteen,' he shifted about in his chair.

Thirteen, the same age I ran away from home. Perhaps it was the age when kids stopped accepting abuse and took action instead. It was obvious the subject was making him uncomfortable, and I knew I should stop asking. I decided I would, after one more question.

'What happened? After I mean.'

'I had to have a psych evaluation and I changed schools. The girl died, and I changed schools.' He looked at the floor. His shoulders rose and fell in a slow rhythm.

I broke the silence. 'That was my brother's wife on the phone. The funeral's tomorrow. Will you come with me?'

Scott nodded.

'We'll go from here, after our ... session. Is that okay?'

'What time is it?'

'Two, at Cadford.'

'It'll be fine.'

'I guess I'd better buy something to wear?' I sighed.

'Do you have any money?' he asked. He looked at the array of food we had been devouring then my face. 'I thought you were skint.'

My cheeks burned and I turned away. 'I got some more.'

I felt the weight of his stare and wished I had kept my mouth shut about clothes. I'd probably end up wearing my t-shirt and combats anyway - why not? Or I could lift something black from Vivienne's wardrobe just as easily.

He watched me carefully. 'It just doesn't seem like a priority you'd have, Crow.'

He was right. I felt his disappointment and wanted to explain. 'I don't want to offend anyone with my clothes.' It was a lame excuse, but the only reason I could dredge up to offer him. I felt ridiculous, after punching him and hearing his painful confession, I had talked about what – clothes? What was happening to me?

Scott sighed. 'I guess I'd better go then. Thanks for lunch. Eleven again tomorrow?'

I nodded. 'Thanks Scott. Really thanks for everything ...'

He shrugged and left.

After closing the door behind him, I returned to the kitchen and sat at the table, cradling my head in my hands. I thought of the watch I had sold and wondered whether I felt guilty, but that didn't make sense. It was just a thing, a worthless possession, probably a gift from a man who wanted more from Vivienne than it was worth. That's why Mother never wore it, but Scott was right - my priorities had become skewed. I shook my head and tried to remember what was important – freedom, equality, love. My thoughts sprinted towards my sister. Would she be at the funeral? Did she even know Vivienne had died? I thought of my brother. He would be dressed in a black suit and tie, his wife also shrouded in mourning garb, would he care if I wasn't? My relationship with him felt more precarious now than ever before. I could lose him so easily and the thought terrified me. I justified my desire for sensible funeral clothes by thinking of him. I wanted to make it easier for him and that, at least, was important.

37

I woke, clutching my head, and heard people moving around downstairs. Panicking, I searched my heavy head for an answer. Perhaps the sounds were ghosts or maybe burglars were robbing the house. I wasn't even sure whether it was morning or night? A bright shaft of sunlight, poking its way through the gap in my curtains and into my brain, was the painful answer. It was definitely day time.

I pulled the knife from my backpack and pinpointed the source of the sounds: the kitchen. I crept down stairs, knife ready in my fist. Adrenaline twitched through my muscles as I paused outside the kitchen door. The voices were female and unfamiliar. I strained to see, but had to nudge forwards, my knuckles white around the knife-handle. There were at least two in the room, but my foggy head prevented me from understanding their words. I wanted to return to bed. What did it matter if the place was being robbed? Maybe the voices belonged to squatters moving in to what they thought was vacant property.

I inched forward. The room was so bright it was hard to focus. I heard a gasp then a shout.

'Giselle!' A woman rushed towards me. 'What are you doing, Giz?' asked a voice so shrill and loud it threatened to shatter my skull. 'Put the knife down.'

I narrowed my eyes to restrict the light, but it was still too bright. I retreated into the shadowy hallway and the noise followed. It was Catherine.

'Cathy,' I gasped. 'What are you doing here?'

'Vivienne's wake,' was the contemptuous answer. 'Well you didn't think our house would be big enough did you?'

'But, but ...'

'Put the knife away please, then you can come and make yourself useful.'

I loped away, returning to my room, feeling like a chastised puppy. Resentment bubbled inside me and I wished my head didn't hurt so much. Going back to bed seemed like the safest option. When I woke again, hopefully, Cathy would be gone. I curled up under the covers and begged for the pain to subside. Hurtling adrenaline denied me my return to sleep and my quickening heart felt like a tribal beat inside my head - a deafening drum roll. I felt sick.

I ran to the bathroom, bent over the toilet bowl and emptied my stomach. In the distance I heard someone call my old name, but I didn't care. Let them call. I flushed and washed my face, feeling a little better, but still unable to stop my body shaking. I squinted at the contents of the medicine cupboard and pushed a couple of white tablets through silver foil then rinsed their bitter taste from my mouth with a palm full of water.

I returned to my room and hunched under the covers, trying to ignore the sounds from the kitchen. I managed to doze in and out of consciousness for a few hours and, when my headache started to subside, I opened my eyes. I stared at the door, searching my head for echoes of the earlier pain, but there were none; the pills had worked. It seemed quiet downstairs too. Maybe the women had left?

My mouth felt cracked and dry, in desperate need of water. I forced my stiff and awkward body downstairs. My dull head warned me to be careful, promising pain if I moved too fast. I clung to the banister and descended. My perception of distance felt warped and I could not trust the stairs would be where I anticipated. I stumbled at the final step and turned towards the kitchen unable to hear any sounds.

It was empty. I poured a mug of water and gulped it down, then another, and another. My stomach sloshed about, threatening to erupt. Ignoring it, I put the kettle on and concentrated on rolling a cigarette, but my vision cheated and the paper moved, doubled then moved again. I closed my eyes to concentrate on the breath moving in and out of my lungs then opened my eyes and tried again. The cigarette was messy but stayed intact while I smoked it.

The doorbell rang. Reluctantly, I shuffled towards it, dragging a funnel of smoke behind me. I greeted Scott with pathetic puppy eyes and he responded by petting me, stroking my hair and asking if I was ill. I relayed my headache and the strange events of the morning and he frowned.

'Maybe we shouldn't send you in today,' he said.

Disappointment crushed my features as if they were made of waste paper. He seemed to soften.

'Look, have something to eat then we'll see, okay,' he said. 'I'll get smudging. Clear some of this hostility.'

I nodded and returned to the kitchen. In the fridge, I saw the fruit of Cathy's labours. It was packed solid with sandwiches, salads, vol-au-vents and more. I didn't want to eat any of it. Where was my hummus? I glanced towards the bin near the back door. No, she wouldn't have. Stuffed inside the black bin bag was all my food. I growled, *fucking bitch*, gathered my food and stuffed it back into the fridge, crushing dainty triangles of bread and cheese.

Sage smoke wafted through the kitchen door and before I realised what was happening I was in my sacred space. The woodland around me looked menacing. Shadows moved within it, prowling around the edges of my circle.

I headed towards the pathway, pushing past branches obstructing the route. The shadowy path seemed alive and dark patches moved like heat haze. I stepped cautiously over them, trying to walk only in the light.

There was my stag. I wondered whether I should name it, or whether it already had a name. It took mere moments to decide the stag's name was Scott. I stroked his face as his gentle eyes looked into my soul. I kissed his nose then we walked together along the path.

Sounds of frantic crying escaped from the shadows between the trees. I turned toward the noise, trying to make out its source, but the forest was too dark.

'I'll be right back.'

The stag nudged me with his soft nose. He seemed agitated as if he didn't want me to leave his side, didn't trust the sounds.

'It's okay. I've a great sense of direction. I'll be back.'

Again the stag pushed me to the centre of the path. His flanks blocked my way. I growled, darted past him and ran into the darkness. The crying echoed between tree trunks making it hard to pinpoint its origin. I walked straight ahead, only deviating to avoid the trunks of trees that blocked my way. I felt the path and my stag fade behind me until the forest was everything and the track, mountain and pool were nothing. The crying got louder and I saw a teenage girl curled up beneath a tree, hands covering her face. She grew quiet as I approached.

'Who are you?' I asked. 'What's wrong?'

'They won't let me keep my daughter,' she wailed.

A twig snapped behind me and I spun around. A heavy hand slapped me across the face. My jaw shifted sideways and I fell to the ground. I curled my body tight, to protect myself from being kicked, but no kicks came and after a time I unfurled and pushed myself up. The aggressor had vanished and so too the girl. I moved my jaw, trying to establish whether it was broken. It burned, but the pain was bearable. I stood in silence, part of me hoping to hear the cries again, but all I heard was the lonely caw of a crow. No that wasn't all I could hear - there was a low humming sound, getting closer, moving through the trees towards me.

I saw a shifting ball of black. The noise grew clearer, a buzzing that took on a higher pitch like a power tool until the mass of insects were almost close enough to make out each wing, every antennae. I turned and fled from the swarm, but the bees gained on me. I felt their wings beat against my face and their tiny legs alight on my scalp. I screamed and the furry bodies rushed to fill my mouth then pain, like ten-thousand electric shocks, hit every inch of my skin. I toppled over and hit the ground in agony as my throat swelled and I tried to cling to consciousness until absolute blackness took over.

Hands landed on my shoulders again and I struggled, unable to hold back my panic.

'Open your eyes,' a familiar voice called.

I shook my head. I didn't want to see. If I couldn't see what was happening then perhaps it wasn't real. I whimpered and tried to push the heavy body away.

'Crow, it's okay. Just open your eyes.'

I knew it was a trick. I must keep them tightly shut and wish the pain and fear away, but he never called me Crow. It was always Petal or Princess – we were his little prince and princess, his secret toys. I opened my eyes, shielding them with my eyelashes, trying to keep my curiosity secret. It wasn't him. It wasn't Granddad. I opened my eyes fully.

'Scott!'

He was trying to cling to me, but I couldn't stop my body from jerking against his hold.

'What happened?' he asked.

My forehead felt cold and wet and I realised Scott was holding a damp towel against my brow.

'I went there, except, except it wasn't there ... or maybe it was. I don't know. I went into the woods. You told me not to, but I heard something. It was a girl. Then he hit me.'

'Who ... who hit you?'

'I didn't see him, not really. He was huge. I felt so scared, but, but I knew him. I know when I lost myself.' I shook my head, trying to put together the fragments of a memory long buried, but they felt slippery in my fingers. I knew where the answer lay: in those books in my bag, but maybe the memory should be buried, along with the man. The memory of him hanging from that rope stirred in my mind. He did this to me. I didn't know how, perhaps I didn't want to know, but he had made me incomplete. Granddad had stolen my power and only I could recover it.

'I want to go back,' I said.

He shook his head. 'I'm sorry, Crow.' His eyes were full of concern and his damp touch on my head was gentle. 'It's too late. It's almost time to leave for the funeral.'

I nodded and tried to stand up, but my legs wouldn't stop shaking and my head felt hollow.

Scott held my elbow to support me. 'Maybe we shouldn't go.'

Not go? I had to go. I looked at him and knew he understood my plea.

'I'll call a taxi then,' he told me. 'Can I use your phone?'

I nodded and he lowered me back into the chair then I remembered the fragments of my phone lay shattered on the kitchen floor.

'The land line's dead,' he called back from the hallway.

And the mobile's fucked. I tried to stand up again.

He opened the front door. Where was he going? As I waited for him to return I felt my mind wandering. Not back to that place not now. Biting my wrist, I concentrated on the pain. He was taking too long. We would never make it there in time.

38

Scott ran back into the kitchen. 'Fifteen minutes.'

'Taxi?' I asked, picking up my bag.

He nodded.

'Let's wait on the front step,' I said.

We waited in the garden for the taxi to arrive. I remembered sitting there before, on the day I arrived back at the house. The flowers looked bigger and brighter. The weeds and wild blooms had won the battle and raised their proud heads above the defeated flora. For a moment I felt like one of those wild flowers and hoped I was close to my own victory.

We sat in silence. The buzzing of bees around the garden and the occasional hum of a car engine pacified us. The air was hot, but dark clouds threatened a storm.

'What time is it?' I asked.

Scott shrugged. 'Do you want me to check?'

I shook my head. It wasn't important. Knowing the time wouldn't make the taxi arrive any earlier.

At last, a burgundy saloon with a prominent aerial pulled up beyond the gate. Scott helped me to my feet. I felt much stronger; the fragrant air had revitalised me. I pulled my elbow away and walked towards the car unaided. Scott followed behind and closed the gate.

'Where to, love?' the taxi driver asked.

'Cadford.'

The taxi smelled of sweat and spice. I tried to roll down a window but it stuck a few centimetres down.

'Hot day,' the driver remarked.

I nodded. Scott tried his window and a sliver of breeze snaked into the car. The soft suspension rocked my body and I felt the insistent tug of exhaustion. My eyes started to close although I tried to keep them open, blinking frequently, heavy lashes rested against my cheeks for longer each time my eyes closed. I leaned back against the hot leather seat and tried to focus on Scott as he stared out of the window, hands balled into fists. He hated this. I could see how distressed he was. Was it the car or the thought of the funeral? I wanted to ask him but didn't, realising he might not want talk about it.

I touched his arm, but if he noticed he didn't show it and I moved my hand away again. I felt awkward, unsure of myself and him. Was he thinking about my mother? What was their relationship? Did he miss her? They weren't lovers, I was certain of that now, at least.

What then of our own relationship? Scott and Crow, Crow and Scott. Did we have one? Were we friends or were we lovers? The ambiguity of our friendship bothered me. It made me think of my other interpersonal relationships, all seemed empty, transitory. People wandered in and out of my life, but I never knew them. I never cared enough to try. I was isolated, cut off from everyone, even myself. How much did I know about my mother, Nanny or even my brother? Nothing of substance. They were all ghosts to me. I remembered finding that purple sphere in the clouds and seeing the vicious razor wire wound around it repelling all touches. Had I done that to myself? Had I deliberately separated myself from the world? Was it too late to change?

The taxi pulled up behind a row of parked cars. I saw Tomas cuddling little Missie as Cathy watched us come to a halt.

'That's twenty quid,' the driver said.

Scott looked at me and frowned, mouthing the word 'Ouch.'

'I'll get it,' I offered. He didn't argue.

It felt cooler here. A breeze played with my earrings. Cathy was scowling and I realised I'd forgotten to change for the funeral. I was the only person present wearing a t-shirt and well-worn combats. I blushed, ashamed for a moment before realising the pointlessness of that feeling. I grabbed Scott's arm and nudged him towards the gathering. The hearse was already there. I wondered whether the rest of the mourners had followed the coffin here and why they hadn't invited me to join them. I smiled awkwardly, feeling unwanted, wishing I was brave enough to say something. This new estrangement felt unnatural. Was it paranoia or was I really not welcome here?

Cathy took Melissa as Tomas was led towards the coffin. I started to follow him. The coffin was carried by Tomas and five other men I did not recognise. Stripped of flowers, the burden was borne into the chapel. Cathy followed behind. I hurried to join them, but found myself pushed further and further back as other mourners surged from the lobby and gathered between me and the casket.

The modern chapel attempted to achieve old world sophistication but fell short of the mark. The entrance lobby was panelled, but looked more like a Swedish sauna than an ancient church. I wished I could be anywhere else. The ugliness around me scratched at my paper-thin surface and I wanted to cry or scream or shout, maybe all three. I wanted my brother to hug me and for everyone else to leave so Tomas and I could be alone with our mother.

Thirty or more mourners followed the casket. No one recognised me. I was merely another body to fit into the room. Only two others walked behind me: Clive and a woman I didn't recognise. Clive looked different without the bold coloured shirt or maybe his tears had altered his face, for he was crying without restraint. The woman beside him was crying too. They were trying to support each other and met in the middle like a Gothic arch. I looked at the woman who seemed preoccupied with Clive and her grief; she didn't return my steady gaze. She was around Tomas' age and had very straight black hair cut in a severe bob around her beautiful heart shaped face. She reminded me of a younger Vivienne, her delicate frown a perfect match. I couldn't see the woman's eyes but believed they must be grey. My heart leapt towards her. She couldn't be ... could she?

I tugged Scott's arm and pointed towards the couple. Scott nodded towards Clive who fawned and preened under Scott's gaze. It sickened me how Clive's dignity could be so easily shattered. The woman seemed unaffected as if she didn't recognise Scott or care about his presence. Clive whispered something in the woman's ear and her hazel eyes rose to meet mine, staring at me and offering a weak smile.

The mourners moved further into the chapel. Clive and the woman sat a little behind Scott and me. I could hardly concentrate on the service. The vicar's words washed over me; none of it mattered. What did I care of God's grace? I could only think about the woman sitting behind me. Was she Vivienne's daughter, my sister?

My throat felt dry. I wanted to shout out and yet at the same time curl up and hide. My brother and my phantom sister pulled me in opposite directions. I clung onto my wooden seat, head swimming. I saw trees ... no, not now. I bit my wrist again and returned to the chapel and the deep, dark groaning of machinery. Everyone bowed their heads and I saw the coffin beyond them, dark, polished mahogany; resting on the lid was a pair of ballet shoes. The coffin shuddered then started to descend. I swallowed painfully. Goodbye Mum. Half of me hoped this wasn't a final farewell, that the spirit of my mother would live on in the house and we could have the relationship I had always wanted.

Flames roared, either real or imagined, and with eyes tightly shut I watched my mother's desiccated body explode in fire. She was consumed quickly, painlessly, but it felt as though one thousand cigarettes had been stubbed out simultaneously across my own skin. Pressure mounted behind my eyes, my face stung and my mouth filled with an unvoiced wail: *Mummy.* I covered my face with my hands and wept hot tears that scalded my cheeks. *Mummy, why did you have to leave me? Why now?* I felt Scott's arm around my shoulders and was thankful, pressing my body closer to his.

I rubbed my eyes dry with my sleeve and glanced over my shoulder. Clive and the woman were getting up to leave.

'I need to know who that woman with Clive is,' I whispered to Scott.

He didn't move so I pushed past him. Stumbling into the aisle, I felt everyone's disapproving eyes on my back. I shrugged them off and pushed the chapel door open. Clive and the woman were already beside the row of cars. The woman paused to light a cigarette. Her pose and facial expression reminded me so much of my mother. I ran over.

'Are you my sister?' I asked.

The woman coughed, spitting cigarette smoke in all directions.

Clive answered for her. 'Giselle meet Anna. Anna, Giselle. Yes you are sisters.'

I grabbed Anna's hand and shook it. 'I knew it,' I said, triumphantly. 'Does Tomas know?'

Anna shook her head.

'No, we thought it best to disappear. We don't want to cause any problems. Have they told you about the will yet?'

'No, I didn't go.'

'I did,' Clive said.

'And ...'

'Tomas and Cathy aren't too happy about it. Look we'd better run. Come round to the shop later. Say six o'clock ... we'll talk then.'

'Will you be there?' I asked Anna.

'Yes.' Anna looked at her feet as tears splashed onto shoe leather, but her voice was soft and musical, like a ballet and I wanted to hear more. I opened my mouth to engage her with more questions, but Clive shook his head and Anna retreated into the car.

'Six o'clock,' Clive said again then, to my complete shock, he winked playfully at me. 'And bring the hunk. I'll cook.'

I watched through the windscreen as Anna patted Clive's shoulder. He smiled at her and reversed out of the parking space. I waved at the back of their car as they hurried away from the funeral party.

'Anna.' The word felt rich and sensual in my mouth. I heard the crunch of gravel behind me and spun around to face Scott.

'She's my sister,' I told him. 'Anna.'

He smiled at me, the look in his eyes more eloquent than any words.

'Do you think she is my missing piece?' I asked him.
He looked at me and shook his head.
'It's a start though, isn't it?'
'Yes and you'll recover the rest. Just give it time.'

39

No-one offered us a lift back to the house. I sat, bubbling with resentment on the chapel steps while Scott talked to the vicar.

'There isn't a phone we can use,' Scott told me. 'But there's a bus-stop just at the end of this road. He says they're regular.'

Standing up, I brushed stone dust from the back of my trousers and imagined Catherine, back at the house, hosting the wake, full of smiles and courtesy. Smiles that were so fake they had to be polished each morning. I didn't know whether I was being fair and I certainly didn't care. As far as I could see it I was here at their request. I had done everything Tomas had asked of me and this was my reward, abandonment. What did they want from me, really? Why did Tomas even ask me to come back to Bristol when he would have been happier keeping Vivienne all to himself?

Clive had said my brother wasn't happy with the will, and I wondered why. Perhaps they were expecting to inherit Mum's house. It was a great house in spite of the bad memories and ghosts dwelling within, large and expensive. Selling it would have set them up for life. Tomas, in his line of work, would have set up an insurance policy or two on Vivienne, so I was sure he'd be okay even if he and Cathy didn't get the house. But if Tom didn't, who did? Anna? That would be a kick in the gut for the brother who refused to listen when I'd tried to tell him about our sister. Yes that really would hurt. My hand tingled as I thought about her, my big sister, another chance to have a family, to love and be loved.

I walked beside Scott away from the cemetery. We strolled down the driveway in silence while I looked around at all the shimmering, white tombs and imagined their occupants bidding us farewell. My life had changed so much in these past weeks. Before I had known only righteous anger and basic survival, but my feelings had become more complicated and harder to untangle. I still felt anger, but it had become more confused and its target less clear. It was hard to hate my mother now I knew many of the problems she'd faced were greater than my own. Some of my anger transferred to Catherine, but I knew that was transitory, meaningless. The woman had too little impact on my life to warrant my hatred. I could still see the unfairness of this world and rage against it, but I felt tired. I wasn't sure I wanted to fight any more and that thought scared me more than any other. Without the fight, the struggle, what did I have left – an uneasy void I must fill with something, but what?

It would be easier to return to London and put all this behind me, keep the anger inside my stomach and not repair my broken soul. My existence there was simple. I fought tyranny and helped people who couldn't fight their battles alone. It was worthwhile and it didn't confuse my senses in the way Bristol seemed to. I had dedicated my life to continuing the fight against oppression my father had fought before me, or so I'd been taught, but even that seemed to hang under a cloud of doubt. Was my father a South American revolutionary or was that fairy tale, retold by my dear, sweet Nanny, also a lie? Did it matter, really, who my father was? Surely it was more important to know who I was, but I had no clue and to find that out I would have to continue this journey with Scott and, if I did, would I remain the same person at the end of it?

'What about ghosts?' I asked Scott.

'Huh?'

'Are there ghosts in the dream world?'

'Only ones you bring there. The ghosts have their own plane of existence. It's the spirit world. You get there by spirit walking.'

I stopped walking and grabbed Scott's hand. My eyes blazed with a strange excitement. I could speak to Nanny, to Vivienne even to my father perhaps. I could untangle the puzzle and set myself free. 'Can I get there?'

'Do you want to end up like Vivienne?'

I shook my head.

'Then no, not without years of training and all the right equipment. Listen Crow, I taught you how to visit your dream world so you could heal yourself. That's great, that's healthy, or it should be, but already you've been dragged into it kicking and screaming and today I found you unconscious on the kitchen floor.'

'But ...'

'Please, Crow, let me finish.' He stared at me and I closed my mouth. I could feel his power radiate around us both. 'A shaman walks a fine line between sanity and insanity. A shaman has to be strong or lose his or her mind. I've battled all my demons, but not in the spirit world. They would overwhelm you, Crow. Promise me you won't follow in your mother's footsteps. I see so much more in you.'

Two weeks ago I would have agreed. I had considered myself worth one hundred of my mother. But now ... things were different. She wasn't the crazed demon I had known, she was more than that, and I felt her tugging me, drawing her into her world?

'Promise me,' he said again.

I nodded. Staring at me, he looked incredulous. I could feel him trying to dig beneath my façade to learn the truth, strip me to the bone. I tried to walk away, but he grabbed my wrist and held me back.

'Say it.' His voice was a low, threatening growl.

Inside, I felt something grow, a new strength and my old defiance combined. I felt my power unfurl in my chest. My eyes flashed with anger and indignation. How dare he? I pulled my wrist from his grasp and marched towards the bus stop.

'Fuck off,' I shouted over my shoulder.

My body grew lighter as I strode away from him. I

didn't need his help and I wouldn't promise him anything. He wasn't hurrying to catch me up. He strolled purposelessly, as if on a summer jaunt through the countryside. His bare feet sounded like dead fish as they slapped against the tarmac and I realised I hated him. He didn't know me at all. How dare he pretend to know what was best for me? It reminded me of Vivienne and her assertions that mother knew best, and perhaps she did protect us the best way she could. She certainly made huge sacrifices to keep us safe. Thinking back on all her suffering, I wanted to hold Mother in my arms and tell her I loved her. My stomach ached with the loss I felt. *Mummy!*

The bus stop was empty and there was no timetable to check or sign of the bus arriving. Scott would catch up with me; would we feel compelled to talk? I could run to the next bus stop, but that seemed childish and, anyway, he would simply get on the same bus when it reached this stop. I stared at him in silence when he reached the bus stop, feeling petulant, warning him not to say another word. He stood apart from me, rolling a stone between his toes, not glancing up at my face. I heard the heavy splutter of diesel that suggested a bus was climbing the hill towards us. As the roof came into my line of vision, I held out my hand to stop it. When I checked behind me Scott was gone. Maybe he'd decided to walk home after all.

The bus was almost empty and the route was quick. As it turned the corner into Vivienne's street I saw dozens of cars parked outside the house; guests for the wake, I assumed.

I opened the unlocked door and stepped over the threshold, into a crush of black. So many people, had they all been at the cemetery? I looked at a group of girls near the front door and examined their delicate features and long hair pulled back from their faces with Alice-bands, knots or ponytails. They could have been miniature Viviennes, perhaps they were her ballet students. Maybe Vivienne had gone back to teaching.

'How did you know my mother?' I asked one girl.

The girl was achingly beautiful and her skin glowed with health. Her perfect face recoiled from me as repulsion added a new layer to her features - ugliness.

I caught a glimpse of Catherine watching me from the doorway of the old drawing room. As our eyes met she looked away to lavish her attention on the old lady beside her. That woman was holding a plate full of cakes, her fingers covered in gold rings and she wore a single, prominent cross on her chest.

I wondered how all these people knew Vivienne. On the stairs two men were discussing one of Vivienne's portraits, smiling and drinking. I imagined them discussing their conquest of my mother - how easy she had been, how needy.

I pushed past bodies in the hallway, ignoring complaints as drinks were spilled or food fell from heavily laden plates, and headed to the kitchen to grab a glass of wine or something stronger and my own plate of food before stepping out into the garden and away from the ravenous strangers.

No ghosts haunted the open space. I looked for Nanny, but the garden was empty. I opened the shed door, hoping for a glimpse of Mother, but it was dark and still. I sat, alone, on the raw floorboards and sipped warm white wine. 'I wish you were here, Mum.'

'I'll always be here.'

The back of my neck prickled as I looked all around me, but it was only an echo inside my mind.

I wondered what time it was. I had no watch, no phone and the only clock was inside the house. It could be almost five by now. I downed my drink and stuffed mushrooms into my mouth. Crumbs covered me, but I didn't bother to brush them off. Taking my glass back to the kitchen for a refill, I checked the clock - five-fifteen. I gulped down two more glassfuls and left the house without speaking to anyone. I didn't see my brother or spot Catherine on my way out. I vaguely wondered where they were and imagined them complaining to other guests about the injustice of the will, or even rifling through Vivienne's jewellery box, just as I had before them.

I walked towards Healing Ways and ordered a portion of chips from the neighbouring takeaway. The stodgy potatoes felt heavy in my throat and burned my chest like acid as I swallowed, but I devoured them all, wondering how many bags of chips it would take to shift this feeling of emptiness.

40

Shafts of evening light caught by hundreds of crystals, behind Clive's door, gave the effect of a new age disco. Clive reminded me of Vivienne: the crystals, their flamboyance and their mutual interest in men. I wondered why it was easier to accept such things with Clive than my own mother. What if I hadn't left home at thirteen and had grown up beside Vivienne? Would I have understood her better, accepted her, loved her?

I wiped a tear from my eye with a stinking finger, rang the doorbell and waited. Clive, still wearing his widow's weeds, swept through the beaded curtain and across the shop. His face lit up as he saw me. He opened the door and grabbed my hand.

'Crow, my dahling girl, I am so sorry. Come in, come in. Anna is waiting upstairs.'

He let go of me to lock the door behind us then took a lilac handkerchief from his pocket and wiped his fingers, fastidiously.

I blushed, guessing his reason. 'I'm sorry. I was hungry and ate chips. Can I wash my hands?'

'Of course. We are so glad you came … Where's Scott?'

'Ahh, we had an argument.'

'A lovers' tiff. No need to say any more. Clive understands the affairs of the heart.'

He walked back through the beaded doorway before I could think of a smart-ass retort, so I followed him in silence, planning to set him straight later.

'The bathroom.' Clive flourished a hand towards a door at the top of the stairs.

'Thank you.'

'Crow?'

I looked at him and saw him properly for the first time since Vivienne died. He was truly the widow and the pain in his eyes was more profound than any I had seen before. Our mutual loss drew me towards this funny old man and I felt comforted by his presence.

'We'll be through there ... when you're ready.' He kissed me on the cheek and stumbled towards a door at the end of the narrow hallway.

I took a deep breath and washed my hands. My face looked puffy in the mirror so I washed that too. Noticing a heavy smell of sweat, I lifted my arms in turn, wishing I'd taken the time to change when back at Vivienne's; I couldn't stop thinking of it as her house, to me it always would be. I stripped off my t-shirt and washed my armpits. The fabric still stank, but at least my body was clean. I dressed and left the bathroom. The doorway at the end of the hallway stood ajar, but there were no sounds coming from the room. I opened it fully and stepped inside. Anna looked up at me, her face as puffy as mine.

'Thank you, Giselle.' Her voice sounded shaky as if each syllable was an effort.

'It's Crow now.' I smiled and walked towards her. 'You look so much like her, but I didn't even know you existed until a few days ago.'

'It's been hardest for you,' Anna said.

I shook my head. 'No, I, I don't mean that.'

'It's okay. I'm okay. I know she loved me, but she felt so sorry for the rift between you.'

'When did she find you? How?'

'I found her, about five years ago.'

A year after I left. Why hadn't they told me? 'Does Tomas know?' I sat down on the chair nearest to her while waiting for an answer.

'Yes. Sort of.'

Something inside my stomach twisted uncomfortably and I tried to steady my breathing, biting hard into my bottom lip. He knew.

'But he refused to see me ... I'm so glad we, at least, might be friends. I need that. I want it so badly.'

'When I ... no it's not important. Of course we can be friends. No not friends, sisters.' The word felt wonderful so I said it again. 'Sisters ... Don't worry about Tomas. He can be a selfish git when he puts his mind to it.'

Anna nodded. 'I think it hurt him too much to think about it. He's buried everything he'd prefer not to recall.'

Clive arrived with cocktails: colourful concoctions brought in for sampling. After a few of them we found ourselves laughing wildly.

'That's better,' Clive said. 'My favourite girl's beautiful

children laughing and joking like six year olds. It's what she would have wanted.'

I choked on my drink and my nose burned as liquid spurted out of it. 'Vivienne laugh? I don't believe it.'

Clive smiled sympathetically and moved beside me, patting my knee softly. I didn't have the heart to tell him his touch made me feel uncomfortable.

His voice, cracked and raspy from crying, was frequently interrupted by sniffing. ' ... sniff ... She often laughed. She cried too of course, but she wasn't a stern woman, not since I've known her. I think she ... sniff ... struggled with motherhood ... She used to tell me it was the one thing ... sniff ... she never felt in control of, but boy did she love you, all of you. She never forgave herself for letting them take Anna or for making you run away, Crow.'

I looked at Anna who smiled and nodded. I guessed they knew a different Vivienne from the one I left behind. Anna's face glowed bright red, the alcohol was working its magic on her and she relaxed into her chair, body slumped, eyes open but glazed. I glanced at Clive who was blowing his nose.

'Why was Anna given up, but Tomas kept?'

'She said it was what her parents demanded. He wanted a son.'

'It took a lot of getting used to,' Anna said. 'I'm still not sure I really understand. I guess some things can be accepted as facts even when they can't be understood and, maybe, this is one of those?'

'Anna?' I asked.

She focused on my face.

'Did Vivienne ever tell you about my father?'

I thought I saw her shudder, but a smile took hold of her lips too quickly for me to be sure. 'Ricky?'

I felt my body shaking and reached for the back of a chair to steady myself.

'What do you want to know?'

'Where did they meet?'

'Birmingham. She danced in one of his clubs.'

'Clubs?'

She cocked her head. 'She never told you?'

'I was told a very different tale.'

'Does the tale you know make you happy?'

'Yes.'

'Then keep it.'

I shrugged, tightening my grip on the chair. 'Okay,' I squeaked, knowing I could ask again later. From now on Anna and I would be inseparable, I could feel it. I turned to Clive instead. 'You were going to tell me about the will.'

'Oh yes,' he said, laughing again. He looked across at Anna, who had closed her eyes, giving in to the soporific embrace of the alcohol. 'You're gonna love this.'

'What?' My heart hammered as I wondered what it said and regretted my absence at the reading.

'Tomas ... Anna ... and you each have a one third share in Vivienne's house and it can't be sold unless all three of you agree. Your sister-in-law was furious; she stormed out, but not before growling in my ear.'

'What did she say to you?' I asked.

'She said, "You did this."'

'Did you?'

'Oh no, it was all Vivienne. She wanted to give you something you didn't have while she was alive – a family.'

I sat, quietly nursing my half-finished drink.

'I thought you'd be delighted,' he said.

I shrugged. 'Have you been in the house?'

'Of course.'

I looked at my drink, wondering how to explain the cruel joke. My eyes stung and my body felt heavy, exhausted. It was a trap. Vivienne hadn't changed. She wanted to continue her reign of terror from beyond the grave, taunting me, laughing at my clumsiness, my stupidity. I wouldn't let her. I'd move on, back to London, back to the real world of hopeless battles with faceless foe.

Clive touched my chin with a fingertip and tilted my face upwards. 'My dahling child, what is it?'

'The place is haunted. Restless fucking spirits or whatever you want to call them. Her gift is a Trojan horse.'

He paused for thought. 'But what about Scott? He's a shaman you know. Can't he ... sort it out?'

'He tried. It helped a bit, I guess, but they're still there. They're still waiting. Clive if I tell you half of what's happened to me in that house, you'll think I'm crazier than my mother.'

'Vivienne wasn't crazy.' Clive stood up and took his

glass back to the kitchen.

I rushed after him. 'I'm sorry ... I didn't ...'

'Everyone says she's crazy, but it isn't true. She's the most amazing woman I ever met. Sometimes, she made me wish I wasn't gay and other times she made me wish I was her. I miss her so much.'

The old man wept into his empty glass. I didn't know what to say or do. Moments drifted by in silence and the scene didn't change. Tentatively, I placed a hand on his shoulder and he half-fell into my arms, hugging me tight. I gasped for breath and he released his grip a little; resting his head on my shoulder, he let tears jerk out of him as I patted his back. It felt like burping an infant.

'I miss her so much,' he said between sobs.

His grief soaked into me, saturating me, making my mind blank. I felt swallowed by his pain, engulfed by his need for comfort. We stood together for what could have been minutes or hours until, eventually, Clive released his hold on me. He looked at my top, drenched with the saline of his tears and blushed. 'I'm sorry, let me get you something to change into.'

He handed me his empty glass and squeezed past into the hall. I put it down on the kitchen counter and wondered whether he'd want a refill. His array of spirit bottles was as colourful as his shirts and I felt out of my depth.

He returned, handing me a magenta shirt and insisting I change into it. I disappeared around the corner to do so, throwing my dirty t-shirt on the floor. The silk of the shirt smelled wonderful, like a summer garden at night. I pressed the collar to my face and breathed deeply.

'Do you like it?' Clive asked as he walked out of the kitchen holding two refilled glasses.

I nodded.

'Keep it. It suits you better anyway.'

'It's the smell,' I said. 'I've never smelt anything like it.'

'Ahh, I use my own special blend of scents when I do the washing. You really like it?'

'It's wonderful.'

'Then bring me all your clothes and I'll wash them for you, but the formula never leaves these four walls.' He tapped his swollen nose.

Clive grinned, transformed again, like an actor moving from tragedy to farce with a few dainty steps across the stage, yet he seemed sincere. I could sense his pain, just below his cheery surface, waiting for the opportunity to overwhelm him again.

Careful not to disturb Anna, Clive lifted a blanket from the sofa. I repositioned my sister's legs so they rested on the arm of the chair and we covered her in soft, fragrant wool.

'I think Anna should be comfortable there, don't you?' he asked.

'Yes, she looks very comfortable.'

'Would you like to stay here tonight, as well?' he asked me. 'You could use the spare bed. I'm certain Anna wouldn't mind.'

The idea of sitting here with Clive, drinking cocktails until the early hours then crashing out on my sister's bed, felt very appealing. 'I'd love to. Thank you, Clive.'

He lifted my drink from the coffee table and held it towards me. 'Chin, chin!'

'Tell me about her, please. If it won't upset you too much,' I asked.

'Vivienne or Anna?'

'Vivienne.'

'All right, but you must forgive an old man's tears.' He prepared his hankie with a flourish that made me smile in spite of my sadness. 'I met Vivienne almost twenty years ago, way before I first opened Healing Ways ... She was a ballerina then and the most beautiful woman I had ever seen. You were only an infant, Tomas had started nursery school and, of course, I didn't know about Anna. She'd come back from Birmingham and had a small council flat. You probably remember the place.'

I nodded.

'When she walked into a room it was like she absorbed all the light then filtered it through herself and radiated it into everyone else around her ... Later on, probably five or so years ago, she started working in my shop, reading Tarot and palms. She would hold séances sometimes for our older customers ... She had time for everyone. She helped people get their lives back together after losing a loved one, or a messy break-up ... and she always knew the right thing to say. The customers all adored her.'

'Did she change so much, after I left?'

'No, not really, not for me. Maybe she was just different with me than she was with her ... family. She called me her safe space.' The sniffing started again, harder this time and he struggled to control his emotions. 'I'm sorry. Excuse me a moment.'

I nodded and sipped my drink. It was strong and the liquor warmed me. I felt myself drifting, away from the warm room and the soft sofa, towards my dreams. In the shadow of an oak tree, I saw my stag again, Scott, and told him I was sorry for not listening to his warning. I stroked his ears and let my tears fall on his nose, kissing him between his soulful eyes. My body felt strange and my limbs stretched, bending and changing direction beneath my bent torso. I felt no pain, it was more like unfurling. My posture altered and I fell onto all fours, but remained as tall as the stag. I looked at my arms, but saw forelegs. I kicked out each leg in turn then pranced around in a circle. I pressed my nose against his and shook my muzzle. Excitement made my heart race; I needed to move, to dance about and stretch my limbs. I darted away from him and into the woods, but he followed in close pursuit. This was freedom, complete and absolute liberty - no fear, no insecurity just perfect happiness.

41

When I woke up I felt torn. I wanted to contact Scott and tell him how sorry I was, but I also wanted to stay with Clive and Anna and hear more about my sister and Vivienne.

'What should I do, Clive?'

'Have breakfast with us then find him. We can all catch up later, but anger and resentment should never be allowed to stew.'

I nodded. We had fruit for breakfast, Clive and I; Anna was still fast asleep when I left. I kissed her forehead and she made a strange snuffling sound that reminded me of a hedgehog. Clive and I embraced and kissed each other's cheeks in the Continental fashion and I promised to hurry back, bringing Scott if I could.

At eleven o'clock I reached Vivienne's house and, to my delight, I saw Scott at the doorway, scribbling a note.

'What does it say?' I asked him.

He jumped, startled and pushed the paper into his pocket. 'Just to call me if you want to carry on with the ... lessons ...' He said the word lessons as if it felt wrong in his mouth, but he couldn't think of a better word to use. Of course they were not lessons, I was my own teacher in this, but I felt I knew what he was trying to say and understood his awkwardness and his fear of offending me.

'Thank you,' I said. 'Can we carry on today?'

He smiled and his face lit up. He looked beautiful, holding his heart in open hands and offering with it a complete acceptance of me; no shame and no mistrust, only respect and love. I opened the front door and found the house in chaos. Paper plates, half eaten sandwiches and discarded glasses covered the floor. A picture of Vivienne had been knocked off its hook and wobbled precariously against the wall.

'What the fuck?' I whispered.

Scott followed me inside. I picked my way through the debris towards the kitchen. Nothing had been washed up. Dirty glasses, serving dishes and cutlery filled every available surface. 'Bitch!'

'I'll help you,' Scott offered. 'It'll be done in no time then we can eat and you can travel this afternoon. I promise.'

I turned to him. My face felt cold and drained of colour and I wondered how I appeared in his eyes. I took a deep breath and swallowed my anger not wishing to direct it towards an innocent target. 'They did this on purpose, because of the will.'

'The will?' he asked.

'Vivienne left the house to Tomas, Anna and me.'

'Who's Anna?'

'My sister, she's my beautiful, wonderful big sister. You saw her at the funeral and you really must meet her properly, Scott. Come with me tonight, to Clive's. She's staying there, for the short-term at least.'

'Of course. That's wonderful, Crow, a big sister. Now, let's get this place sorted out. Shall I do the washing up?'

'Scott, I wanted to say ...'

'You don't need to say anything.'

'But ...'

'It's okay. I understand and nothing is ever broken that cannot be mended.'

I wasn't convinced he did understand, but I left him to his somewhat Zen thoughts. Cleaning the house took hours, especially with my frequent cigarette breaks, but eventually the downstairs of the house was tidy again.

'Do you think they went upstairs?' Scott asked.

'I hope not. I don't think I should check. It would be too much to stomach if they messed up my room.' I opened the refrigerator door. 'I'll make us some lunch then we can start ... Mmm left overs. I wonder whether any of it's vegan.'

Scott squeezed next to me and looked in the fridge. 'They look okay, and those. Are you gonna throw the rest out?'

I shrugged. 'Probably.'

Scott grabbed a tray of the garlic mushrooms I'd sampled the day before. I picked up some sliced salad vegetables and started shovelling them into my mouth before we reached the table. Scott fetched a couple of glasses of water and joined me.

'I need a coffee.'

Scott stood up.

'No, I didn't mean that,' I said, laughing. 'I'll get them. What do you want?'

'Just some green tea, please.'

'Assuming we have any. Maybe Cathy left some.' I took the kettle to the sink and stared out of the window. 'Do you like the garden?' I asked, gazing out into the sunlight.

'It's great. You could grow all your vegetables out there.'

'There's no tree,' I said.

'You could plant one.'

'Will it take long to grow?'

'That depends on what you plant and where, but yes, it'll take some time. Are you in a hurry?'

'I'd like a tree.'

'So, will you stay?'

'I don't know, maybe. What do you think?' I looked at him. He seemed surprised to be asked, as though everything I did confused him and each time I said or did something new he needed to get to know me all over again.

'I don't know. You seem troubled here. Maybe you'd be better elsewhere.'

'But when I'm whole again, Scott?'

He shook his head. 'Let's see, okay? Only you can decide. Would Anna stay here too?'

'Ooo, do you think she might?'

He shrugged. 'Maybe,' he said, chuckling. 'Does she have family elsewhere? Kids, a husband?'

'I don't know,' I told him. 'We just got drunk last night. She hardly said a word.'

'Are you ready?' he asked me.

I nodded and followed him into the living room. He started the ritual from the beginning: spreading out the mat and the, as yet unlit, candles and lighting his stinky smudging stick.

'You feel okay today?' he asked.

'I'm fine now,' I said, taking off my boots. 'What is it I'm doing? Where am I going? Who will I meet there?'

'You're communing with the source of everything - a great wisdom, the energy from which we all originate.'

'Do you really believe that?'

'Of course.'

'It feels like I'm just tapping into my subconscious, if I'm honest.'

'You can do that in your dreams.'

'I do. It feels the same, although it's easier to direct what's happening when I do it this way rather than when I'm asleep. Like lucid dreaming, I guess.'

He frowned, but didn't answer. I supposed it didn't matter really, where I was going or whether I was communing with some great source of energy or simply myself. What was important was the work. I was making myself better, reshaping my internal landscape into a place where I could feel more comfortable.

I stepped onto the mat and sat cross legged, hands resting on my thighs, palms open and facing upwards. I breathed in the pungent smoke and the smell of burning sage enveloped me. He lit the candles, one by one, then sat in front of me in full lotus position and waited. I closed my eyes and started counting. When I reached three I was by my oak tree, the air chill and refreshing like the mist from a waterfall. In a perfect circle full of peace, I faced the tree and smiled to see how much it had grown. Its leafy canopy hung above me, protecting me like a patient parent, even though it was really my child, wasn't it? I stroked the trunk and it felt warm to the touch. I could sense sap flowing steadily beneath its bark, feel its life force and its enduring strength. I wrapped my arms around it, pressing my body against its rough surface as it let its energy flow through my soft flesh and into me, filling me with power.

'Thank you,' I whispered.

I felt I should give it a gift as it had blessed me with this power. Spotting bluebells growing in the grove, I picked them and placed them among the tangle of roots at the base of the great oak then realised, in so doing, I had cut short the lives of those flowers and hung my head in shame, but it was all one, wasn't it, the tree, the grove and the flowers? They were all me. When tending to a garden it was important to know what should live and what should die back and I suddenly saw how the same theory could apply to my life. Some things should be nurtured and others allowed to wither and die; that was what I was doing with this journey, choosing what to keep and what to let go.

I turned to walk away and saw the stag waiting for me at

the mouth of the pathway. I called to him, but he didn't come closer. So I went towards him, greeting him warmly and teasing his ears. He licked my face and I kissed his nose. 'Back to the mountain.'

He walked beside me through a forest filled with bird song. There were no menacing shadows and I could hear nothing to disturb my wonderful sense of calm and well-being. Even climbing the mountain filled me with joy and each handhold was cushioned with moss while a benevolent sun warmed my spine.

I remembered my way, back to my soul. It shone brightly, more vibrantly than before. It was truly beautiful. I studied the gash. Part was still missing, but it looked less angry as if it had already started to heal. The cruel steel of the razor-wire tangled around my soul, looked out of place now. It distanced me from myself. Perhaps I had needed it once, to protect me from harm, but now it seemed as though it was simply cutting me off from the world. I thought of Anna and of Scott, wanting to love them – wholly, completely. My hands trembled as I reached out to touch the wire. Pain sliced through my fingers and I pulled back, sucking the tips of my bleeding digits. Holding them close to my face, I inspected my hands, but no wounds remained. I tried again and the pain felt even more intense. I screamed. I needed gloves. Wandering across the misty landscape with cloud billowing across my bare feet and calves, I passed my granddad's old chair, my mother's bed and a noose suspended from somewhere too far up to see.

Ahead, I saw the garden shed and strode towards it, pulling open the door.

Inside there were no shadows. Everything was bathed in white light just as it was outside, as if the structure had no roof and yet I could see wooden slats above. I rummaged through spades and bags of seed, peered behind bikes and the lawnmower until I found a pair of green gardening gloves and pulled them onto my hands. They felt warm, as if Nanny's hands had been inside them moments before. The smell of mint and lavender wafted from the fabric and I felt protected, as though Nanny had taken my hand and would help me finish what I had started. On a hook at the door was a pair of red handled secateurs. I took them with me. What would happen when I freed myself? Kneeling down in front of the vicious steel, I made the first cut. The metal sprung open and lashed at my thighs. I moved carefully around the barrier, snipping as I went. I felt pain, but the physical discomfort of invisible cuts across my legs was overshadowed by my raging emotions. Tears of anguish rolled down my cheeks and I considered rebuilding the fence so I might never feel this vulnerable again, but I was determined to be free, however high the cost. If freedom meant heartache then so be it. I refused to remain caged.

As the final joint was broken, the wire transformed into shell-pink ribbons that fluttered like autumn leaves to the floor, making way for the new buds of spring. I stood up and reached towards the sky, stretching. Tears fell like rain, but their loss made me lighter and I rose above the cloud, spreading out my arms like wings and soared. When I heard Scott's voice say 'ten,' I was ready to return, excited to test my new found freedom.

'Four, three ...'

I opened my eyes. Scott's face filled my vision and I devoured his image, hungry for more. Like a tiger stalking its prey, I crouched on all fours and crawled towards him. His pulse quickened and trembled beneath the skin of his throat, but his eyes were full of wonder. I lay at his feet and kissed his filthy toes without fear of rejection. His muscles tightened then relaxed.

'Crow, what happened?' he asked, pulling me upright.

'I freed myself,' I said, returning to his feet and lavishing my attention on the base of his toes.

'Stop it please,' he said, giggling.

I laughed, but my laughter crossed the border into hysteria and when I tried to stand up I fell to the floor, shaking uncontrollably. He leaned towards me and touched my forehead. I could smell his breath as I inhaled between laughs.

'You're burning up. I'll get a cold cloth.'

As my laughter subsided, I couldn't even remember what I had found funny. He returned to my side, pressing something damp against my forehead. I had a flash of deja-vu, but couldn't remember whether life was repeating itself or I'd had a premonition.

Cradled in his arms, I closed my eyes and breathed

deeply. His smell surrounded me and I ached for him, wondering whether this was madness. What had I done? Giving no thought to the consequences, I had pulled away my spiky armour. Now what would happen? I didn't speak. I let him lull me to sleep while I wondered whether this was what it would have been like to have a father.

My legs started to relax and deaden until I could no longer feel them. The numbness spread up my body, but it didn't frighten me. It felt right, blissful even, allowing sleep to simply overtake me. My eyelids felt heavy and I yawned then a warm darkness, like a burrow filled with feathers and moss, surrounded me.

42

When I woke again I was on top of my bed. In the soft salmon light everything resembled a prop in a classic fairy tale. I wondered how long I had slept and whether Scott was still in the house. I sat up, head throbbing and licked my lips, but my mouth was so dry I couldn't moisten them. Unsteadily, I stood up and stumbled downstairs, knocking into walls and furniture on the way. A light emanated from the open kitchen door and exotic spices drifted towards me tickling my senses.

Scott was there, stirring a steaming pot of what I presumed was curry. He looked up as I joined him.

'Feel better?' he asked.

'Thanks, yeah.'

I walked towards him and grabbed a glass from a cupboard beside the oven, filled it with water, downed it in one greedy gulp then refilled it. The cold water refreshed me and my brain started to work again. I looked at the clock - seven.

'Clive and Anna,' I said.

Scott looked confused for a moment then seemed to remember. 'I'll run over there, explain you're running late. Can you keep an eye on the pot? It's got about twenty minutes left, but it needs stirring.'

Left alone, I heard the house creak, but dismissed the

sound as noise from the ancient and juddering water pipes. Those were not footsteps above, but wooden floorboards contracting in the cool evening air. I hovered over the pot for a while, stirring. Vegetables, beans and lentils rose to the top then became submerged again. Shades of green, brown, yellow and orange peeked through the surface as I rotated the wooden spoon. My stomach groaned.

I removed the spoon and rested it on the draining board then made myself a cigarette. I blew my smoke away from the food in the way a mother might blow smoke away from a pram, feeling strangely guilty. I walked away from the pot to open the back door and finished my cigarette under the lintel. When I returned the food felt much thicker, harder to stir. Each rotation required an almost Herculean effort and I wondered whether to take the pot off the heat. I dipped the spoon into the curry and pulled out a mouthful. After blowing on the terracotta pulses I slid the spoon into my mouth. It tasted wonderful and made my tongue dance to the music of the spices.

I turned off the heat and gathered together bowls and cutlery. When the table was set I checked the cupboard for wine. Only a few bottles remained; guests must have consumed the rest at Vivienne's wake. I pulled the cork from a bottle of red and left it near the pot to warm then stood on a chair and pulled wine glasses from the cupboard. As I placed them on the table I heard the front door click open.

'It's ready,' I called into the hallway.

The slow movements by the door did not sound like Scott. They sounded heavier. I crept to the kitchen door and looked out into the shadowy hall. They were all there: Scott, Anna and Clive. Anna was shrugging out of her jacket. When she freed herself Scott took it and hung it over the banister finial for her. I watched Anna in silence as she turned her head this way and that to look around the hallway, standing in the middle of a dozen perfect-looking mothers. She spun slowly, looking at each portrait in turn before her eyes met mine. Anna ran towards me, arms wide open, for a hug.

'Sister,' Anna said.

'Sister.' I smiled. 'I'll get some more dishes.'

'Shall I set the dining table?' Clive asked as we walked into the kitchen.

'Okay sure. Thanks Clive,' I answered.

'It's okay, Crow. I'll do that,' Scott said, grabbing an empty bowl and filling it with curry.

I reached for two extra wine glasses and turned towards Scott smiling. I was filled with joy and wondered whether it was love. From an early age my mother had taught me love and sex were inseparable yet here was that wonderful feeling, radiating from my stomach into every sinew of my body, and I just had to accept it, enjoy it. I didn't have to run from it, push it away or hide and I didn't have to strip naked to embrace it.

I took the glasses into the dining room where Clive had already spread out a table cloth, and Anna was laying out cutlery. They both looked up at me at the same time.

'Thank you,' Clive said.

I returned to the kitchen for the wine bottle and stepped aside to let Scott through the door, laden with bowls of curry. I remembered the strange sensuality of the first time we passed in this doorway and thought of how much had changed since that moment. The noise of conversation filled the house and I could hear no other sound.

'Crow,' Clive said, standing up as I entered the room. 'Let me get that from you.' He ushered me towards an empty chair at the head of the table. 'Anna and I were just telling Scott about the last time we were in this room.'

'Yes. Mum had a party and there were all these men. Of course, Clive was in his element, but I found it strangely creepy.' Anna winked at me.

'Vivienne did like men.' I gulped down my wine. The others laughed as if I had made a hilarious joke and I found myself joining in with their laughter. 'To Mum,' I said, lifting my glass.

'To Vivienne.' The toast echoed around the room.

'My Nanny used to tell me a fairy tale about Mum, called the Ballerina and the Revolutionary. Have any of you heard it?' I asked.

They shook their heads so I relayed the tale. They watched me intently as my face burned with happiness. For the first time, I felt the thrill of being the centre of everybody's attention.

'The daughter of a revolutionary ...' Clive nodded, a

knowing look in his eyes.

I shrugged. 'Maybe.'

'That figures,' Scott said. A fierce pride glowed in his eyes.

I looked at Anna. 'Do you know who your father was, is?'

Anna's face darkened and she looked at her bowl, stirring her food and acting as though the question was never asked.

Clive spoke for her. 'We thought you knew.'

Anna shushed him.

I licked my lips, feeling cold. The brightness of a few moments ago had vanished and a sense of dread crept across my skin before crouching in my stomach. I did know, didn't I? Filthy, Filthy ... one step forward, run back, hide. I shuddered and bit my lip, tasting blood. I stared pleadingly at Scott who shrugged and shook his head. Anna seemed absorbed with her food, but Clive was staring straight at me. When, at last, my sister looked up her cheeks shone with tears.

'I'm so sorry, Anna, forget I ever asked ...'

'Anna,' prompted Clive. 'Anna if you don't tell her ... the secret will always come between you.'

I shook my head. Panic rose from my stomach into my throat. *The secret.*

Anna looked from Clive to me then back again. She lifted her glass and finished her wine. 'Can I have another?'

Scott leaned across and refilled her glass. The room was

silent except for the creaking of footsteps in the room above. I tried to shake the sounds from my ears. No one else seemed to have noticed them. Scott reached across to squeeze my hand. I looked at him, but his face melted like candle wax and instead I saw Grandfather's grotesque features swinging from a noose. Pages from Vivienne's diaries fluttered around my head like moths and I knew. Without being told I knew.

'Granddad,' I said.

Anna stopped drinking and nodded.

'Excuse me. I feel sick.' I darted out of the room.

A gentle tapping on the bathroom door tugged my head out from the toilet bowl.

'Are you okay?' Anna asked.

'I'll be fine,' I said. 'I'm sorry.'

'Don't be. I had pretty much the same reaction when Mum told me,' Anna said.

'How do you feel about it now?' I sat up with my back to the porcelain and stared at the door, visualising my sister's face beyond. The image was fuzzy, but I could make out Anna's silhouette crouched on the other side, close yet untouchable. I stretched my fingers towards the shape, but didn't risk moving away from the toilet.

'I try not to think about it,' Anna replied. 'They say you can't choose your family.'

'Do you have any other family: husband, children?' I asked.

'There's no one. You're all I have.'

I didn't answer. I just sat there, pressing my shoulders hard against the cold bowl, separated from my sister by three inches of wood and a lifetime of secrets. At last sympathy took control of my body as the nausea subsided and I inched forwards, crawling towards the door. My head felt too much like whipped cream to risk standing up. I reached for the bolt, pulled it back and opened the door. Anna tumbled into the bathroom.

'It will be enough,' I told her. 'I promise. You can live here with me. Tommy will come around eventually then we'll all have each other.'

'Do you want to know about your father?' Anna asked.

I shook my head and swallowed vomit, grimacing. 'Not now.'

She patted my hand. 'It isn't like that, I promise.'

My eyes prickled and I lifted her fingers to kiss them. 'Later. I should process this first.'

She shrugged. 'Do you feel well enough to go back down?'

'I think so.'

Anna rolled back to a seated position and grasped my hand. With an elegant unfurling of back and legs she rose to her feet, pulling me with her. Less graceful than Anna, I stumbled, but she caught me. I felt as clumsy in my sister's presence as I had in Vivienne's, but I brushed the feeling aside. Who cared if I favoured Doctor Marten boots to ballet shoes? Grace wasn't everything.

I strolled into the dining room and asked everyone

whether they wanted coffee. I felt there was no need to explain my actions and nobody chose to mention my brief absence. Both Anna and Clive offered to help, but I told them I was fine and headed into the kitchen to switch on the kettle and roll a cigarette.

'Can I have one of those?' Anna hovered in the doorway, awaiting permission to enter. I smiled and passed her the first roll-up. 'Thank you.' Anna folded her lips around the cigarette. I lit it for her and started rolling a second.

'Mmm, nothing better than fresh tobacco,' Anna said.

I leaned against the kitchen counter and inhaled. Heat filled my body, but the drug did not give me pleasure, it just removed my cravings, temporarily. The kettle clicked off and I grabbed four mugs and put coffee granules into three of them, a green tea bag in the fourth and waited for the water to cool a little. Anna came over and peered into the cups.

'The coffee tastes better when you wait,' I told her.

She nodded and offered me a gentle smile. 'Everything in its time.'

When the drinks were ready Anna and I carried them into the dining room.

'Should we move into the lounge?' Anna asked.

'Just a minute ...' I said and whispered into Scott's ear.

Scott nodded and left the room, closing the door behind him. I shrugged and tried to mask the sound of wheels scratching across the parquet hall with an enquiry about

Clive's shop. When the noise receded, we walked together, shoulders brushing against shoulders, into Vivienne's drawing room, my living room, Anna's lounge. Granddad's chair had been removed. Scott appeared behind us, slightly warm and sweaty. I squeezed his hand. 'Thank you.'

He nodded. 'It's in the garden. Hopefully it won't rain. I couldn't get it in the shed.'

'Hopefully it does rain. Let the old bastard get wet,' I whispered in his ear.

We settled ourselves onto the settee and remaining arm chair. The room looked larger without the tatty old chair dominating one corner. I sipped my coffee as my eyes kept wandering back to that spot, as if a ghost of the chair remained before I found myself distracted by my guests' animated chatter. Sitting between Anna and Clive on the sofa felt like sitting at the back row of a cinema with the cool kids and I felt years of forced adulthood fall away as my world began to feel full of possibilities and potential.

'Do you remember that time Vivienne rode a horse naked around town?' Clive asked, fighting for breath between bouts of laughter.

'When was that?' I asked.

'You must have been four or five. She was a celebrity even then ... Christ! I remember when she came back from Birmingham with you in her arms and everyone was gossiping, mainly because of the colour of your skin and she told us you were an African princess.'

'You what?'

'Because of the mixed race thing ...'

'So my father wasn't a South American revolutionary.'

'Oh yes ... of course ... sorry.'

'Does it matter?' Anna asked.

I nodded. 'I centred my life, my dreams and aspirations around being a revolutionary's daughter. I needed to feel part of something and my dad provided the key. I'd never be a ballet dancer, but I could fight. I could right wrongs. I could make a difference.'

'You do that. You,' Scott said. 'Whether you're inspired by your father or not.'

I shook my head. 'Everything is meaningless in the end, isn't it?'

'Crow!' Scott said, sharply. 'That's nonsense and you know it.'

I shook my head. 'Sorry too much wine, too many stories. I should shut my mouth.'

The silence in the room grew so thick it was hard to reach through it 'Will you open the shop tomorrow?' I asked Clive, not caring about the answer but trying to change the subject.

'No, I'm taking the week off. There's a number for anyone who wants to contact me urgently. I'll deal with those people, but really I just want time to reflect, to remember ...' His voice trailed off.

'Do you work?' Anna asked me.

I couldn't think of a decent answer. I sat, fiddling with my hands in my lap. The portraits I sketched for tourists, they were work, but I'd hardly touched my charcoals since arriving back in Bristol. Too many distractions drew my attention away from expressing my creativity. 'I guess I sell the pictures I draw.'

'Ooo, I'd love to see some of your work,' Anna said, squeezing my forearm. 'I never had the eye for it myself.'

'I'll sketch you tomorrow, if you like,' I answered. 'I'd paint you, but I don't have any paints right now.'

'Do you prefer to work in oils or watercolours,' Clive asked.

'It's been a long time since I've used either. Oils are more fun, but watercolours are more within my budget.' My hands and feet itched. I wanted to sprint out of the room, grab as much of my work as I could find and throw it at the feet of Anna and Clive like offerings to my gods, but worried it might seem too needy and self-involved, so instead I snuggled further back into the sofa, nesting between my sibling and potential-future-father-figure, feeling happy.

Scott sat alone on the armchair with his feet tucked beneath him and seemed very serene. I wanted to be able to accept and enjoy things like he could. People were chatting around me, possibly to me, but I didn't hear them. I closed my mind off and concentrated on the feelings inside - my beating heart and the blood pulsing through my veins, rushing around my body, the breath entering and leaving my lungs and the way a hair tickled my forearm as it grew. I felt warm, soft and empty, yet full. It was a strange, conflicting feeling that didn't settle me at all. I looked at Scott again. He seemed distant, his eyelids heavy. He was probably just falling asleep.

'Crow, if you're tired maybe you should go to bed, dahling.' Clive nodded towards Scott's sleeping body. 'Maybe you should take him with you.'

'Clive, stop it. Don't embarrass her.' Anna patted my hand. 'Maybe you should go upstairs though. It's been a long day.'

'Will you stay here tonight?' I asked Anna.

She shook her head. 'No I'll go back to Clive's tonight, but we can come back tomorrow. Maybe we could discuss the house and what we want to do. Do you think we should ask Tomas to join us?'

'I dunno. I guess ... we'll have to at some point. It's just ... to be completely honest ... it's Cathy. I don't wanna deal with her yet.'

Anna and Clive stood up. Anna bent over to sort out her handbag and Clive gave me a kiss. He nodded towards Scott and smiled. 'Maybe get him a blanket if he's staying down here.'

I embraced Anna and kissed both her cheeks before they left. I smoked a final cigarette in the kitchen and took a blanket from Tomas's old bed and draped it gently over Scott's body. He had curled himself up so his head rested on his knee. It looked uncomfortable and I wondered whether I should wake him to move, but decided not to disturb his rest. He was probably supple enough to get over it tomorrow. I turned off the light, blew Scott a kiss and retreated upstairs.

43

In spite of relentless searching, sleep evaded me and I lay in my bed, willing my mind to switch off for a few hours. Instead my thoughts kept returning to the living room and Scott, asleep in my house. Eventually, I did manage to grab a few hours of sleep. I wrapped my arms around it and pulled it tight across my face and chest, entering dreams that were as full of Scott as my waking thoughts. I was back in the woods. Leaves lay scattered on the ground and he was there, lying in a nest of yellow and orange oak leaves. Between the leaves I caught glimpses of his pale flesh. I wanted to join him, to roll in the leaves together, laugh and tickle his skin, but when I touched his shoulder and he opened his bright eyes and stared at me, I kissed his feet instead. He sat up and leaves fell from his body. I moved my lips to his chest and kissed him there. Grabbing my arms, he flung me away from him and his face twisted into a cruel laugh.

'Do you think I could ever be interested in you?' he asked. 'You're not even a woman. Not like your mother or your sister. What are you? You're damaged; you're filthy, filthy.'

My body jolted and I sat up. My face was hot and moist and the bed covers clung to my skin. Shaking, I tried to catch my breath. It was just a dream. It was just a dream. It wasn't real. I could see through a gap in the curtains it was still dark outside. I bent down, held my ear to the floor and listened. I pretended I could hear Scott's gentle purr as he slept then I returned to my bed, adjusted the covers and closed my eyes.

If I fell back into another dream, I didn't remember it when I woke. Sunlight filled my room, softened by the curtains and I lay in bed, wondering whether Scott was still there. I crept down the stairs, wanting to catch sight of him asleep in the chair again, half-tempted to wake him with a kiss as if we were in a fairy tale. Half-way down the stairs I heard noises from the kitchen and realised he was already awake; the moment was lost.

'Good morning,' he said to me as I marched into the kitchen.

'Hi,' I replied, hunting for my tobacco tin.

'Want coffee?'

'Yes please. How did you sleep?'

'Surprisingly well, thanks. Hope I didn't cause you any trouble.'

'It was no trouble,' I answered, rolling a cigarette. 'I would have moved you, but you looked strangely comfortable curled up in the chair.'

He passed me a mug of coffee.

'Thanks.' I nursed my coffee and smoked a cigarette. A thousand thoughts flitted in and out of my head. Most were stupid, like imagining a domestic bliss scenario between me and Scott as if either of us were made for such mundane lifestyles.

My thoughts shifted to the bricks and mortar around us, binding us to this space. Would I stay? It was a beautiful house and living here might mean living with Anna; I was certain that would be fun for a while at least. It would also please me to piss Cathy off, but there was an atmosphere within these walls that kept me on edge and had me checking over my shoulder at odd times. The house was menacing and even while the ghosts were quiet, I knew they were still there, waiting for me to let down my guard. I had heard them last night, warning me not to be complacent. Not for the first time I wondered whether the ghosts caused Vivienne to lose her sanity and now Mother might be one of them: those terrifying shades creeping over from the spirit world, the gates to which Scott jealously kept locked. I felt frustrated and restless and I decided I would finish this psychic journey, heal myself then leave. There was nothing keeping me in Bristol except three strangers and a backpack full of bad memories.

I sipped my coffee and rolled another cigarette. 'I want to go back to the dream world today.'

'I guessed you would,' Scott answered. 'I've got to be somewhere else this afternoon though, so it'll need to be soon.'

'Do you have your kit with you?' I asked.

'Always,' he replied.

I believed him and suspected his mat and smudging stick

were his comforters, like my back pack and knife. One minute he seemed so at peace and the next it felt a sham, a front, as if he was no more confident in this world than me - two awkward souls in the maelstrom of life. Was that why he still lived with his mum? Did he need her security to spread his wings? Not just her money, but her presence - her physicality, someone to ground him if he soared too high. I didn't want to be grounded. I wanted to fly. I wanted to light the world on fire and watch it burn. I wanted to get back to London and rejoin the fight. All this nonsense about wills and houses, it wasn't my world. I was a revolutionary, my father's daughter? He would never have settled down.

'Okay, I'm ready,' I said.

I found my place on the mat as smoke from burning sage wafted around the room. It felt different without Granddad's chair crouching behind me, easier. I was in my dream world before I started to count. Sunlight warmed my face. I greeted the great oak and took the path to my waiting stag; he wanted to play and to be caressed so I stroked his cheek and kissed his nose. Reaching the mountain took no time at all and when I stepped onto its towering side, I found myself at the top, quick as thought. I made my way towards my soul. The purple looked brighter now and my energy more apparent. The pink ribbons were scattered around it; I gathered them in my hands and blew them into the air removing all traces of my imprisonment. A beautiful rainbow appeared across the sky. But the pulsing wound remained, darker than before. A piece was still missing. Was time running out? All around, icons from my childhood and adult life were littered. With a sense of dread, I knew where I must check first. The chair looked bigger than the one Scott threw into the garden and, as I stepped towards it, I realised I was shaking. I looked to the rainbow for reassurance and knew I must face this, knew I could face this. I could do anything here.

I walked clockwise around the chair, but as I walked the chair moved too, always the same arm facing towards me, until I gave up, feeling dizzy. I gripped the arm of the chair and tried to yank it towards me.

Tomas was crying. I sat on the floor, my small arms around his slender frame, trying to comfort him. He kept pointing at the armchair unable to say anything between his violent sobs. I hugged him, wondering what had frightened him - a spider maybe. I walked towards the chair. Granddad's hand was resting on the arm and his fingers were twitching. It looked as though he was playing the piano. I loved to hear him play, but there was no music now, only strange grunts and wheezes.

He must have sensed that I was watching him because he leaned forward to look at me through glazed and rheumy eyes. He smelled of cleaning fluid and soured milk. 'Hi Princess,' he said. 'Come and sit on pappies lap.'

He grabbed me under my arms and lifted me. As he moved me across his lap, I saw something strange, a one-eyed, purple worm or snake, fatter than anything in

Nanny's garden. It twitched and I screamed. Shaking, I clung to the side of the chair as my head threatened to implode.

I needed to do this. I pulled the heavy thing on its rusted wheels, turning it. Almost there, I would see it soon, whatever it was. As the chair turned I realised my eyes were closed. I forced them open, keeping them narrow at first, hooded by my eyelashes. The chair looked empty until I spotted something tucked deep behind the cushion. The fabric reeked as I leaned across it and I felt bile rise into my throat. Perhaps I looked distressed, down there, or wherever my body was, because I heard Scott's voice start to count backwards.

'Ten,'

'No!' I screamed, reaching behind the cushion. I drew it out, the damp, long and unhealthy-looking purple grey thing. I knew what it resembled, but also what it really was, not part of Granddad at all, but part of my self, lost more than a decade before. I ran with it towards my soul.

'Eight,'

I started to panic. My body urged me to return to my sacred space, but my mind wanted to finish this for once and for all. Pieces of my dream-self tore from me as I ran. I reached my soul and pushed the slippery member into the break. I turned back to the chair, squatting like a malevolent toad. My hand extended to my right and I felt a heavy weight. I glanced across and saw a bottle with a petrol soaked rag, pushed partly into its throat. The rag became a flame and I hurled it towards the oppressive armchair. I would be free. A burst of bright light dazzled me and my eyes filled with tears then I was rushing downwards.

44

'Three, two ... one,'

I opened my eyes.

I scrambled on all fours across the room and crouched before Scott, trembling. 'I did it. I found my fragment. I'm whole.'

'Crow, that's fantastic! I'm so proud of you.'

It felt as though we should embrace so I wrapped my arms around his neck and kissed his cheek over and over again. 'I feel ... I dunno ... I feel alive. Like the earth was burying me and I've dug my way out.'

Scott nodded. 'That's it exactly! We'll make a shaman of you yet.'

'I don't want to be a shaman,' I said grinning. 'I want to be a revolutionary.'

'Will you go back to London?'

'Yes, of course ... probably ... eventually.'

'I'll miss you.' His words stole my breath and my chest felt deflated.

'I'll miss you too. Look Scott, can people come into each other's dream worlds?'

'Yes. Not into your sacred space, but the forest and the mountain. There will be many travellers. Who did you see?'

'I want you to come with me,' I said and bit my lip

waiting for his reply.

He sat, grinning at me. 'Ahhh. You do, do you?'

I blushed. 'Yes, I do. Will you?'

He paused then nodded. 'Yes, I'll come.'

'Now?' I asked, eagerly.

'I can't now. I have an appointment in an hour,' he said. 'I could come back later.'

'I'm gonna visit Anna this afternoon,' I said. 'I want to talk things through with her.'

'Tomorrow then?'

'Yes tomorrow.'

I wondered what Scott was thinking. He looked happy, excited even. What would happen in the dream world? Would I try to seduce him? Would he seduce me? I felt tempted to cancel my plans to visit my sister, but no, that would seem too eager, too clingy and I didn't feel like being either. I was free now and planned to remain that way.

When Scott left, the house felt empty. I wandered into every room, pulling back the curtains and opening windows, letting the lazy summer air fill the house. I gathered flowers from the garden and filled two vases: one for the dining room and the other for Vivienne's old drawing room - my living room - the room where I learned to live again.

I wanted to dance so I rummaged through Mother's CDs and vinyl collections and found some old music of my own tucked towards the back. Placebo filled the room as I spun round and round, feeling graceful for the first time in my life. I imagined Vivienne's approving gaze, but I didn't feel her watching me. That was okay; I had reclaimed the authority to approve of my new-found grace for both of us.

'I am beautiful,' I told myself, watching my slender arms whirl around me. 'I am lovable. I am whole.'

When I felt too dizzy to dance, I sat on the floor with my open backpack in front of me. The diaries waited patiently. I lifted each of them out and turned them around in my hands, inspecting their covers then I took them into the garden and burned them.

'I love you Mum,' I shouted into the smoke. 'Whatever mistakes you made, I forgive you.'

Wandering from empty room to empty room, nothing disturbed my peace, no menacing shadows, no creaks or groans. I closed each window and left. Instead of walking to Clive's I found myself bouncing, almost skipping along the streets, attracting looks of wonder from strangers. At first, in response to their confused stares, I moderated my movements so as not to disturb their peace, but I was full of music - the rhythm of my blood, the percussion of my steps, and the melody inside my mind. Eventually I realised the world outside my skin was insignificant in comparison to my internal landscape and I ignored it.

Clive opened his door and embraced me. 'What's happened? Did you guys ...'

I laughed, delighting in the tinkling sound. 'No, I did this all by myself. I'm free Clive. No more ghosts. No more fear.'

'Come in, my dahling child, my butterfly. Tell me how you achieved this miracle of transformation.' He stepped aside and waved me into the hallway. I saw Anna waiting for me at the top of the stairs.

'I hoped you'd come,' she said.

I smiled and felt the narrow staircase reflecting the warm glow of my energy.

'Wow, was he that good?' Anna asked, giggling and moving away from the staircase.

I followed my sister into the living room in silence and sank into an armchair, but soon realised I was unable to keep still. My hands moved around me and my feet tapped a rhythm in the air. My skin tingled and it felt as though I was conducting a huge electrical current from every hair into every follicle. 'It was magic.'

'What was magic?' Anna asked.

Clive handed me an ice-cold glass. 'Elderflower,' he said and passed another to Anna. 'The suspense is killing us, Crow dahling. You simply have to tell us what happened to you.'

'I found myself. I don't know how else to explain it,' I said, giggling.

'Tell us everything,' Clive pleaded.

Anna nodded. 'Please. We're desperate to know. You, you just don't look like you did yesterday, not at all. If it isn't sex we need to know what your secret is.'

I told them everything, carefully describing Scott's ritual

and explaining about dream space. Anna questioned every detail, but I didn't want to paint a word-picture of my sacred space, it was too personal. Instead, I described the pathway and the wood and told them about the mountain and my damaged soul. I chose not to mention the razor-wire or precisely what I found in my grandfather's chair.

'I found the missing piece, and now I'm whole. I'm the 'me' I was always supposed to be.'

'I'm so proud of you, little sis. So what now? What will you do now you're whole?'

'I'm leaving Bristol,' I said. 'Going back to London. I want to help people who need me. There is so much to do there, so much unfairness, so much poverty.'

Anna frowned and shook her head. 'You can't. You said we'd live together.'

'You never even said you wanted to, Anna,' I answered. 'I've got what I came back for – answers and understanding. Wherever I go, you'll always be my sister. We'll visit each other, write letters, chat for hours on the telephone. I won't disappear.'

Anna turned away.

'I'm sorry, Anna, but for the first time in my life I'm not running away; I'm walking towards something great. This is important to me.' I hugged her and kissed her cheeks.

Anna nodded and wiped her eyes. 'Of course, I'm sorry, but I'll miss you. We have so much to catch up on.'

'And we will,' I whispered into her thick hair.

We spent a lazy afternoon together. Clive brought us

coffee and food while we snuggled together in an armchair. Clive offered us the settee, but we declined. It was strange but wonderful this closeness - the innocent melting of two bodies into one. I wondered whether Vivienne ever held me like this. I was sure Nanny did. Anna smelled of flowers and holding her reminded me of Nanny's garden and summer days spent digging up weeds with my grandmother and watering flowers, while Tomas rode his bike around the grass in circles, blowing raspberries at us and trying to get me to chase him. I had loved that garden. It was the only place I had felt happy until now.

'Should we phone Tomas?' Anna asked.

'What for?' I sat up and tilted my head.

'To let him know we're okay to sell the house.'

'Are you okay to sell it?'

She nodded. 'It isn't even part of my history. If it isn't part of our future I'd rather have the money, to be honest.'

We looked at Clive who was absorbed in a book. He must have sensed our examination, because he looked up. 'Sorry?'

'We need to phone Tomas. Can we use your phone?'

'Of course, although it's only four o'clock. Will he be home from work yet?'

I shrugged. I didn't know whether he would go to work this week. 'I'll phone later.' I sank back into my sister's arms, half-hoping the idea would be forgotten entirely. I didn't look forward to hearing Cathy's voice. 'Actually Clive, would you do it?'

'Phone Tomas? Of course, dahling,' Clive replied.

He returned to his book and I returned to my happier childhood memories, slotting a young Anna into each of them. I remembered the garden always felt warm and was always filled with sunshine. I couldn't remember ever making snowmen or raking up autumn leaves, but I remembered digging up potatoes. The dark earth covering my fingers felt warm and smelt like sunlight. I would mould it into statuettes of the family and rest them against the garden wall. Nanny used to frown at the dirt beneath my nails and I winced as I remembered how fiercely she would scrub them.

I drifted off to sleep in that warm cocoon of a chair and when I woke Anna was still curled beside me. I heard a nervous flurry of movement behind me and Clive's voice, raised slightly, but I was pinned in place and couldn't turn to see what was happening.

'Hello Cathy, it's Clive. Can I speak to Tomas please? Good evening, Tomas ... Yes it is ... Yes she is ... Tomas calm down. Do you think this is what your mother would have wanted? Yes ... They would like to meet with you ... Would Vivienne's house be neutral ground? Okay ... how about the solicitors? It really isn't like that at all ... I think you should ... Tomas there is no need to insult me ... It's all right, I understand ... Yes, we've all been under a lot of strain. Shall I tell them tomorrow then? ... What time can you get there? I'm sure seven will be fine. Thank you, Tomas.'

Clive crossed the room and sat back down on the settee. He looked older, more fragile. His face was blanched and he was shaking.

'What did he say?'

Clive jumped. I guessed he didn't realise I was awake.

'He will meet you at the house, tomorrow evening at seven o'clock. Please tell me that's okay.' Clive wiped his face with his handkerchief.

'It's fine. Thank you, Clive.' I tried to get up without disturbing Anna but our limbs were tangled together. 'Thank you.'

He smiled at me and on his pale face I superimposed the features of my imagined father. I wondered how Clive would cope without Vivienne in his life. He looked as fragile as the kitsch ornaments and music boxes that filled the room. Not strong like I imagined my father. Clive was just a frightened child who missed his mummy, like the rest of us.

'Are you okay, Clive?'

'I am top notch, thank you, dahling.'

'You know it's all right if you aren't.'

'I miss Vivienne. I will always miss her, but having her two beautiful daughters keeping me company is compensation enough.'

I nodded and ruffled Anna's hair. My sister stirred but did not wake. 'Do you think you can help me out of this chair?'

Clive moved Anna's leg while I lifted her arm and

twisted out of her grasp. Standing in the centre of the room, I stretched my limbs. My arms felt stiff and my feet prickled in that dead flesh sort of way as blood returned to them.

'May I?' I asked, waving my tobacco tin at Clive.

'Anna smokes in her room by the window.'

'I remember the way.'

I kissed him on the cheek and walked into the dark room. Stumbling over discarded clothes, I crossed to the window and pulled back the curtains. Anna's room looked like the squat might have done had Chrissie not been a compulsive cleaner. I laughed as my eyes roamed over the debris: magazines, clothes and dirty coffee cups everywhere. I rolled a cigarette and flung open the window.

The street was noisy and sounds of children's play echoed up from the alley below. The hum of traffic was almost constant; it must have been be rush hour already. I wondered whether I could see Scott's house and leaned out of the window as far as I dared, but couldn't see his ribbon covered tree. Disappointed, I smoked my cigarette and returned to the living room.

Anna's eyes were open and she stretched her arms above her head, yawning. 'So we're meeting the bruvva tomorrow?'

I nodded. 'I hope Cathy doesn't come.'

'Strange woman that one. She always seems full of smiles.'

'Seems is the operative word. If you piss her off she'll

make you pay,' I answered. 'Which of course makes it all the more fun.'

'But we're not going to piss her off are we? You want out of the house - away from Bristol.'

It was impossible to gauge what Anna was thinking. My sister's face confused me. One moment she seemed tranquil and the next, agitated. Vivienne's face would do the same when she was feeling vulnerable, usually just before I would find myself on clean up duty, washing blood or pill-peppered vomit from the bathroom.

'If you need me to, I'll stay until you're okay. You're my sister.'

'It's fine, honestly. I'm sorry if I ...' Anna stood up and walked towards the kitchen. I started to follow.

'I'm making tea,' Anna said, dismissively. 'I'll bring one in for you.'

I returned to the living room. 'Do you think she'll be okay?' I asked Clive.

Clive shrugged. 'She reminds you of Vivienne as well, does she, dahling?'

I nodded.

'Vivienne was tougher than you gave her credit for. She survived a long time, but she followed her heart more than her head and I am certain if she was given the choice all over again she would do exactly the same. That woman knew how to live for love - an inspiration to us all.'

Clive looked at me, his frank eyes told me to follow my heart and in his narrow mind I think that meant choosing

Scott, but he didn't understand. Love wasn't always about sex. It was about making a difference and choosing to fight for what you believed in. I shook my head, doubting I could explain the way I felt to him even if we had one hundred years.

Anna returned with steaming cups. 'Talking about me, were you?' She frowned at Clive.

'No, my dear. We were talking about Vivienne, and I suppose about Crow as well,' Clive replied.

'What will you do?' I asked Anna. 'Where do you live? Do you work?'

'Wow, all the questions.' Anna laughed. 'I move around a bit. I live in Bath right now. I do charity work, mostly. At the moment I run a shelter for women who have to disappear.'

'A shelter, a safe place! Anna, that sounds wonderful. I could do that in London – unofficially of course. It's perfect.'

Anna's eyes clouded and she frowned. 'You could help us.'

'I could.'

'But you won't.'

'I don't know, Anna. I need some time to find my place, I reckon.'

Anna looked at me strangely and I felt something important was not being said. My neck prickled, and I searched for an appropriate question that might shed light on the mystery, but I didn't have enough information to find it. I looked to Clive for support, but he was reading again. There was something amiss though and it nagged at the back of my skull. I regretted burning the diaries; maybe Vivienne had written something which could have helped me to join the dots Anna had sketched out for me.

I left soon after and the same nagging feeling followed me back to the house. The streets were quiet. It had been raining steadily and the pavements shimmered in the twilight. My footsteps echoed between rows of houses. I pulled my jacket tightly around my body, glad I had brought it. Vivienne's house was the only one in the street in complete darkness. Every window I passed revealed the flickering light of a television or the warm yellow glow of a lamp. In contrast my family home looked cold and empty. Pacified by Scott's smudging, it waited quietly for its mistress to return. I wondered whether I might ever miss these walls and stroked the brick-work with my fingertips. There was no life in them. I could leave and not regret it.

The door groaned as I opened it and the shadows of the hallway rushed to greet me as if they wanted to convince me to stay and become one with them, but I knew to do so would be to fade a little more with each day. I was alive and this was a house of dead things. Even if Vivienne's will had said it belonged to me, I did not belong to it.

I shrugged off the darkness and headed for the kitchen. Listening to the hiss and bubble of the kettle, I dragged on a cigarette, feeling heavy. I had lost the lightness of being I'd felt earlier. I was worried about Tomas and concerned about Anna. Maybe I was also worried about what tomorrow would bring. Would Tomas even come to the house? I had loved and looked after Tomas throughout our childhood and I came back when he said he needed me and now, after everything, he had rejected me. With a sinking feeling I realised he was a spoiled brat, incapable of considering my feelings on any matter and wondered whether it had always been that way.

45

My body was tingling again. It was impossible to get used to this nervous excitement. Unable to settle, I moved from room to room, cleaning the living room and vigorously polishing the windows until the sunlight streamed through them uninhibited. The crystals did the rest, breaking open the light into a myriad of colours. The space looked magical.

I felt like Cinderella, faced with my golden carriage but still dressed in rags. I found the perfect outfit in my mother's wardrobe: a silk jersey t-shirt and a simple black skirt. I had to lift the bottom a little to walk safely so I discarded that skirt and chose something shorter. I swirled in front of a mirror and the hem opened out around my knees like a morning bloom.

I checked the clock for the twentieth time that morning. He would be here soon. When the doorbell chimed, I rushed towards it. Scott hovered at the doorstep, shifting his weight from foot to foot. He managed a smile. We drank tea and spoke of my plans. I wouldn't be a stranger and he would have my address as soon as I knew it. I told him Tomas was meeting with Anna and me that evening and asked Scott to stay. He said he wasn't sure it would be a good idea. I asked him to stay anyway, for me and he reluctantly agreed.

We stood up ready to move into the living room. My legs shook beneath me and I clutched the table. Scott noticed and frowned. I watched his slender body as he crouched down to spread out the mat and arrange the candles. He made the circle wider this time to fit us both. It looked like a gateway to another world and maybe that's what it was. He lit the sage and smudged the room, cleansing every corner. It seemed to take forever and I felt impatient, but chewed my nails rather than disturb him.

At last he sat in the circle and I joined him. We faced each other, two sides of a magic mirror. Scott sat with his feet resting on his knees. I crossed my legs and rested my hands on my thighs. He closed his eyes, leaving me behind. Racing to catch up with him, I let my eyelids close and started to count.

My circle danced with reflected light and I wanted to dance with it. I twisted my body in time to imagined music and presented all I was to my silent tree. My body felt warm and my breath ragged. I felt wild and free. Bending over, I became a stag and rushed into the trees. I didn't know where I was going, but my body took me there anyway. When I reached a silver tree with a carpet of Autumnal leaves beneath it, I knew I'd reached my destination. My body changed back to human form and I sat beside the tree to wait. The leaves on the ground rustled. They were piled high and as I leaned towards them I saw toes and fingers peeking out from beneath. I brushed the leaves aside any my hands revealed a face: Scott's face, his eyes closed and darting from side to side as if in a dream. I kissed his lips and he opened his mouth so I could fill it with my eager tongue. His breath was like warm soil and I breathed it in.

My body hardened as I kissed him. Looking down at my naked self I realised I was not the shape I had inherited from my mother, but sleeker, more sinewy and most definitely male. I brushed dried leaves out of Scott's hair and showered him with kisses. His eyes gleamed in the soft light like torches to lead me home. I traced the shape of his ears with my fingertip and watched him shiver with pleasure. He stroked my throat and my pulse quickened. Pleasure spread down my body and the skin stretched outwards at my groin trying to accommodate my growing desire.

Our tongues danced together again and I rubbed my body gently against his. My pelvis stroked his stomach and my chest drew circles across his shoulders. His hands grasped my waist and he turned me over so I was pinned between him and a bed of prickly leaves. He looked at my face and smiled. My limbs felt like liquid, only my penis remained solid, the rest of me became soft and yielding. Scott closed his eyes and covered my mouth with his own. His kisses became deeper, more urgent. With one hand he stroked my chest while the other moved tantalisingly downwards. He stroked my stomach; it tickled and I wriggled and squirmed deliciously beneath him. At last his fingers were cupped around my manhood and I felt like a puppet as he expertly tugged at strings which controlled the very essence of my soul. I thought my body would explode in pleasure as he rubbed against me. I knew I loved him, but words were irrelevant, our pleasure below language, to be felt, not discussed. Squeezing my eyes shut, I moaned as flames of desire licked my flesh until I felt so hot I wanted to tear the skin from my body.

Scott's blond hair was alive with red and orange flames; he looked like a god. The skin on our bodies blackened. I rubbed my bicep and charcoal scales peeled off revealing an angry red blister beneath. I looked around; the trees were aflame and thick, black smoke surrounded us. I coughed and Scott opened his eyes. He moved away from me and I writhed about in the pile of burning leaves overwhelmed with pain. 'The house is on fire!' I said.

'The candles?' Panic mastered Scott's face contorting his beautiful features. 'Count backwards, quickly!'

'Ten ... nine ... eight ...'

I looked at my body. Fire had become my skin. I shook my head. 'We're already dead.'

He kept counting. I took his hand and led him through the flames.

'Five ... four ...'

In spite of the black smoke I found the pool easily. As Scott said one I pulled him down under the dark surface. Water washed the pain away. He was inches away from me, treading water and I swam towards him.

46

The water drained away and we were in Vivienne's house, surrounded by flames. A candle had been knocked over and the mat was alight. Coughing and choking, I grabbed Scott's hand and we staggered out of the house and stumbled through the garden. Sirens grew louder; I could hear them over the agonised screaming of my flesh. I felt something heavy being wrapped around my shoulders, covering my head and I was forced to the ground and rolled until I lost consciousness.

In a way the fire might have been a blessing. There were no arguments as to whether the house should be sold. It was beyond repair, structurally unsound. The ghosts were gone and so was everything that might tie me to my past. I was completely unburdened.

Anna's love was a beacon guiding me to a better future. I felt no fear; only excitement and wonderful potential remained. I saw Vivienne's love in Anna's eyes and knew she was proud of what I'd become. I'd taken my chance to see and forgive my mother. Tomas was distant, unwilling to play a role in this new family, but it was his choice and in time he might want to repair the wound. If so Anna and I would welcome him with open arms.

Until then I had the family I had always dreamed of.

Scott and Anna filled my heart. The only thing more important than them was our work, the fight, justice and equality.

www.ingramcontent.com/pod-product-compliance
Lightning Source LLC
Chambersburg PA
CBHW020929120726
47905CB00008B/2444